P9-BZE-713

26a

26a

DIANA EVANS

wm

WILLIAM MORROW

An Imprint of HarperCollins*Publishers*

Grateful acknowledgment is made to reprint the lyrics from the following: "One Day in Your Life," words and music by Sam Brown III and Renee Armand. Copyright © 1974 (renewed 2002) Jobete Music Co., Inc., and Stone Diamond Music Corp. All rights controlled and administered by Emi April Music Inc. and EMI Blackwood Music Inc. All rights reserved. International copyright secured. Used by permission.

HarperCollins books may be purchased for educational, business, or sales promotional use. For information please write: Special Markets Department, HarperCollins Publishers, 10 East 53rd Street, New York, NY 10022.

FIRST EDITION

Designed by Chris Welch

Printed on acid-free paper

Library of Congress Cataloging-in-Publication Data

Evans, Diana.
    26A : a novel / Diana Evans.— 1st ed.
      p. cm.
    ISBN-10: 0-06-082091-8 (acid-free paper)
    ISBN-13: 978-0-06-082091-6
    1. Twins—Fiction.   2. Sisters—Fiction.   3. Young women—Fiction.   4. Identity (Psychology)—Fiction.   5. Racially mixed people—Fiction.   6. Separation (Psychology)—Fiction.   7. Nigerians—England—Fiction.   8. London (England)—Ficiton.   I. Title: Twenty-six A.   II. Title.

PR6105.V345A613   2005
823'.92—dc22   2005043414

05   06   07   08   09   WBC/RRD   10 9 8 7 6 5 4 3 2 1

For Paula

Contents

The
First
Bit

Ham

Before they were born, Georgia and Bessi experienced a moment of indecision. They had been traveling through the undergrowth on a crescent moon night with no fixed destination and no notion of where they were, whether it was a field in Buckinghamshire, the Yorkshire Dales or somewhere along the M1 from Staples Corner to Watford. Night birds were singing. The earth smelled of old rain. Through scratchy bramble they scurried, through holes that became warm tunnels and softly lit underground caves. Their paws pressed sweet berries in the long grass and they sniffed each other's scent to stay together.

Soon they began to sense that they were coming to a road. One of those huge open spaces of catastrophe where so many had perished. Squirrels smashed into the tarmac. Rabbits, badgers, walking birds—murdered and left for the flies. Bessi thought they should risk it and cross, there was nothing coming for miles. But Georgia wasn't sure, because you could never be sure, and look at what the consequences might be (a little way up the road a bird lay glistening in its blood, feathers from its wing pointing stiffly up to the sky).

They crept to the roadside to get a closer look. Nothing coming at all. No engine thunder, no lights. It took a long time for Georgia to come around. Okay then. Let's be quick, quicker than quick. Run, leap, fly. Be boundless, all speed. They stepped onto the road and shot forward, almost touching, and then the engine came, and for reasons beyond their reach, they stopped.

That was the memory that stayed with them later: two furry creatures with petrified eyes staring into the oncoming headlights, into the doubled icy sun, into possibility. It helped explain things. It reminded them of who they were.

A slowness followed the killing. While their blood seeped into the road they experienced warmth, softness, wet. But mostly it was brutal. There were screams and a feeling of being strangled. Then a violent push and they landed freezing cold in surgical electric white, hysterical, blubbering, trying to shake the shock from their hearts. It was a lot to handle. Georgia, who was born first, forty-five minutes first, refused to breathe for seven minutes. And two and a half years later, still resentful, she was rushed back to St. Luke's Hospital with dishcloth, carpet dust, half her afro, and tassels off the bottom of the sofa clinging to her intestines. She'd eaten them, between and sometimes instead of her rice pudding and ravioli. The ordeal of it. Ida running around the house shouting "Georgia's dying, my Georgia's dying!" and the ambulance whisking her off and Bessi feeling that strange sinking back toward the road (which, when they were old enough to explore the wilderness of Neasden, they decided could well have been the North Circular that raged across the bottom of their street).

There is a photograph of them seated at a table in front of their third birthday cake, about to blow, three candle flames preparing to disappear. Georgia's arms are raised in protest of something forgotten and across her stomach, hidden, is the scar left over from where they'd slit her open and lifted out the hair and the living-room carpet like bleeding worms and then sewed her back together. The scar grew up with her. It widened like a pale smile and split her in two.

As for Bessi, she spent her first human month in an incubator, with wires in her chest, limbs straggling and pleading like a beetle on its back. The incubator had a lot to answer for.

SO GEORGIA AND Bessi understood exactly that look in the eye of the hamster downstairs in the sun lounge. He was ginger-furred with streaks of white, trapped in a cage next to the dishwasher. *What is it?* the eyes said. *Where am I?* The view from the cage was a hamster blur of washing machine, stacked buckets, breathless curtains and plastic bags full of plastic bags hanging from the ceiling like the ghosts of slaughter. People, giants, walked through from other parts of the house, slamming the door and setting off wind-chime bells. A sour-faced man with a morning tremble. A woman of whispers in a hair-net, carrying bread and frozen bags of black-eyed beans.

What *is* it?

Feebly he poked at the plastic wheel in the corner, looking for motion, hoping for escape or clarity. And the explanation never came. It was deeper than needing to know what the wheel was for, where the cage had come from and how he'd gotten there, or in the twins' case, the meaning of "expialidocious" or why their father liked Val Dooni-can. It was more of a What *is* Val Doonican? And therefore, What am I? The question that preceded all others.

The hamster was alone, which made it worse. Alone with a wheel on a wasteland of wood shavings and newspaper. Georgia and Bessi did everything they could: stuffed him with grapes and cleaned his mess, gave him a name. "Ham," Georgia said, her eyes level with Ham's because she was only seven, "be happy some days or you might not wake up in the morning, isn't it. Here's a present." She'd pulled a rose off the rosebush in the garden that was Her Responsibility (Aubrey had said so, and Ida had agreed—so Kemy could shut up) and laid it, the ruby petals flat on one side, a single leaf asleep in the sun, on a saucer. She opened the cage and put the saucer next to Ham.

He sniffed it and then was still again, but with a thoughtful look on his face that wasn't there before. Georgia thought that sometimes flowers were better for people's health than food. She often spent entire afternoons in the garden with a cloth, a spade and a watering can, wiping dirt off leaves, spraying the lawn with vigor, and pulling away the harmful weeds.

The twins lived two floors above Ham, in the loft. It was their house. They lived at 26a Waifer Avenue and the other Hunters were 26, down the stairs where the house was darker, particularly in the cupboard under the stairs where Aubrey made them sit and "think about what you've done" when they misbehaved (which could involve breaking his stapler, using all the hot water, finishing the ginger nuts or scratching the car with the edge of a bicycle pedal). Other dark corners for thinking about what you've done were located at the rear of the dining room next to Aubrey's desk and outside in the garage with the dirty rags and turpentine.

On the outside of their front door Georgia and Bessi had written in chalk 26a and on the inside G + B, at eye level, just above the handle. This was the extra dimension. The one after sight, sound, smell, touch and taste where the world multiplied and exploded because it was the sum of two people. Bright was twice as bright. All the colors were extra. Girls with umbrellas skipped across the wallpaper and Georgia and Bessi could hear them laughing.

The loft had a separate flight of stairs leading up from the first-floor landing and an en suite bathroom with a spaghetti-Western saloon door. Because of its intimacy with the roof, it was the only room in the house that had triangles and slanting walls. The ceiling sloped down over Bessi's bed and made her feel lucky. There was no other bed in the whole house that the ceiling, that God, was so close to, not even Bel's, who had the biggest room because she had breasts. That meant that Bessi's bed was the best. She wrote it down in yellow chalk: BESSI BEST BED, on the wall where her eyes landed in the mornings, just by the attic cupboard where things could be hidden, whole people could be hidden and no one would know to look there because you couldn't stand up in it and it was full of old books and buckets and spades for the holidays.

At the end of Georgia's bed next to the window—a whole upper wall of window that gave them church bells and sunsets and an evergreen tree in the far distance—was another triangle, an alcove, for thinking. Two beanbags whose bubbles smelled of strawberry were tucked into the corners and that was where they sat. Not many people were allowed to sit there too, just Kemy and Ham. But absolutely no one was allowed to sit there with them when they were thinking, especially when they were making a decision.

Late in the summer of 1980, Kemy knocked on the door (that was a rule) when the twins were trying to decide whether Ida and Aubrey should get a divorce or not. Georgia had put a jar of roses on the windowsill so that she could picture them while she was deciding, and sliced a nectarine for them to share afterward—the nectarine was their favorite fruit, because its flesh was the color of sunset. Bessi had wrapped her special duvet around her because she couldn't think when she was cold. Sky-blue slippers on their feet, they sat down in the strawberry corners and shut their eyes. They thought long and hard about it, drifting through possibles. Five minutes passed and ten minutes. Then, into the silence, Georgia said, "Mummy can't drive." Bessi had not thought of this. It was definitely important because they needed a car for shopping and getting Ham to the vet next week to see to his cold. A cold could kill a hamster.

That was a No.

What Bessi had been thinking about was the apple trees that were Her Responsibility. Ida liked to make pies, and Aubrey liked to eat them, so Bessi had to watch the apple trees all year round until the apples started thumping to the ground in September. Then she'd make the announcement, projecting her voice: "APPLE PIE TIME!" And everyone had to follow her with their baskets and stepladders and Safeway bags, even Bel with her hips. Bessi didn't know whether she could give up this position because she felt, in some way, it was important training for the future. And it was almost September. So now she murmured, "It's almost apple."

That was another No.

But if they *did* get a divorce, thought Georgia, they'd all get more sleep, wherever they were, and surely that was a yes.

But not if they ended up sleeping in Gladstone Park. And that wasn't definitely impossible.

Then Kemy knocked on the door, which was irritating because they hadn't gotten very far.

"*What?*" they moaned.

"Can I come in?"

"No," said Bessi, "we're deciding."

"What about?" Kemy was disappointed. "I want to too."

"*No.* Go away," said Georgia. "'Simportant."

Kemy was five and didn't know what *simportant* meant, so she started crying. "I'm telling Daddy you're deciding," she shouted, and stamped downstairs.

Georgia and Bessi adjourned the divorce decision, agreeing that it would be best to wait until after the vet and after this year's apples. And anyway, "It's not up to us," Bessi pointed out, taking a piece of nectarine. "No," said Georgia, "it's up to Bel."

IN THE MORNINGS they went first into the sun lounge to check on Ham and then out into the garden for the apples and the roses. They put their anoraks on—Georgia's red and blue, Bessi's yellow and green—over their pajamas when it was cold. It was usually cold because heating was expensive in the sun lounge (thin walls, a plastic corrugated roof) and there was no heating outside unless it was summer. They understood that. It would be a waste of money to put heaters along the fence outside. Imagine how much it would cost to heat all the outsides in the world. Probably more than three hundred pounds.

Georgia climbed the stepladder and unhooked the hose from the wall. Ham watched. He'd been awake for hours watching the hazy dawn pull in the morning. Today, a Wednesday, he was especially not happy. Wednesdays were hard and the twins understood this too. It was the being in the middle of the beginning and the end when things tumbled, things tossed. The day was reluctant and didn't know what to wear. It dreamed and reached out for dusk, but people carried on as if it was Tuesday, or Friday, as if time's moods didn't matter. This was confusing for Ham and the twins, but they did the best they could to join in.

With the hose over her arm Georgia peered into Ham's cage. It smelled of dry wood and droppings. He blinked very slowly and looked at her chin. "Chocolate drop for brekky treat?" She rustled in the food tray under the table. "Cheer you up today." There was no noticeable response, not even a quicker breath or a quiet sneeze.

Georgia stepped out into the crispy sun and studied Bessi through the bushes that separated the front back garden from the back back garden. The back back garden was wild. Aubrey only mowed the lawn up there once a year because no one ever showed an interest in shaking out a mat and lying down. It had shadows. A hulk of old grass turning to straw by the back wall. A shack next to it full of incredible spiders. Bessi shone through the leaves like stained glass. Very still. She was waiting for thumps with her eyes closed but none had happened yet. She felt that if she concentrated hard enough something would, right in front of her.

The apple trees, who were very pregnant now, creaked and swayed into another long Wednesday. They were twins too. So far this year they'd released three unblushing apples between them. Not nearly enough for Bessi to say Apple Pie Time. There had to be at least four each, with rosy cheeks. And then the things could happen. The

ceremonial march into the wild, the picking, peeling, boiling and baking, apple pies and applesauce with inside sugar and all of it up to her.
Dear God, she thought, please help them drop the apples so that we
can pick them up. Thank you. Amen.

Georgia went and stood next to Bessi and their knuckles brushed
together. There was a shiver on the wind. Bessi opened her eyes.

"I think Ham's d'stressed," Georgia said, staring through the grass.

There was a pause. Sometimes, when Ida hadn't gotten enough
sleep, she closed the bathroom door and locked it. She had a bath for
five hours, during which time they would put their ears up against the
door and hear her talking to someone in Edo (usually Nne-Nne, her
mother, whom she missed). When the bathroom door finally shuddered open, Ida would wander out into the hall as if it were a dirt
track into a whole new country and she'd arrived at the airport with
nothing but her magic dressing gown and a toilet bag. Georgia asked
Bel what it meant because being clean didn't usually take that much
time. Usually it took twenty minutes, or an hour if they had bubble
bath. Bel had lowered her voice and told her that Ida might have
d'stression. When Georgia had asked her what that meant she'd said it
had to do with being sad, that being sad could be like having a cold if
there was enough of it.

And Ham had a cold.

"Is he in the bathroom?" asked Bessi.

"No. He's in his room."

Bessi frowned. "But if he's not in the bath, how can he be
d'stressed?"

"You don't have to have a bath. You just have to have a cold."

"Oh."

They stared at the base of a thumpless apple tree. A sparrow who
nested in its branches peeked down at them and waited.

"What shall we do?" said Bessi.

"Gave him a chocolate but he doesn't want it."

"What about Vicks? On his nose."

"Have to ask Mummy."

"Okay."

Georgia went quiet. She fell into deep thought and put her hand on her stomach over her scar. She said, "What if he dies, Bess?"

"Don't know. We might have to put him in a box and have a funeral."

NEASDEN WAS LIKE the high heel at the bottom of Italy. It was what the city stepped on to be sexy. London needed its Neasdens to make the Piccadilly lights, the dazzling Strand, the pigeons at Trafalgar Square and the Queen waving from her Buckingham balcony seem exciting, all that way away, over acres of rail track and miles and miles of traffic. The children of the city suburbs watched it all on TV. It was only very occasionally that the Hunters ventured past Kilburn because most of the things they needed could be bought from Brent Cross, which had all the shops. And when they did go into town the Little Ones (Kemy and the twins) bumped into things and someone always got lost (Kemy in the bedding department of the Oxford Street branch of Debenhams, Georgia at the Leicester Square fair one winter, underneath an orange polka-dot horse with wings).

Neasden was easier. A little hilly place next to a river and a motorway with nodding trees and one stubby row of shops. One bank, one library, one optician, one pharmacist, one chip shop, one Chinese takeaway, pub, hairdresser, liquor store, cash 'n' carry, greengrocer and two newsagents, a full stop at each end of Neasden Lane. There was also a chocolate-smelling chocolate-biscuit factory said by the older locals to have driven people to madness. Schoolchildren were given unforgettable guided tours through it, the chocolate warm, melting, over freshly baked biscuits on conveyor belts. Georgia and Bessi had been there, and afterward they'd laughed a lot.

The place had clean air and history. Its hills were the result of Victorian golfers who'd whacked their golf balls toward far-off holes that now were tiny memories underneath houses, alleyways, wonky car parks and Brent Council bus stops. It was a place where cyclists' legs started to hurt, where they stopped and swigged water in the summer, leaning on their bikes halfway up Parkview and breathing in the chocolate air (which deepened in the heat). The roads snaked and dipped and wound themselves around the hollows and windswept peaks in dedication to the open countryside, now lost to concrete. Except for Gladstone Park with its ghosts, and the Welsh Harp marsh, where the river rushed on.

Gladstone's house was still standing at the top entrance to the park. It hadn't been *his* house exactly, Georgia knew, he'd just stayed there sometimes with his friends the Aberdeens when Parliament got too much. But as far as she was concerned, it was Gladstone's house. The duck pond and the lines of oaks, the reams of gleaming green grass had all been his back garden. Bodiced ladies in ruffles and high hats used to sip wine there under their parasols, and children hid in the shade of trees. Gladstone liked parties, but he also liked peace and quiet, a dip in the pond, and lying in his hammock between two trees. Georgia had seen a picture of him. Serious eyes in a fleshy face, a clever mouth, long white sideburns and white wispy hair around his balding crown. He looked nothing like her father.

Last Christmas, when Gladstone's garden was thick with snow, Aubrey had taken his daughters to the park with sleighs. They'd dragged the sleighs to the top of the hill where the ducks were shivering and whooshed back down again and again. Aubrey had decided to join in, even though Bel warned him not to because of his bad back, which he often suffered from in winter, or when he felt particularly agitated. In his long navy trench coat, the thick glasses slipped into an inside pocket, he'd sat down on a sleigh and pushed himself out into the soft slide down. Bel said in a foreboding voice, "He's going to hurt himself." They all watched and thought about what would happen if Aubrey hurt himself. At first it was a good thought. But then Aubrey began to scream and despite everything Kemy said, "Don't hurt himself, Daddy!" and the four of them began to run. He screamed a deep, toneless man's scream, all the way down and they ran after him call-ing, frantic, afraid for his back and even his heart. He looked strange, a grown man on a sleigh with his short legs out in the air. When they reached the bottom, touching his arm, pulling him up, Kemy in tears, he said he was fine, his back was fine, and stop fussing, goddammit. He had stayed in bed for a week afterward drinking Ida's milky tea and not speaking much. This had been a very good week for the rest of the family, who spent it catching up on sleep, not standing in cor-ners, and watching forbidden television.

It might not be *that* bad, Georgia was thinking now, if they ended up sleeping there, in the park, after divorce. They were driving around the edge of it on the way to the vet in the royal-blue estate with three rows of seats. Ham was next to her with the *What is it?* still in his eyes. Aubrey was at the wheel.

Georgia imagined it like this: She and Bessi would knock on the door of the house and one of Gladstone's great-grandchildren might open it, or better still, Gladstone himself looking sweetly ancient in a waistcoat. He'd ask them what he could do for them and it would be at this crucial point that Georgia would tell him that she and Bessi were in his class at school, green for Gladstone, and she'd show him her badge. He couldn't refuse. He'd say, Well, I was just serving tea to the haymakers, but do come in and make yourselves comfortable. And he'd let Ham in too. They'd all wake up the next day to the silver kitchen sounds of an oncoming party and wait for the ladies to arrive for their wine.

So that was a Yes. That was an Oh-yes. She nodded.

Aubrey, at this moment, was not in the best of moods. Last night he'd stayed up shouting about the boiler being broken and how his family were a bunch of ungrateful sods, especially Bel because she'd started to wear lipstick. No one had slept much; they all, regardless of age, had bags under their eyes. And to make things worse there was a traffic jam on Dollis Hill Lane, and there were never traffic jams on Dollis Hill Lane. It was "preposterous," "damnable" and "a flaming nuisance." That's what he said. Kemy, sitting on the other side of Ham, asked what pre-pos-ters meant, thinking it was possibly something to do with Michael Jackson, but Aubrey ignored her. Georgia stepped in, for she had been pondering this too, arriving at the conclusion that it was something to do with extra. Extra posters. Extra normal. Extra or-di-na-ry, which was the same as normal, she knew this, she was "a very clever girl" (her teacher Miss Reed had said only last week). So she said, "Extra posters and more ordinary." And Kemy looked at her for a while with her shiny brown eyes that throbbed for being so big.

The traffic had advanced and the car in front was failing to keep up. Aubrey beeped and raised his voice, "Come on, woman! What are you waiting for!" Bessi was stuck fast to the passenger seat by her seat belt, feeling sorry for herself after a fight with Kemy about not sitting in the front. She studied the outline of the head in front that Aubrey was come-on-ing. It definitely looked like a man to her, lots of grizzly hair and massive shoulders. "I think it's a man, Daddy," she said. Aubrey dug the end of his Benson furiously into the ashtray, blowing out smoke from the very back of his throat. When the smoke was fresh, when it drifted, it resembled the eventual color and texture of his hair, which was also fading away.

They stopped on a hill and Aubrey had to use the hand brake. He jerked it up with such force it shook the car and made a loud ugly squeak that made Kemy laugh. "Ha ha! do that again, Daddy!" Her skinny legs flippered and she kicked the back of Aubrey's seat. "Do it *again*!" He threw a glare over his shoulder. "Will you settle down, bloody hell, just settle down!"

Ham sneezed softly in his cage and closed his face.

THERE'D BEEN AN accident at the lights. The police were clearing the road and as they drove past they saw a red, ruined car smashed up against a lamppost. The hood was crumpled. The lamppost was lean-ing away from the windshield, away from the death, who was a woman, who was dying in the ambulance flashing toward the hospital. Georgia caught a wisp of her left in the front seat, a cloudy peach scarf touching the steering wheel, and a faint smell of regret.

FOR TWENTY YEARS Mr. Shaha had been the only vet in Neasden. He'd come to London from Bangladesh after the bombs of World War II. "They destroyed Willesden completely," he told people (his grandchildren, his wife's friends, his patients—the dogs, hamsters, budgies, cats, gerbils, and the occasional snake), "terrible, terrible things. But life must always go on, that is the way of the Shaha." There were two framed documents on the wall of his waiting room, which radiated the permanent stench of animal hair and animal bowels: his creased veterinary certificate, and a misty black-and-white photograph of his mother, with a folded letter written in Bengali, hiding her neck.

Ham scowled and chattered his teeth as they waited amid the meows and grunts. He shuffled around in his cage picking at dried rose petals, while opposite him a panting Labrador winced and scratched its balls. When Mr. Shaha called them in, Kemy had fallen asleep and Aubrey had to carry her. Mr. Shaha, old and fat, atrocious eyebrows, with his crooked spine only suggested beneath his lab coat, slowly took Ham out of his cage and looked him straight in the eye. "Now, what's the matter with you?" he said. "Hmm?"

"It's Ham. His name's Ham," said Georgia. "He's d'stressed."

"He's got a cold," Bessi added.

"And he doesn't want chocolate."

Ham was airborne, on a warm free hand. Mr. Shaha's breath smelled of kippers from his lunch. He put Ham down on the examining table and Ham kept bolt still.

"Is he going to die?" Georgia asked.

Mr. Shaha gave her a serious look. "Little one, we are all going to die one day, and I suppose it is better if you are prepared."

There wasn't much he could do for Ham. He checked his mouth and his eyes, one of which was closing, and recommended warmth and lots of sunlight. "Try to keep him active," he said. Aubrey bought a checkered tie-on body blanket from Mr. Shaha's accessories cabinet (which had proven to be quite lucrative over the years), and on the way home Georgia secured it under his throat and belly. "There," she said. "Isn't it better now. You won't die anymore."

But Bel had another one of her dreams, and Bel's dreams were never taken lightly. She had once been told by a fortune-teller at the annual Roundwood Circus that she possessed "the powers of premonition," which had made her shudder, as she was only ten at the time. Ida, who had been harboring suspicions about Bel's psychic status on account of a certain piercing mystery in her eyes that reminded her of her paternal grandmother, Cecelia Remi Ogeri Tokhokho, who had also been prone to clairvoyance, had held Bel's hand and looked at her very intensely. "Don worry," she'd said, "it means you are a wise one and you will know many secret things." As she got older, Bel's dreams became more and more reliable, to the extent that sometimes Ida would consult her on matters such as forthcoming natural disasters in Nigeria or whether Kemy would catch chicken pox from the twins (which she had—they had scars on their backs).

The night after the visit to the vet, Bel dreamed of a wedding held in a muddy field. She tossed and turned. There was no bride and groom. There were no guests. There were only a few waiters wandering around with stacks of empty plates, and the only sound was a dog barking frantically outside the tent. Bel woke up and rubbed her temples with her fingertips. She knew what was coming.

Over the next two weeks Ham moved less and less. The apples began to thump and Bessi was joyous. She banged a frying pan with a wooden spoon and led her army of harvesters up into the wild. Under Ida's supervision they peeled and chopped and mixed, frilled in aprons, getting sweaty. And while Bessi was standing at the stove, busy with the applesauce and the future, Georgia walked silently out into the sun lounge every hour to check on Ham. She felt, in those last days, that she and he were traveling together to the end of *What is it?* and there was only so far she could go.

Ham sat through the days with his nose glistening. He was making a decision, and when the decision was made, he simply stopped moving. And closed the other eye.

Then it was possible, Georgia noticed, to choose the time, to leave when you were ready. The heart sends a message of surrender to the brain and the brain carries out the formalities, the slowing down of blood and the growing cold, the gathering of stillness and the inside lights retreating. Ham's fading vision caught the angry man walking about in the middle of the night and shouting something. There were tender strokes along his back from the little girls, and roses, new roses. He could hear the faint echo of bells. But it all was history. He had decided and it had happened and now he was ending toward what was next. Toward another shock, another scale. It had been very small, this life.

The last thing he saw: the two of them enclosed in a yellow hula hoop, edging out into the garden.

The Wedding

Diana Spencer steps from the glass carriage, holding her skirts, and lifts her head in the way she has of still keeping it down. Her veil is silk taffeta, as long as centuries and just as heavy. She steps into a July full of kisses and dares not look all the way around. Because the universe is watching her, and she is just a shy young girl from Norfolk. Her tiara is leaping with diamonds. Into the cathedral she walks, slowly, in case she falls, which would be dreadfully unforgivable. Her prince is waiting. He seems to wait—he and God's creatures on the ceiling and the Archbishop of Canterbury and Lord Nelson in the crypt, the city, the half of England outside and the other half along with the rest of the world in the cameras, and her almost mother-in-law, Queen Elizabeth II—for eternity. She needs her whole blood family to ease the weight of the veil.

Most of Neasden was inside the cameras. It was the same with the Queen's Silver Jubilee. There had been street parties elsewhere, in Kensington and Clapham and the East End, as there were street parties now, local carnivals with orange squash, dirty aprons and soggy barbecued drumsticks; but save for the rare adventurer who sped into town on the tube to join the fans and tourists straining their necks and sighing outside St. Paul's, the folk of Neasden stayed at home. That year there were other things to think about. The Brent depression and the increase in muggings down the alley that led to the shops, the roadworks on Parkview and, for the Little Ones, how they'd get ice cream if the ice cream van's speaker wasn't working, which it wasn't. It arrived with a loud wheezing engine instead of the much more alluring "Sing a Song of Sixpence." The Hunters stayed at home and ate chicken.

In the kitchen there was a lone shelf stacked with books on English cookery that Aubrey and his mother had bought for Ida since her arrival in London. Some of them had the corners of pages turned down, suggesting an interested reader, but Ida rarely looked at them. She preferred to follow her own way, within the confines of roast dinners and bacon and eggs and onion-soaked liver on Mondays. Her roast potatoes were sometimes burned at the edges, her boiled vegetables were soggy on occasion, particularly after a long bath, but when it came to chicken, Ida was beyond the teachings of any book. Ida knew what to do with chicken. She did not seem to add much seasoning, nor did she cram the insides with year-round stuffing or cloves of garlic. Bel and the Little Ones believed that Ida spoke to the chicken. As she basted it with oil in the sun lounge and sprinkled the skin with mysterious grains, she bent and whispered, "You are delicious, you are tender, you are the chicken of kings and queens." And the chicken obeyed. It swelled and juiced in the oven on its journey to food, it gathered in its flesh all the bliss and passion of taste, and it fell lusciously into their mouths, brown and moist and holy.

Bessi was busy with the parson's nose. It was the best bit of the chicken, Aubrey said. All juice and salty tantalizing squidge. She ate it (Bessi's Best Bit) every time they had roast chicken, which was every fourth Sunday and on special days such as this. A fairy-tale wedding, and for Georgia and Bessi, a possible sway against divorce.

Much later, too late for Bessi to get over it, it emerged in conversation that the parson's nose was actually the chicken's bum. The arse of the chicken. Bessi was dismayed. It had never occurred to her before, but of course, it had always been far too big to be a nose. She would blame the onset of her eczema on the bums. She'd calculate that in her lifetime (that is, between the ages of six and fourteen, because thereafter another parson's nose would never pass her lips), she would have eaten approximately one hundred and sixty-eight chicken buttocks and fourteen turkey buttocks. These were drastic proportions.

As Diana negotiated the red carpet, Bessi munched innocently on a buttock. There was no bacon anymore for her and Georgia. Not now. The death of Ham had been the end of bacon, the delicate curls of it cooked with the chicken, the end of sausage rolls, the end of Spam, the end of pork itself. (Though Bessi *had* secretly eaten a pork sausage at Christmas, but that was all, just once. She loved pork sausages. She was ashamed of herself. She'd savored every delicious moment of it.)

Ham had been buried by the apple trees in a ceremony solemnly led by Georgia—she'd been the one to find him, slumped to one side in petals and droppings on a Sunday morning. The funeral was also attended by Bessi, Kemy and Bel (who was late). They'd sung "Kumbaya" and Hot Chocolate's "No Doubt About It," the only song Ham had ever responded to, up on to his hind legs, staring into the music. They dressed in the black they had, which wasn't much—knee-high socks, school shoes, leggings and tight tops of Bel's which were baggy on them—and prayed for Ham's safe journey to the road: "We know, Lord, why Ham had to go," Georgia had said with her palms and her eyes squeezed together, feeling hot. "Please let him be happy now, and tell him we love him. Thank you. Amen."

For today, a tossing sweltering Wednesday with heat showing on the roads, everyone was allowed to eat in the living room so they could see The Wedding better. Eating in the living room meant that when they'd finished they didn't have to say, "Please may I leave the table thank you for a good dinner," because there wasn't a table. Kemy was sitting between the twins, the three of them in a line on the sofa being careful with their plates and by now assuming more and more the condition of triplets—although there was only so far Kemy could go, there were twin things she could never understand, and this made her snug up to them closer still, wanting to know, wanting to see. She tried to decode their looks over dinner and was still hoping to be included in one of their deciding sessions at 26a.

Diana had reached the top of the stairs. Her bodice gripped her waist and her arms were ivory balloons. She looked like a princess snow woman who was getting lost in her ruffles.

"Her dress is silly," Kemy said, swallowing cabbage (there was no point in arguing) and looking at the twins. "Isn't it."

"No," said Bessi, "but a bit because she can't walk very fast."

"You don't have to walk fast when you're getting married," clarified Bel, who was secretly wearing eyeliner and, less secretly, a miniskirt that showed leg when she sat down. "You're *supposed* to walk slowly. Like Mum." Ida walked slower than anyone else in England and Bel was the only person in England who could bear to keep pace with her.

"Not that slowly," Bessi said. "When *I* get married, I'm going to walk faster than that anyway."

"So am I," said Georgia. "Look, she's going to take all day."

"Bloody hell!" Aubrey's carrot wouldn't stay on his fork. The bank had given him the day off work and he was sitting over there in his chocolate armchair with the corner of a paper napkin tucked into his collar. He managed to get the carrot into his mouth and leaned back, looking relaxed again. There were little silver men on the mantelpiece next to him which he had been collecting for years. They were a comfort and a source of fascination for Aubrey, braced as they were in various states of movement, a horse rider bent low into the wind, a helicopter and pilot on an axis. One of them, recently pushed, was doing full swings on a crossbar.

On the other side of the room, in her rocking chair by the curve of windows, was Ida, her glasses and earrings shining in Waifer Avenue sunlight, across her shoulders a red crocheted shawl.

Like Georgia, Ida gave the impression—the quietness, the sideways look—of someone who was always leaving and had never fully arrived, only hers was a different place altogether. It was on the map in the hallway, with Italy, in yellow, and British Airways could get her there. Nigeria and Ida, parted now for sixteen years, with one two-week visit with baby Bel and a new British passport in 1969, had never let each other go. There was red dust still in her eyes. It got in her way when she ventured farther than Neasden Lane without Aubrey, and when she asked directions from passersby they never understood what she was saying. So she didn't go out much. Sometimes to the cash 'n' carry for birthday presents, very slowly, wearing her nearly black wig with the fringe, but mostly she stayed in, wrapped up, shaded, talking to Nne-Nne, who often made her laugh.

Ida was usually the last to finish eating because her food was special. She had to do things to it. First, she preferred everything stewed—fried up, mushy, with added beans and chili. She liked to be able to pour her roast dinner, steak and kidney pie, rice and stew, sausage and chips, with the beans, onto her plate. And this took time alone at the cooker, stirring and seasoning, and sometimes sitting down to eat at the kitchen table as if she'd forgotten everyone else in the other room. She'd chuckle with Nne-Nne between mouthfuls, and if anyone came into the room the laughter would stop. Second, because Ida often felt cold, what she ate had to be warm, preferably hot. She warmed everything up, including salad, cake, bread, cheese, coleslaw, Safeway's black-currant cheesecakes (which she was fond of and got agitated if Aubrey forgot to buy them), apples, biscuits and ice cream, until it was almost but not quite liquid. She had her own separate salt and pepper pots that she'd adapted herself with a darning needle from empty tubs of Vicks, which was the sole medicinal substance she believed in.

The two things Ida said most commonly were "You better ask your daddy" and "Have some Vicks."

Since Diana had gotten out of the carriage Ida had stopped eating. Her lunch was going cold. She was leaning forward with her head to

one side, gazing at the bride. Almost there, with all of her veil and sequins and flowers intact. Georgia and Bessi watched their mother
carefully and looked at Aubrey, who was having a fight with his peas.
"Look, Daddy," said Georgia.

Now she arrives and her prince holds out his hand. The earth has
hushed. There they are, a pool of perfect, shimmering, unbreakable
love, ready in God's greatest UK branch to receive his divine blessing.
Diana's lifting her luscious eyes and they shine out through the veil in
their cases of dark mascara blue. Charles, in his medals and buttons, the
dashing groom, one of the world's most eligible bachelors, keeps turning his face to Diana's because he can't help it. She sends back shy
smiles and concentrates on becoming a princess. She is doing everything right. Love will last when it begins like this.

"Is there any pud?" asked Aubrey, who smacked his lips and
smoothed out his napkin. He liked pudding. All kinds of pudding.
Sponge cake, rice pudding, trifle, fruit salad with golden syrup,
bakewell tart (invented in Bakewell, Derbyshire, Aubrey's hometown
and origin of the parson's nose). Layers of pudding were lining his
stomach. That's what happens when you get "over forty-five," Bel had
recently told the Little Ones. The things you like start showing on
your body and it becomes harder and harder to get rid of them. You
had to do two hundred sit-ups and a hundred push-ups *every day,*
which Aubrey didn't, which was why he had custard and syrup and
sponge on his stomach and red bits of vermicelli in his eyes. Over
forty-five sounded horrid. Georgia and Bessi thought that thirty-six
might be the best time to stop (they would stop at the same time, they
had decided during a particularly long session on the beanbags, of
course they would—like husbands and wives who didn't need di-
vorces, until death do us part).

Today was rice pudding with optional ice cream, but Ida ignored
Aubrey's question by pretending she hadn't heard him, which was un-
likely because his voice, the only male voice in the Hunter household,
was the loudest. Couldn't he smell it? Rice baked in milk on a low heat

for an hour and a half until the top was skin only had one smell. What he really meant was, I am ready for my pudding now; when I am ready, the pudding is ready. Ida took up her knife and fork and returned to her stew. Georgia and Bessi said, "It's coming, Daddy," and Bessi felt annoyed a bit and wished he'd be more patient. Bel got up to fetch more gravy, because the room was full of things about to snap and the sniggering accusation of a perfect wedding.

In real life weddings were different. There were no television cameras and no archbishops. People came as they were, in not-new suits, with stubble, and behaved as they behaved. Ida married Aubrey in a drafty church in Sudbury in the spring of 1965. The vicar couldn't pronounce her name and there were six guests, some of them sneering, none of whom she knew. Aubrey's parents, Judith and Wallace (also on the mantelpiece, looking historical and dusty), one of his brothers (the other absent because he didn't like Africans and particularly ones that were joining his family), an old school friend called Arthur who sprayed spit when he spoke, his new Spanish girlfriend Monica, and a sad old woman at the back in a purple coat who'd wandered in off the street. "Tokhokho," Ida said to the vicar as he struggled with the three staccato, fearless, perfect Os. "Er, yes," said the vicar, "To-cocoa." He couldn't do it. Irritation feathered his nostrils (he'd missed his breakfast and resented Saturday-afternoon weddings because it meant he missed the horse riding). And it didn't matter anyway. The name was about to be lost, sent drifting out to sea on a raft made of yesterday.

Ida the bride was slim and delicately muscled and the tips of her shoulders had a sheen. Her forearms were a circus of bangles. Behind each set of thick, skyward lashes she'd dabbed a fingertip of indigo and wrapped her hair in a white scarf laced with copper. Her body was brown all over and there were wide black tribe tracks down her cheeks. The dress—simple, cream and sleeveless with a slash of peach across the middle—stopped at the knees and her bare calves dipped into a pair of tiny white shoes. Throughout the ceremony Aubrey's brother William, with the stubble, kept looking openmouthed from the swarthy brown calves of his almost sister-in-law to the flushed pink neck of his little brother. He had never seen anything like it.

"So . . . the pudding, then?" prompted Aubrey.

"It's not ready yet," Ida muttered.

"*Wait*, Daddy," said Bessi. "Mummy hasn't even *finished*."

"*And* they're asking her the question," Georgia added.

Aubrey sighed to himself and sipped Liebfraumilch. Everyone wished he wouldn't.

The twins were hoping that The Wedding might make Ida and Aubrey remember things, that they loved each other, that Ida was very pretty indeed and Aubrey was a nice man sometimes, sometimes lots of times. They wanted their parents to look deeply at the picture of them on the mantelpiece beside the dusty relatives, standing arm in arm behind confetti (how pretty, how pretty she is), and walk back into each other's eyes with an "ahhh, remember our day" look, and beating hearts. Because then they'd be able to adjourn the perplexing divorce decision for good and Aubrey would go to bed at night cuddling his wife instead of marching up and down and making lots of noise. There was always something, they were finding, that made divorce out of the question—apples, new school uniforms, the Brent d'stression, which would make it hard to find somewhere to live.

But so far, Ida and Aubrey hadn't looked at each other once, not once, not even a glance. In fact, there seemed to be nothing less they'd rather do, particularly now, during the question. "Listen, Daddy; listen, Mummy," said Georgia.

"Do you, Diana Frances Spencer, take thee, Charles Philip Arthur George, to be your lawful wedded husband?" asked the archbishop.

The photographers run into her eyes. St. Paul's is ablaze. It is hot with hymns. They have sung "I Vow to Thee, My Country" and she is leaving herself behind. She wants to take one last look back there, where everything was loose, uncertain and recognizable, but the cameras are marching. There is no more time. It is past. She will wake up tomorrow morning on a cloud of majesty, scores of maids at her feet, mosaics and angels on the ceiling, and dear Charles at her side snoring.

She says: "I do."

"Are they going to kiss each other now?" asked Kemy.

"Yeh, in a minute," Bel said.

"Is he going to use his tongue?"

Georgia and Bessi had just done the wishbone and Georgia won. She wished for Aubrey to look at Ida deeply and lovingly, and if not, Neapolitan ice cream. Bessi made a wish too (what was Georgia's was also hers). She wished to be famous one day but only for two weeks because it might get irritating after that. Two weeks was how long their holidays were for—so far Corfu, Tunisia, and the Canary Islands, on the burning beaches (which was another No).

Kemy sniggered. "They're kissing. Look!"

"He's no good at it," Bel said, looking at the kiss sideways. "He's not moving his head."

Cameras cannot catch the inside of a kiss. Charles's head stays still and Diana receives him obediently. It is not a passionate kiss. There is no tender hand pressing into the small of her back, no arching against him and the round of her breasts seeping into his rib cage. Their lips shake hands. It is sealed. She belongs to him and he belongs to his mother. There are bright sighs and chatter from the congregation and then they are singing again, the hymn "Christ Is Made the Sure Foundation."

Ida was trying to remember how she'd felt at that moment, after the kiss. Aubrey had gripped her shoulders as if he'd been practicing how he'd do it. He'd looked about him first, into the congregation, bashful. Here goes. Left or right. Right. No, left. His face descended and then disappeared. Someone coughed, his father, who had come wearing an old green suit that gave the impression he might be at that moment turning into something mightier than a man. A long, growling, nicotine cough and Aubrey finished it there, half holding her hand, perspiring, and they looked back at the vicar, into the new country of their marriage.

It was now that Ida finally looked over at her husband. Georgia and Bessi sat forward. Her eyes left Diana and Charles walking back up the aisle, and traveled across the carpet to Aubrey's chair. They moved up his legs, over the mound of stomach waiting for dessert, lingered briefly on the crowded mantelpiece next to him, the foggy old photographs and the silver men, and arrived at his face. Aubrey was no longer handsome, and perhaps he had never been handsome. He had barrels of exhaustion under his eyes from the long sleepless nights, ridges in his lips from sucking cigarettes, and a mottled pallor to the skin from not enjoying life (Bel said). Ida had not looked at him this closely in a long time, and it was a disturbing sensation, their children present around them, that she did not in her heart feel a faint recognition of desire.

Aubrey may have sensed that he was being observed by his wife, because he glanced toward the armchair and up into her face. Georgia and Bessi were encouraged by this, though it was not the kind of look they had been hoping for. It was a brief, disappointed moment in which Aubrey's eyes said, "Where the fuck is my pudding?" and Ida's eyes said, "Get it yourself and who the fuck are you anyway?" It was broken by Ida taking off her glasses and laying them on the windowsill. She got up and said, "Bel, come and help me in the kitchen," and left the room.

DIANA'S BOUQUET HAD six different kinds of flowers: gardenias, white freesias, lilies of the valley, golden roses, white orchids and stephanotis. She and Charles were on the Buckingham balcony now, after their kiss, and another glass ride, and another kiss. They were facing the cameras waving and the bouquet looked heavy. Georgia studied it carefully and decided, a quick one, that there should be less because flowers were not meant to be a burden. If she had done it, she would've made it less.

From the palace they were going to Hampshire. Then they'd fly to Gibraltar for a twelve-day cruise through Egypt on the royal yacht, for romance and making children. Ida and Aubrey had returned to their planets. There were three thousand miles between the rocker and the chocolate armchair. Georgia and Bessi were sensing that it might take more than a royal wedding and a red carpet and the Archbishop of Canterbury to close the distance.

So for now, everyone ate rice pudding. There was no Neapolitan so they had choc-ices instead, which wasn't bad. This combination of ice cream with something warm meant that Ida didn't have to heat up her ice cream and they could all eat their pudding in unity. They arrived together at the end of dessert when the crystal bowls were empty apart from shallow puddles of ice cream which had to be scooped in vanilla strips into the spoons, so that the Hunters became an orchestra.

When the pudding was finished, Georgia went outside to water the rosebush. She didn't have to say, "Please may I leave the table thank you for a good dinner." She liked it when she didn't have to say this.

While Georgia was in the garden, Bessi went into the kitchen, still hungry because there hadn't been enough roast potatoes. She was ashamed. She opened the oven and saw three curls of bacon left around the remains of the chicken. It's not Ham, she thought, it's bacon. She ate one of the salty pink curls, hoping Georgia wouldn't know.

"You're eating Ham!"

Kemy was there suddenly at the kitchen door. "I'm telling Georgia."

"Oh, don't!" Bessi pleaded. "Please don't! She'll be ashamed at me!"

"Only if you make me a chicken sandwich." Kemy was also still hungry.

Bessi thought about it. "Okay," she muttered.

"Toasted," said Kemy. "But only a bit."

"I'll do it."

"And with the crusts cut off."

"All right."

"And mayonnaise."

Bessi nodded bitterly and made the sandwich, with mayonnaise and salt and pepper. Sandwiches were very popular in that house. They'd all inherited a taste for chip butties from Aubrey and most of their meals were accompanied by a plate of bread in case anyone wanted a rice sandwich or a baked-bean buttie.

Kemy ate her sandwich. Twice while she was munching, Bessi said, "You better not tell."

THAT NIGHT, THE twins lay in their beds in the dark. The umbrella girls on the walls had gone to sleep. The loft was silent.

"It didn't work," said Georgia, into the black.

"No," said Bessi. "What shall we do?"

"I don't know. Maybe we could get a tea towel with Diana and Charles on it and put it in the kitchen."

"Yes. That's a good idea," said Bessi. "You're clever."

"We'll have to ask Daddy for some money."

"Yes . . ."

"Good night," said Georgia. "I'm going to see Gladstone."

"Good night."

Bessi heard Georgia falling asleep. She always fell asleep first. She listened to Georgia's breathing getting deeper and heavier.

In her dream, Georgia walked to Gladstone Park. It was a warm night. She reached up and knocked on Gladstone's door.

"It's me again," she said, "green for Gladstone."

Gladstone was in his dressing gown. His hair floated around his head like a halo. He invited Georgia to sit down in the elegant armchair and tell him all about it over a cup of hot chocolate. She warmed her hands around the mug and asked Gladstone if he'd watched the wedding today. He said, "No, dear, I don't have a television."

"It was a lovely wedding," said Georgia. "We wanted Mummy and Daddy to like each other again, but I don't think it worked. What shall we do now?"

Gladstone sat smiling up at the ceiling. "Ah, my wife and I had our anniversary here, back in '89. What a breakfast!"

They talked about the roses. He told her to keep them moist. He knew a lot about growing things from planting trees. Georgia liked sitting with Gladstone, and she began to feel that there was nothing to do at all. She felt sleepy. In a slurred voice she said, "It feels like there's someone missing all the time, when everyone's together at the table. Is it because of Ham?"

She heard Gladstone's voice in the distance. It said: "My dear Georgia, the future has already happened, just like the past. And one day you will see that there are no answers, only the places we make."

Escape

One floor down from the loft, in the master bedroom, Ida turned her back to Aubrey. She began to drift. She wandered back toward home and on the way she remembered again the kiss, Aubrey's face disappearing into hers, the sunshine afterward as they stepped outside. Maybe a little bit happy, that's how she'd felt. Aside from feeling lost. As new countries, new beginnings, always give the sensation of being lost, of blindness. You step into a boat after midnight and the waves take you out. You drift. The horizon is anywhere and the morning never comes. Not until something inside is quietly shattered and it feels like relief. Then the lights come on, and you can see what has happened.

That was how it began. Before Aubrey, before England, even before Lagos, Ida's adventure started two hours after midnight, not on a boat, but on a bicycle. She was fifteen when she left Aruwa. Where the dust on the ground was red and inflamed, where the singing tree sang from the center of the village and the air was sticky. It was a deep dark blanket night and she was discovering loneliness. There were devils hanging upside down from the stars and they were shouting Go home! Where are you running to! She slowed down when she reached the singing tree, its trunk swollen from ancient sunshine and the yearly lashings of ferocious rain. There was a strange thickness to its leaves, an infinite green, and its branches stretched outward and forever. This was where the spirits lived and wisdom was woven, where children climbed branches in pursuit of magic. She'd climbed it often herself, all the way to the top, and sat there on a big blue day hearing voices, whispers. She walked into the world of it now, bowing her head, and prayed a farewell.

In her bag she had a ruby cotton dress, two wrappers and T-shirts, a tin of shea butter, some underwear and a few niara from Uncle Aka for the bus to Lagos. Her mother's beads were around her wrist. And everything else was under her skin.

She ran and the crickets screamed. "Stop at the pump," Uncle Aka had said, "wait by the pump and he will come." The bushes twisted in the breeze and the bush rats scuttled as she stood there with liquid knees. The stones on the road rolled toward her by themselves. Darkness had always been her friend, something to walk in feeling safe, wrapped up in mystery, the speckled silver of the universe the only light she needed. But tonight the sky was against her. Bats and devils. A skinny moon. Moths and mosquitoes and tumble-fly sifting about her ankles. A half hour passed and no one came. No bicycle, no Sami. "He is very tall and very black," Aka had said, "about nineteen. And he makes plenty cash from the bicycle." Sami, who was from the next village, was well known for riding women back from Ighetu Market with melons and bunches of plantain, the old and crippled to engagements at their relatives' houses, and occasionally, for a higher fee, he colluded in great nocturnal escapes such as Ida's. Always at two in the morning at the same pickup point, by the water pump at the edge of Aruwa.

She heard no one. She stood in the middle of the road, turning, panicked, her bag swaying, and searched through her choices.

Nne-Nne and Baba would still be asleep, Baba on his back with his royal mouth open and Nne-Nne in the space left over. She could go back now, creep back past the clay pots along the mud-pressed wall and the tiny doorless room where they slept and pretend she had never been as brave as this. Unpack her shabby things and lie down in the dark. The night would pass by and as she slept she would lodge her dreams back into the corner where they were dreamed, on a three-legged stool in a web of shade with the wooden shutters closed. In the morning she would start preparing to marry the man with the puckered face. There were things to do. Baba, Aruwa's chief tailor, the first person in the village to own a sewing machine, had to start on the dress. She'd stand by the crooked coffee table with her arms raised and stare out of the window while he took her measurements. Nne-Nne, under the baseball cap she wore every day that stole from the world her cheekbones, would scribble it all down with her quick, diligent hand while giving Ida the occasional acquiescent nod. And then there'd be the long walk to Ighetu for the shopping, the visits, the meetings for the final negotiations and the exchange of capital. The day would come and never go, like bitterness. She would disappear into Thomas Afegba and join the chickens, goats and tomato shoots in his colony of property.

Or she could walk. If Ida was the true worthy grandchild of Cecelia Remi Ogeri Tokhokho, buried next to her husband under the washboard in the backyard, the only woman in Aruwa history to shrink the world, to have made it alone to Lagos and come back twenty-three years later rich and self-made, smoking a cigar, wearing scarlet lip gloss and cackling, she would walk. And walk for all the days it took.

Cecelia had left designs on Ida's future. When Ida was thirteen she had asked her parents if she could stay on at school with her brother so that she could become "a big businesswoman like Granny." Nne-Nne had chuckled, looking up from her weaving in front of the house, and said, "Ida, we are not in city." "I don care!" Ida shouted. "I wan to learn." Nne-Nne was taken aback. *The cheek,* she thought, *the backchat of this child.* Ida stood over her in front of the sun with one hand on a skinny hip, glaring, and it struck Nne-Nne, as it often did, how much she was like Baba, with her temper and her fire, and like Baba's mother before him. Nne-Nne imagined that Cecelia was just the same when she was a young girl. The stubbornness, the big ideas; things that only sons could use. Nne-Nne had lived in Aruwa all her life. She was married at sixteen, children quickly followed, she had never questioned what God had given her. If there was a slither of curiosity about the things she had never seen or done, Ida dramatized this for her, with her tantrums and her foolish dreams, and Nne-Nne had a special affection for her because of it. Eventually, she was sure, Ida would come to understand that here, in Aruwa, life was only as wide as the village and in the end women always became their mothers. That was how it was.

Nne-Nne had tried to sound sympathetic. She'd said, "Ida, my child. There is only one Cecelia."

Baba had also refused, his belly falling over his drawstring, fiddling with the aerial on the radio he'd recently acquired as part of his eldest daughter Marion's dowry. "For wha?" he grunted. "Your motha can teach you anyting you ave to kno." The radio scratched across the airwaves unable to latch onto anything coherent and Baba seemed to forget she was there, standing aching in a trail of light that fell across the room. Ida begged. "Two years more," she pleaded, raising her voice, and Baba shot back with, "Child! You wan to mek trouble!"

Since then Ida had lain in dreaded wait for the Thomas moment.

While the shifty radio crackled across Nigeria and the rest of the world, she cooked, sewed and cleaned, walked the roads to the fields and picked vegetables after the rain. She ate little and developed a frown. Daydreamed on the three-legged stool about Cecelia, and lip gloss, and taking giant steps across whole countries. She washed clothes and killed chickens, she learned from Nne-Nne how to cook moi-moi and egusi stew the way they were meant to be cooked, with acceptance, conviction and instinctive amounts of crayfish and cayenne pepper.

When Thomas Afegba came for her she was in the kitchen stran-
gling a chicken. He was talking to Nne-Nne and she noticed, through
the curtain of beads, that he was big and stout with a large mouth,
wearing an expensive *agbada* that was tight around his chest. He
lacked youth, grace, beauty and tenderness—all of them. Nne-Nne
had one of her best wrappers on and no baseball cap, which was not a
good sign. She only wore her best wrappers and no baseball cap at
weddings, initiations, village meetings, funerals and preliminary negotiations with suitors for her daughters. As the sun lay down and
stroked Baba's sewing machine, Thomas Afegba whispered with Nne-
Nne while Ida squeezed the chicken's neck. It squawked and flapped
and Ida wondered, seething, what Baba would take for her. Would it
be another radio, with a clearer sound? A goat or even a bull? Was she
worth Aruwa's first television? The chicken, hysterical now in its final
struggle, battled with Ida's hand. Its feathers were taking flight. She
slammed it down on the table and brought the knife down, sending
blood splattering up onto her face.

A week later Baba came to an arrangement with Thomas, whom
Ida had not yet been introduced to. Two goats. Four hundred niara.
And a portable television from England.

Up close Thomas was dented, she could see, in the cheeks, but this
was not the central problem. Neither was he entirely lacking in charm,
of a gruff and aging kind. The problem was that as he leaned into her
she discovered that he smelled of peanuts and tobacco like Baba,
which couldn't be right, your husband to smell like your father. When
she looked up into his stranger's face she felt the weight of his shadow,
and she knew that underneath that shadow no businesswoman and
no new Cecelia would be nurtured.

She refused him. With a fever in her gut and a stare past his temple,
she refused him, and told the hand he held in his to be cold.

After Thomas and Baba had shaken hands and Thomas had
strolled away, Baba sat down and went back to his sewing as if there

was nothing wrong with buying a television with your daughter. "Don worry," he said with his back to her, "Thomas will look afta you very well."

The rage made her run and she landed on bony Uncle Aka. He was emerging from his house in a topless straw hat and a thin white shirt, slightly drunk from palm wine, light rain on his roof, and an empty afternoon. Ida came hurtling toward him and it was hard to make her out. She looked like a lunatic, or a hurricane. He said, "Child! You no look fine-o," and Ida gabbled, her face soaking wet from tears and rain and refusal. "Oncle!" she cried, "I no go marry him, I run away, I run away dis night!" Aka hugged her and took her in. He sat her down and gave her wine. "Thomas Afegba?" he asked. "You mean de big Thomas from Inone? Your fatha kno im at all?" Because there were also the rumors (which Aka was always privy to) of the occasional beating which, although this was not unheard of, would not sit well with a girl who carried fire inside her like Ida did. It called for action, something severe and immediate.

"You bin to Lagos city befo?" Aka asked, looking sly.

Ida stopped sobbing. "No, Oncle. Neva."

Her choices. Thomas and puckers, or Lagos and hope and maybe love. It was not so far from Aruwa to a dream and Ida's legs were strong. She started walking and in the dark trees Cecelia's ghost blew her onward. Cecelia sang, "Go and find it, child, your dreams are down that way, go and find them, child." The water pump became a fresh memory. She bounced over the potholes and cracks and puddles of the only road she'd ever known and thought about the bright heaving city at the end of it. Big sturdy houses, music everywhere, a college. A cinema where a man in a canvas suit and hair the same color would buy her a Fanta and she would sip it slowly, through slick, saxophoned love scenes, while he looked sideways at the sepia glow on the high curve of her cheek.

Sami saw the solitary figure in the road with the swish in her skirt. The way she walked could only be the walk of a woman traveling alone to Lagos in the middle of the night. He pedaled toward her, the tires growling through the stones, the bicycle wheezing with age, and when she heard him she turned and flashed a smile and her hand flew to her chest. "Sista, you are brave-o," said Sami. "Get on." Ida sat down on a wooden slab over the back wheel and stuffed her skirt behind her knees. Twice it got caught in the spokes, much to his irritation. She held his waist as lightly as she could and they didn't speak much. Ida thought about Nne-Nne, lying asleep in that small space. She wished she could have told her she was going and said good-bye properly. She briefly touched the beads around her wrist. The bicycle dipped and lumbered, Sami's long thighs like spider's legs walking through the fading night, all the way to Ighetu, where the bus picked her up at dawn.

AUBREY DREAMED OF another kind of escape, not from a future but from a past. He and Ida met somewhere in the middle, in Lagos, a hundred miles from Aruwa and three thousand miles from Bakewell (because the past was a lot farther to run from). Dean Baxter, his mother, his father, his shame—all of it had left Aubrey with a fascination with movement. He loved airports, train stations, bus stops, highways, even car parks (multistory, the top floor) for their eternal promise of departure. The silver men on the mantelpiece who never actually went anywhere, that silver horse galloping, the swinging and spinning and rocking, they kept him aware of the comfort of journeys and their power of erasure. A new place, a new face.

When Aubrey was a boy, too young to pack a suitcase and board a train from Bakewell to anywhere, he'd find a spot by the river Wye and seek a new reflection in the rippling gray water. He'd change his name to Paul or David or Anthony and call Dean Baxter exactly one hundred indecent names. Beggar, for stealing his lunch. Lazy sod, for making him do his math homework or else he'd knock his teeth out. Filthy flaming thug for knocking his teeth out, one at the front, one back right, when Aubrey, in a moment of recklessness, had returned to Dean two pages of grossly incorrect sums so that he failed the monthly math test. Bastard, oh yes, you pilching pickled bastard, for tripping him up so that he fell flat on his face, a great palm-grazing, satchel-hurling crash, in front of Miss Jacqueline Flynn, the only girl in school that Aubrey had ever dared to fancy—she was flame-haired and perfumed and well-to-do, way out of his league, but she was new; and anything was possible when things were new.

Stinking louse. Fat-faced dimwit. Pig-breath, dog-muck and bound for hell. One hundred was a nice round number. When he'd finished, Aubrey would stand up a foot taller with a gentler nose and hair that was not the same color as condensed milk, stride back home with a stranger he liked and start again. He became so multiplied he forgot himself. His thoughts were crowds of figures, perfect algebra, subtractions and divisions and multiplications and conversions from inches to centimeters, yards to meters, miles to kilometers, bombing his senses and never leaving space for the true naked feel of inadequacy. He avoided mirrors and they avoided him.

If it wasn't for his mother, who never failed to remind him, with unconditional devotion, with a dangerous love, of what he lacked, he might forever have escaped himself. When Judith Hunter let out one of her throatless, quivering laughs and said, "My Aubrey might not be much to look at but he's my Einstein all right," he'd wince and count the potatoes and pretend he wasn't there. Auntie Mave and Uncle Cyril would be over for Sunday lunch, and Wallace Hunter, the strapping hulk at the head of the table whose brawn had bypassed Aubrey to such an extent that Wallace sometimes wondered about his wife's fidelity around the time of Aubrey's conception, would be sawing into his Yorkshire beef, sleeves rolled up, the table legs trembling, and chew like a starved rhinoceros, pausing sometimes to breathe or ridicule his wife. "Einstein?" he'd shout. "Einstein? I bet Einstein's as poor as muck and impotent to boot!" He'd shake the house with laughter, Harold and William, Aubrey's older brothers, joining in with their biceps and triceps bulging, their mouths stuffed with roast potatoes, while Aubrey sat sweating next to his mother. "Now, dear," she'd say, "you *know* that's not true, don't make fun." Then she'd pat Aubrey's hand under the table and wobble her head, dabbing at her mouth with a serviette and sliding a humble look toward her sister.

But Wallace liked to push things. He liked to drag a joke, a dig, a lifelong humiliation to the very end of possibility (WE ARE HUNTERS, went the family motto on the wall, WE HUNT). "You know him, then, do you? Been to Bakewell, has he, then, eh?" Wallace boomed, throwing a wink at Harold and William, a gotta-keep-'em-in-check-son wink that Aubrey both despised and admired for its effortless domination. "Is there something you're not telling me, Jude?"

The chairs cried out. Three burly men clutched their burly bellies and Cyril and Mave lowered their eyes hoping Judith hadn't bothered with dessert.

"Harold . . . Willy," Judith tried, kneading them with howling eyes. She had a lilac cardigan that she wore on these occasions with an old pair of pearl earrings her grandmother (in sepia on the sideboard) had given her the night before her wedding, and by now the lilac and the sore blush in her cheeks and her seaweed eyes made her look like a fresh bruise. "No, dear, of course I don't know Einstein personally, *silly!*"—the quivering laugh toward Mave—"Oh, isn't he *silly!* No, what I meant was that, well"—a pat on Aubrey's knee—"I'm sure that my Aubrey is perfectly capable of . . . well . . . you know . . ."

Wallace is not helpful. "No, dear, I have no idea what you're on about."

"Well . . . you know . . ."

"Well, well, bloody well what, then, come on, woman!"

"*Performing,* dear, *performing,* you know! *Honestly,* Wallace." And Aubrey would cough suddenly and feel his insides drooping. Seven potatoes left and thirteen sprouts. "Auntie Mave," he'd say over the noise, their best china jug and saucer rattling in his hands, "more spuds?"

Judith meant well and he loved her. She was the only other human being he felt he resembled. From each other they received comfort and a certificate of being. At 9:20 on winter nights Judith slid a hot-water bottle under Aubrey's blankets, for his bones and the aches of isolation. On Saturday afternoons his drawer was stocked carefully, prettily, with clean socks, vests and Y-fronts. And on Sundays, fresh pink tulips from the stall by the cemetery adorned his windowsill.

Aubrey was the daughter Judith never had.

He was fragile and needful, oh, he was practically a *baby*, her boy. "A child's mother is his only safe shelter," Judith often quoted from Hilda Beaty's *A Mother Knows* to anyone who'd listen. It was she who sat with him through the stretching evenings sipping sherry and knitting in front of the telly while Harold and William were out "making romance," she put it, with Linda and Jean from number fourteen; who stroked his milky head and said "They don't deserve you, dear" when Aubrey complained (once, never again) of the girls not being interested in him and having no other option on Saturday nights when the world demanded it was time to party but to trot along with loud, spitty Arthur to a bosomy place where mad old men slumped in corners. "But you will find a lovely girl one day," she assured him. "Be patient. We must face these things with fortitude, and"—she giggled— "a little tiny glass of sherry."

How he needed her. How she obliged. And then one day he left.

She called out from his Ovaltine, "You'll never get it, dear," when he applied for the job that would get him out of Bakewell, out of his mother's clutches, out from under his father's big toe, and away, as far away as a stamp could get him from the teddy bears on the walls, the pink tulips on Sundays, and the sweet-smelling pants in the drawers. "They'd *never* take on a timid little thing like you in *London*, now, would they, silly," the word *London* sounding too heavy for her tongue. Because cities, capital cities in particular, were no place to live, no, not for her Aubrey. They'd eat him alive with HP sauce and chips and then what would she do? Cities were full of animals. They were rude, *rude*, they were colder than a Derbyshire winter. Once in her life she'd been to London, with Wallace on her honeymoon, and she got knocked down at Victoria Station in the pedestrian zone, by the pedestrians, flat on her back with her stockings out.

"Anyway"—she's stirring three spoons of sugar into the Ovaltine— "what's wrong with the post office? It's perfect for you. They'll always need a good head for figures there, won't they, dear. My best boy! Now come and get your nightcap."

Aubrey was twenty-nine. He was losing hair. It was an age when despair either took the mind or changed into determination. The latter was where these words came from: *I am a precise and proficient worker with a keen eye for detail and a good head for figures. I approach all my duties with loyal intentions and am eager to acquire new skills leading to greater responsibility.* The stamp was licked. The Ovaltine had gone cold. Judith Hunter sat downstairs alone in a half-light, the ends of her knitting needles flicking with an unusual speed.

Alders Financial liked his writing. It was not easy in banking to find a numbers whiz with a good hand. And he was a smart fellow, always in a tie well knotted (though perhaps a little too tightly) and polished shoes. They started him off administrating in business accounts and Aubrey moved into a room in Pimlico where, for the first time on winter nights, he experienced the crisp and finite discomfort of cold linen. He read most evenings, spy novels and the banking press, in the pool of a standing lamp. At work, too terrified of getting anything wrong, he was impeccable, infallible; he wasted very little time conversing with colleagues and very little money eating in overpriced restaurants. He got promoted, quickly, first to auditor and eventually to the oil clients at the top of Alders's corporate priority list. They sent him away, much much farther than any stamp he'd ever imagined.

"Nigeria? But where's that, dear?" she asked, sounding older.

"It's in Africa, Mother," said Aubrey, standing in a phone booth on Victoria Street with a nasty draft getting through his socks.

"Africa? What d'you want to go there for? It's full of flies, you know. They get all in your supper."

"Mother . . ."

"You'll starve. They're all starving over there, Aubrey dear. I'm sure I heard it on the news once, little children, all dying of malnutrition, poor mites. And all those flies! There's mosquitoes, too, you know—they bite."

"Mother, I—"

"Oh, are you sure, dear? It's so far away. How far is it, dear? And why haven't you phoned in so long?"

"I phoned last fortnight."

"Well, you used to phone every week. You *used* to phone every *day*."

"I never phoned every—"

"Are they looking after you properly there, dear? Is someone doing your cooking? Oh, I suppose you can cook a bit, can't you, you can make beans on toast and mashed potato. But what about your washing? You can always send it to me, you know, I'll get your father to send it back, I'm sure it won't cost that much, honestly, I don't mind, I don't have that much to do now with—"

"I can do my *own* washing, Mother!" Aubrey snapped.

A fretful silence squirmed down the line and scratched his ears.

"Sorry."

He looked for something to count. There were eleven holes in the telephone dial.

"Don't interrupt your mother, Aubrey. What's happening to my best boy, ay? You'd never've spoken to me like that before . . . your dear old mum. Aubrey? Are you still there?"

"Yes"—he jerked his tie loose—"but I don't have time to chat really."

"You haven't spoken to your mother in *two weeks* and you don't have time to *chat*?"

Aubrey pictured her fingers scuttling around the top button of her housedress. He hadn't the nerve to tell her how long he'd be gone. It could be a year, it could be five. When he went to say good-bye, standing in the hallway in a long winter coat and a new pair of glasses with a softer lens that kept his eyes from her, he told her maybe six months and that was bad enough. Judith burst into tears and shuffled off to the kitchen for another glass of sherry.

He got fizzy with excitement. The very best things about the journey were: (1) that sound, "BA556 to Lagos, now boarding"; (2) the simple freeing fact of flying; and (3) the dinky plastic supper, not least the pudding.

LAGOS WAS THE loudest place on earth. Traffic, markets, dust storms and shouting. Music rocketed out from open windows. Traders wandered through the dust and obstructed the traffic, with trays on their heads selling plastic lighters, broken batteries and peanuts. Bodies and their handbags hung ruthlessly to the outsides of buses. Stout crooked skyscrapers rumbled at their bases and men in open shirts walked by. Children burst out from alleyways and corners and it was chaos. It was heat.

She was seventeen and he was thirty-two then. A shabby cinema with wooden benches on Lake Street. The film was *West Side Story* and Aubrey wasn't the same as the other guys. He had on too many clothes—and a tie! He was white with hair too white to be blond and he had the look of someone who was always alone; as Ida was alone, torn between the home she missed and Cecelia's lofty example. Aubrey Hunter and Ida Tokhokho met in darkness, just as Tony and Maria spotted each other across the dance-fight between the Jets and the Sharks, just before they floated toward each other in dream bubbles and almost kissed.

Ida and her friend Betty had no money and were dying for a drink. Sweat was traveling down from their armpits to their waists. Their mouths were drying and on the next bench Aubrey leaned back with a warm beer, and stole looks at Ida, and swigged. Betty said, "Aks your friend to buy us a drink, eh. My throat feel like desert." When Ida had arrived in Lagos, wild-eyed and wretched, Betty had helped her find her way to Uncle Joseph's street, which Aka had made her write down on the inside of her hem. All the way on the bus Betty had talked non-stop about her brother's new barbershop in Lagos Island and how she was going to help him build it up. And she had. She got free hairdos whenever she wanted them, the most recent, burgundy extensions all the way down her spine. Ida was taking night classes to finish her schooling and sewing the neighbors' tatty clothes during the day. She had not spoken to Nne-Nne or the rest of her family since she'd left Aruwa.

With her head kept down she turned and saw Aubrey watching her. "You aks him," she said to Betty, who hissed back, "It's not me he likes, is *you*. Go na, aks him." As they whispered, huddled together like new-born chicks, Aubrey clambered over. He felt that he was riding a wave, and he could see her waiting for him at the end of a tunnel of water. His hands got sticky. He swigged and then he said, over the music, "Would you like a drink, a drink?" Betty was relieved. Ida smiled (What a smile, he thought) and said, "Please yes, we are thirsty," and he loved the need of it, the thirst, and the idea that he could quench it. He bought her a Fanta and Betty a beer, ice water sliding down the bottles. Ida sipped. He watched. Later he drove her home through the settling evening as a single stroke of night colored the sky indigo. Lagos continued, wide-awake with streetlights, crickets and speeding cars. Before he drove away, Aubrey asked what her favorite color was—red, she said—and could he come back tomorrow.

If love is a quenching of loneliness, a substitute for a dream or a filling of a void, they fell into each other headfirst with their eyes closed, touching each other's different chests and different hair in Aubrey's air-conditioned bungalow. He told her, "I'm no good with people mostly, but you're nice." She showed him the flea markets where lanterns hung against bamboo stalls and they walked through the alleys eating akara cakes. "My mother," she said, "she makes the best akara in Nigeria, believe it." They never held hands or touched in public places; Aubrey preferred to show his increasing affection with gifts. He bought her a whole new red wardrobe and promised, if she returned with him to England, to buy her a sewing machine.

They were married within a year, strangers still, unaware of the knots hidden inside waiting for the right amount of time and neglect to unravel them. He took her home to a hedge-lined house by a river and a motorway with red crinkled windows in the porch, and a loft. Aubrey was glad to be away from the raucous noise of Lagos, and there were times when he thought he could still hear it from Neasden.

Ida's early reaction to England was mostly a prolonged state of shock. She was shocked by the cold and the coldness that went with it. Up and down Waifer Avenue, or along the foggy city streets during their drives to Kilburn, she stared at the way people slid past one another without a flicker of curiosity, at how fast they walked, speeding around trees and lampposts to avoid contact. "How your body?" they asked one another at home. "Where have you been? I haven't seen you." No one asked questions here. They were silent and their joys and hurts were private. She told Nne-Nne (the flame of her, in the mind) everything, how strange it was, how she missed home. She pictured the cheekbones shining in the sun and the battered baseball cap and whispered, "Nobody here know my name, or where I am from."

Opposite the mirror in the hallway, so that you could see it if you saw yourself, Ida put up an ebony carving of an old spirit woman with horns. "It will give us wisdom," she told Aubrey, "and wise children." Aubrey wasn't altogether convinced. He thought it looked mucky, like something off the rag-and-bone cart. In the dining room he lined the main wall with miniature watercolors of the English countryside: the jade ocean at Land's End, a willow tree in a field of buttercups, the misty mouth of the river Wye. "Now that's what I call a sight," he said.

Ida put more heads all over the house, on shelves and windowsills. From the top of the stairs an eyeless black mask with a freakish mane of straw hair "protected them," Ida said, from the evil that was every-where. (*For goodness' sake*, thought Aubrey.) And finally, for the living room, Aubrey chose, very carefully, a large-scale tapestry of the Derbyshire dales. They were colliding, silently, through geography.

In 1967, Bel was born. Isabel. She surprised them both for the canyons of love a child can throw open. She had Ida's temper and Judith's green eyes. "My eyes, fancy that! She's a cute one, oh, she is!" Judith said when she hurried down from Bakewell for the christening (the others couldn't make it). Ida had only met Aubrey's mother twice before, once at the wedding and then a few months afterward when she had stayed for the weekend and given Ida cookery lessons covering Sunday roasts (including Yorkshire pudding) and shepherd's pie. "Got to keep our men happy, haven't we," Judith said slowly, for they had trouble understanding each other's accents. Ida found that Judith made her feel tired, even over the telephone, when she called to check that Aubrey was being looked after properly, and to let Ida know she would be happy to provide more cookery lessons whenever she wanted. Ida told Aubrey, "Your motha fuss too much, it's not right," upon which Aubrey flew to Judith's defense, a little hysterically, Ida thought.

Judith made Ida miss her own mother even more. As she watched her the day of Bel's christening, fussing over the cradle in her old-fashioned pearl earrings, she wished it was Nne-Nne standing there instead. She wished it so hard that she saw it. Nne-Nne, in an orange wrapper and headwrap, in this lonely house in Neasden, gazing down at her new granddaughter. "Welcome, sweet girl," Nne-Nne said, "to our hearts and our home."

It was Bel and Nne-Nne who kept Ida in good spirits through days that stretched for miles, days whose endings began to bring Aubrey home with a bitter smell on the edge of his breath. Aubrey had come to realize that there was a part of him that was a stranger to the world and everything in it, and that was therefore supremely incapable of succeeding as a human being. He was a marvelous failure locked in Judith's love and Wallace's scorn. He complained to Ida about his sloppy colleagues at work, about Bel crying all the time, about his

Yorkshire pudding being subpar. In solitary moments he looked down at the baby as she slept and was terrified by her frailness, and he became increasingly unnerved by Ida's whisperings and cryptic laughter. *We must face these things with fortitude, and a tiny glass of sherry.*

Sometimes he got home late, and sat up with a glass by his side, which he refilled at intervals. Once he woke Ida up in the middle of the night and told her, standing at the end of the bed looking lost and menacing, that the fridge was dirty and tomorrow she should clean it. Then he went back downstairs. In the morning, he was asleep in his armchair and there was a note on top of the fridge. It said: *Clean the fridge. And the floor's dirty too.* He went to work that day later than usual. She made him a cup of tea before he left. He didn't mention the fridge.

It was not often, it was mostly never, that they said I love yous. Instead, after dinner while she was ironing, Aubrey might bolt forward in his chair with an encyclopedia on his lap and say, "My God! Did you know that the blue whale's tongue weighs more than an elephant and it can go for six months without food? Well, I never!"

The lights were on. There were no princes and no angels on the ceiling. But somewhere, he loved her. He bought her a sewing machine with a three-year guarantee from John Lewis. A Singer, like Baba's. And he arranged a short holiday in Lagos for her and Bel, where Ida had a brief, stilted reunion with Baba and Nne-Nne at Uncle Joseph's house. Baba was still bitter; Nne-Nne was still hurt, if covertly overjoyed to see Ida again. It was difficult to say good-bye, and when Ida returned to Neasden, to the clouds and the gloom and Aubrey, her homesickness took on a new intensity and the bath became her refuge. Years slipped by. She soaked for hours as her body swelled with the twins. She told Bel about the singing tree and the millions of stars in Aruwa, and she wrote messy, doleful letters home that she never sent because there was shame in her unhappiness. In return, she received no letters back. Nne-Nne had never written a letter in her life, and Baba, Ida assumed, had nothing to say to her. In the evenings, to keep herself from despair, Ida sat down before the sewing machine in the dining room, to make her magic dressing gown.

She had three pieces of fabric: a white and copper kente she'd brought back with her from Lagos, an explosion of stars on a black background bought from a fabric shop in Harlesden, and the third a design of Nne-Nne's, amber and disco blue shooting through each other like the inside of champagne.

As she sewed one piece to another in cyclical patchwork, she came across a road. Not a strange road, with headlights or danger, but one to take her back, to remind her of who she was and where she had come from. Inside champagne, Ida saw the water pump and the bushes moving in the breeze. There were home skies in her yard of universe; there was ancient bark singing old songs in the copper. She imagined, as she sewed, that she was the needle, walking along Aruwa slopes, back through the village, her footsteps soft and steady like slow rain into sand. Bel was six years old then and already having dreams. She named the dressing gown magic, because it made her mother shine, and probably fly.

Sekon

Would there be television? Would there be *Dallas*? Could they watch Sue Ellen wake up in the morning with her makeup on and would there be music? Did Nigeria sell nectarines? Would there be a loft and could they take the beanbags because three years was a long time, longer than any place they'd ever been, and there'd definitely be decisions. Were they ever coming back? Were they emigrationing? Ida was behaving as if they were. She kept shopping, every day. She wasn't in when the twins and Kemy got back from school (Would there be school? Would there be uniforms?) and Bel had to be their mum and toasted-sandwich provider until Ida came home, laden with plastic bags splitting from the weight. She bought wholesale. Ordinary things that were a part of life, like shampoo and bubble bath, soap bars and clothes and toys, as if this were her last chance to get them. Didn't they sell soap there, or shampoo? She even went south of the Thames to Brixton with Bel on a Saturday and bought fabric and false hair and cocoa butter. Brent Cross, aglow and bulging with Christmas, became a weekly expedition. And Aubrey complained about the money, that he wasn't made of it, and just because Alders was paying for everything it didn't mean Ida could behave as if her husband was an oil tycoon and they lived on a ranch.

Would there be Christmas? Couldn't they go after Christmas? Christmas was meant to be cold and snowy, not hot, and Nigeria was hot. Most of the clothes they were taking and that Ida was buying (the best so far: two identical bow-strap stripy dresses, Georgia's white and turquoise, Bessi's white and fluorescent pink) were for summer, even though it was almost winter. And they'd even had their hair cut, which Georgia was still angry about because of how it went wrong. The hairdresser in Neasden was run by an Irish couple whose two daughters were the stylists. They were not officially trained. They were not up to the challenges posed by afros. The trimming of an afro required an understanding of roundness, which needed to be applied to the scissors. Mandy, the older daughter, snipped at Bessi's hair for a very long time, looking confused, flicking her brown bob from side to side, until it was not the trim Ida had asked for but a full-blown, four-inch transformation that sent Bessi into a torrential grief there in front of the mirror, watching her face getting soggy. Ida and Aubrey were sympathetic. Ida called Mandy useless (the coming of Nigeria was making her vocal, even feisty) and Aubrey refused to pay. Georgia was also sympathetic—"Don't worry, Bess," patting her. "You still look pretty"— until the sacrifice of her own hair was suggested as the only solution. They were twins. They had to look like twins. Georgia's hair must also be cut, to the same length. But not by Mandy, by her sister, the other one, by Emma, who got it wrong, even wronger than Bessi's. She took five inches off and Georgia was bitter, even toward Bessi, probably for the first time.

Georgia and Bessi didn't believe in looking absolutely the same because that was there in their faces, almost, though Georgia's features were fuller, she had rubyness in her lips, and wider, browner faraway eyes with lashes that hit the sky. But these differences were almost invisible to outsiders. They were the same, like dolls. They were twoness in oneness. When they'd started primary school one of their classmates, Reena, got them to stand next to each other on the wall in the playground, not moving, while she counted differences. There were five. Reena wrote them down and put them on the notice board:

1. Georgia's mouth is biggist.
2. Georgia has big ears, Bessie don't.
3. Bessie's eyes are smallist.
4. Georgia is half an inch tallest and a bit fatter.
5. Georgia has a beauty spot by her mouth—she is pretteist.

They got cornered at lunch by people checking, pointing, looking for more differences. Were Bessi's teeth slightly more crooked and was Georgia's face rounder? And Georgia, doesn't she walk with her feet pointing outward, like a penguin or a ballerina, whereas Bessi points hers inward as if she's knock-kneed?

The real differences, the ones that mattered most, were inside, under clothes and in the soul. There was light and there was shade.

If they wore different colors it meant that they could be whole people inside themselves, because people could see that Georgia was Georgia, in turquoise, and Bessi was Bessi, in pink. There were pink thoughts and turquoise thoughts, with white stripes. This meant so much more than a red stitch inside the collar, which was how Ida and the teachers used to differentiate their old green Puffa jackets when they were six, before they'd discovered the ability of color to make a half into a one. A half of green into a whole land of pink. A half a question (for sometimes even their parents couldn't tell one from the other) into a whole turquoise question.

"Who's going to look after the roses while we're away?" Georgia asked in the car on the way to Brent Cross for more shampoo and candles for when the electricity went off. "The roses need water, and what if it doesn't rain?"

The journey was only three weeks away and the questions came all the time now, unexpectedly, to anyone, even to Judith on the phone, who warned them continuously about mosquitoes and malaria and said their father was being extremely irresponsible, dragging them all that way away to the perils of Africa. Aubrey told Georgia he'd ask Mr. Kaczala next door to water the roses. All he had to do was put the end of his hose over the fence. "Every day," said Georgia, "tell him he has to do it *every day*—if he doesn't they'll die."

"*And* the apples," said Bessi, starting to panic, "*and* the apples, *they* need water, too, and Mr. Poland's—"

"Kaczala's," corrected Bel.

"—hose won't reach all that way! Isn't it. And who's going to pick them up?"

"The lodgers can do that," said Aubrey, loosening his tie. "Don't make such a fuss."

Bessi tutted. The Little Ones, especially the twins, were not happy about the lodgers. Who were they? Why couldn't they live in someone else's house? What if they wouldn't give it back? What if they broke things and messed things up, or accidentally burned it down and there was nothing left when they got back but boards and ashes, and holes? "No one's sleeping in *my* room," Kemy declared when Aubrey told them about the lodgers over dinner—he may've been promoted again, he said, but it wasn't cheap, feeding a family and paying the bills, and one day they'd see for themselves. Kemy was also disgruntled about missing the school trip to the chocolate biscuit factory next spring. She wanted to get wild and staggered on chocolate, like the twins had when they'd gone, and now she'd miss it, she wasn't happy at all, and the lodgers were the last straw.

For the twins it was an even deeper violation. "*And ours,*" they said together. "No one's sleeping in *our* room, either." Because the loft was their house, it was full of secrets and thresholds. It belonged to them. The thought of strangers sleeping in 26a and treating it like home was like imagining someone moving into your stomach, into your head, into your dreams.

"Of course they are," Aubrey had said, not understanding the intrusion of it. The lodgers were a big family. Six children, two parents, and a grandmother. The grandmother would live in the loft with the youngest girl (apparently, they were inseparable, and the grandmother liked having a private bathroom); two more girls would be in Kemy's room and three boys in Bel's.

"But *nooo!* They can't," shouted Bessi. "It's *our room.*"

"*Yeah!*" said Georgia.

"Well then, would you like to pay the mortgage while we're away?" Aubrey snapped.

The twins didn't understand what a mortgage was but they knew it was expensive and you had to work, and you had to be older than eight (and nine as well—they were nine in January) to work, unless you became a robber like Oliver Twist, which was definitely impossible because they had parents.

The whole thing was getting out of control. They were losing their home. They were losing Christmas. They were going to summer when it was winter. They were going against the grain of their lives. For three years Georgia wouldn't be able to stand next to Ham's grave and wish him good wishes, or water roses (did Nigeria have roses?), and Bessi wouldn't be able to lead the apple army (apples?) up the garden path. They'd grow older, and become foreign. "Will we be Nigerians?" Kemy asked her mother, sitting next to Bessi on a suitcase that Ida was trying to zip closed. There was too much in it. Ida had emptied the shops. Everything leakable was in plastic bags and Ida was ready. She had written a brief letter to Nne-Nne and Baba to say that she would soon be coming to visit, and she did not want to go empty-handed. She paused to answer Bessi's question: "What do you mean? You are Nigerian now," she said. "But only half," Bessi pointed out. "If we live there, will we be *all* Nigerian?"

The suitcase was almost closed and Ida was bending down and using all her weight to pull the zip. Her belly was full of soft empty spaces that children had left behind. She said, "Nothing will change. It is your home." And then she added, as Bessi was about to ask another question, "You better ask your daddy."

Aubrey wasn't around much. He was working all the hours to "tie the loose ends," so Bessi went to ask Bel, who was in her room packing suitcases with Georgia: "So, what will happen when we get there? Will there be a loft?" Bessi sat next to Georgia on the side of the bed. They both looked up at Bel folding clothes and waited for her to answer. As they waited, Bel was struck by a feeling that she had seen this image before, of these two faces, looking up.

She said, "I don't think there'll be a loft. But let's wait till we get there, and see."

The night before they left, Georgia and Bessi—and Kemy was allowed, too, because it was a big good-bye—stood at the window in the loft and looked out at the evergreen tree. The moon was lying in a silver hammock, behind the tree. They had the same feeling at the bottom of their stomachs, the tremor of an oncoming journey, the feeling that this night was the end of here and tomorrow would be an unknown, a dream that was not a dream, another sun and moon, different trees, different beds. Somewhere in the darkness the world would transform. Their house would go spinning in whirls of tornado and then slow down, and they would drift. They were full of hope, and sorrow. And fizz.

The three of them held hands and Georgia prayed. "Dear God, make the plane get us there safe, and please look after the house and make the lodgers give us it back. And let it rain, in case Mr. Poland forgets." They had already written and signed their instructions to the lodgers on a sheet of paper, assisted by Bel, and pinned it to the door of the wardrobe:

Do pick Apples in Septembers
Do water the Roses if Mr. Poland (Kaczala) forgets
Don't sit on Beanbags

Don't make Anything messy
Don't make Fires

georgia   *Bessi*

They looked out over the chimneys of Neasden and registered the things that were inside them. Over there beyond the fence at the end of the garden, the school playground, where they ran at lunchtime, and shouted, and stood on the wall for differences. To the left in the far distance, the Welsh Harp, the river, with the clearing at the edge where a rope hung from a tree over quicksand and you had to be brave to swing it. The evergreen tree that was high enough to shield the moon and too far away to find.

And the smell of chocolate biscuits, with the chocolate still warm.

THE EXCESS BAGGAGE came to £146.50. Aubrey was not impressed. His back was hurting from lifting suitcases, of which there were seven. He said "Hellfire, woman," "For pity's sake," and "God almighty" to Ida, ripping out his wallet, and everyone kept quiet including the polite lady at the desk. But then he seemed to forget about it. Because he also was fizzy, as Aubrey could not help be in such environments. All these departures, the trolleys and their wheels, the taxis opening journeys, those wonderful spirited planes raising their noses to heaven. The places, he thought, all the places! Aubrey's good-bye had consisted of a study of the silver men in lamplight, the helicopter, a gentle fingertip push sending it spinning, and a last walk through the garden with a cigarette (the Little Ones had seen the glow of the ember from the loft).

They had left the house at five o'clock the next morning, in the dark, the way of beginnings.

The twins were wearing their different-color anoraks with red cords and they both had short, bumpy afros. The Hunter afros traveled through realms of texture between Aubrey's genes and Ida's genes, Kemy at one end, soft and floppy, Bel at the other, thick and coarse. The twins were somewhere in between. Georgia, with outward feet, had a new clip with a plastic daisy on the end positioned just behind her ear, and Bessi, with inward feet, had painted her nails in Glitter Girl nail varnish. Ida made them hold hands with Kemy through the crowds and queues and announcements, down the cold spaceship tunnel that joined the airport to the plane, until they were on board. Kemy refused to put her hand luggage, a Miss Piggy rucksack with hair, into the overhead compartment and started crying when Bel tried to get it off her. "Sindy's in there!" she shouted. Passengers stared, waiting to get past. "Let her keep it," said Ida. "Come, sit down." And she gave Kemy the window of a row of three, her in the middle, Aubrey by the passageway anticipating lunch. On the adjacent row of Flight BA712 Bel sat on the end, responsible for the twins, while Bessi let Georgia take the window on the condition that she would have it on the way back. "Don't forget," she said. "Bel, can you remember for us too? Bessi's sitting by the window on the plane in 1984. Okay? Don't forget." Aubrey, as he always did, told everyone to read the leaflet about what to do in an accident. They stared at the pictures of life jackets that didn't look as if they'd be able to help them if they fell out of the plane, and watched the woman at the front moving her arms around.

Six hours was the longest plane they'd ever been on; even Tunisia hadn't been this far. Georgia was worried they might run out of petrol and there'd be nowhere to stop. There was nothing up here but clouds, which couldn't hold planes, or petrol stations, because they were nothing but white. She stopped worrying when they were in heaven. This was the best bit of flying, when the plane had run off the earth and glided upward and upward right through the clouds, the seat-belt signs were off, and they were sailing. The sky turned to ocean and the wisps and rolls of clouds were its shifting islands. Whenever they were up here, Georgia saw herself and Bessi lying down on the fleecy grasses and sky-bathing. They had bikinis on, and there were

Dr. Orange ice pops for when it got too hot. They had a whole island each and spent time falling asleep, or reading books that turned their own pages, or diving off into the pure saltless blue. *It is so quiet up here,* thought Georgia, *it must be very close to God, to where he thinks.*

Apart from heaven, lunch was the second best bit of flying. The surprise of it, the questions in the flurry of air hostesses shooting up and down the aisle in their eternal lipstick. Will it be chicken? Will it be beef? What will be under those plastic rectangles covered in steamy foil? When it came, Aubrey sat forward and viewed the display. He loosened up his fingers. Beef casserole, boiled carrots and mashed potato. Crackers and cheese to the left. A bread roll and butter. Sponge pudding in the corner (sponge pudding!), and a shallow white cup for coffee. Four courses. "Smacking," he said. He ate everything and so did Bel, because she wasn't fussy. Ida didn't eat the cheese because it was straight out of the fridge, or the pudding. Bessi also left the cheese. She had to be careful. She was getting allergies, so far spinach, which made the inside of her bottom lip go lumpy (the incubator's fault).

Georgia left her pudding. Cakes were fattening. And she was the fattest.

As they ate, Kemy slept, her shaggy hair hanging over the armrest onto her mother's lap. Ida said not to wake her, that sleeps interrupted in the air were bad luck.

"That's nonsense," said Aubrey. "Where d'you hear that from?"

"It's true," Bel butted in. She was learning more and more from Ida about the truths that were called superstition. Eat with your right hand to avoid poison. Don't sleep where a mirror can see you. Turn around once if a cat, any cat, crosses your path at night. The two of them sat on Ida's bed in the late afternoons and roamed the mystical world. Bel was the only one who knew what Ida talked to Nne-Nne about and she would never tell. And last year, a week before Aubrey had received a two-thousand-pound windfall from work, Bel's palms had itched for three days.

So Kemy missed lunch. When she woke up she was furious. "I'm *hungry*," she whined. "I want lunch. I want *plane* lunch and a plane sandwich. Why didn't you wake me?"

"It's for your own good," said Bel. "Mum said so."

Kemy went on whinging. "Off we go," said Aubrey, raising his eyes. "See?"

Ida collected everyone's leftovers—her pudding, Bessi's cheese, one of Georgia's crackers, a piece of tomato in beef juice—and put it on a tray for Kemy, who remained indignant. She wanted a proper lunch. Aubrey had to ask one of the air hostesses for a whole new lunch so that he could have his postprandial nap in peace. When it came, Kemy made herself a beef-and-mashed-potato sandwich and was satisfied.

Then *Grease* came on and John Travolta took them to Nigeria in a pair of spandex trousers.

THE SOUTHERN NIGERIAN heat was different from summer in London, or a beach along the Mediterranean. It was something bestial and extreme. It did not believe in seasons or lapses into coolness, apart from the months of December and January, which weren't really cool at all. Coolness was relative. It was just two months of a lesser humidity, though a heat still thick enough to carry people off planes like floating carpets, even to make them faint. Through the day, through the year, there were simply different levels of extremity. Very warm at dawn, merciless at noon. Heavy rain from March to November, and sunny swollen rainbows waiting in the wings. The air was thermal, and when they emerged from the plane their first instinct was to undress, to undo zips and shrug jackets violently off their shoulders, to carry things, tie them around waists instead of wear them, and surrender to the throbbing four o'clock sun. Miss Piggy's hair trailed along the ground as they waded into the sweaty, shouting airport lounge. The roots of resentful afros became damp.

Aubrey dabbed his face with his hankie and Bel's eyeliner melted down her face. Ida had on a weepy, glossy smile that wouldn't end.

A man who reminded Ida of Sami was waiting for them. Troy, their towering slender driver, dressed throat to toe in white with only his forearms showing, and a beautiful round Adam's apple. He had gold plate in his mouth and a sleek matching grin. Soft-voiced, he said, "Welcome, welcome," and immediately, fourteen and panda-eyed Bel fell in love.

Troy rescued them from a riot of illegitimate porters who were pulling at suitcases to make some cash. They followed him to the carriage: a blond Mercedes parked in the shade of a coconut palm. The Mercedes had silver beams along the sides, a silver ballerina at the tip of the hood, and the headlights were smooth blazed sockets of crushed ice. Troy cleaned it twice a week, every inch, with warm water and a leather cloth, until it dazzled. Had it been made of glass, it would've been good enough to take Diana to St. Paul's.

They drove for two hours, looking for apple trees and roses, asking questions (How far is it? When does it get dark? What's that? What are those?) until the whirl of it spun them to sleep. Bel stayed awake, watching the slope of Troy's neck and the outline of his Adam's apple. They drove southeasterly away from Ikeja toward central Lagos, along the highway through grassland and wasteland and hints of savannah, down toward the coast that stretched for five hundred miles between Benin to the west and Cameroon to the east. Behind the shores where high waves made curls on the horizon was a belt of lagoons and mangrove swamps. Giant kingfishers with huge black bills made solitary journeys through the fifty-foot trunks. Shiny orange-eyed starlings with purple heads searched for wild figs and chattered up and out toward the desert. To the far east were the clustered waterways of the Niger delta, where towns slid about on sewage and watched the great ships carrying oil out into the Atlantic. Over a mesh of islands and mainland and bridges, Lagos spread itself. The traffic slowed as they skirted the commercial center, with its bright yellow buses and shiny skyscrapers and the traders wading out into the queues, and a final bridge crossed the lagoon toward Sekon.

Sekon was a quiet suburb east of Victoria Island. It had low houses and lines of sleepy palms. The houses stood well back from red roads without pavements and the gaps between them were vast, especially at night, reminiscent of an emptier time. Streetlights happened only once on every street.

Troy had put the air-conditioning on during a conversation with Aubrey about the Benin rubber industry, which Troy invested in. Full-blast ice air made a wintry car. Georgia and Bessi woke up cold, on the gravel in front of a strange new house. They were full to bursting with What is its?

"Is this it?" asked Georgia. "Are we here?" said Bessi. The twins were dizzy. Cold and hot and dizzy. It smelled of oranges. It felt as if God had turned the map in the hallway at Waifer Avenue into a liquid reality and was dipping them upside down into Nigeria. Georgia was even a little frightened as she looked around her, and she stayed very close to Bel. The house was big, with a flat white roof and crimson ivy along one side. An old dog was pissing against a cedar tree in the middle of a circular front lawn, and sprinklers around the edge threw out shell-shaped water. Next to the house was a row of tiny bungalows with blue doors. "Can me and Bessi have a bungalow?" Georgia asked. Someone grunted, a man in a string vest grabbing suitcases out of the trunk with Troy. They were carrying them into the house, and at the front door, holding it open, was a very small woman with bow legs wearing a nurse's uniform.

Troy introduced the dog as Beetle and the man in the string vest as Sedrick, the watchman. His job involved sitting in a narrow box by the front gate and opening and closing it. The rest of the time he picked sugarcane strings out of his teeth with one foot up on the wall in front of him or leaned against the cedar tree smoking. His eyes had become yellow and droopy from watching.

As they walked toward the palace the gravel growled beneath their feet. Inside was a black marble staircase speckled with white, with thin iron ankles holding one step to another. It would be a cruel place to fall. At the top of the stairs was a corridor with rooms leading off one side. On the other side were long glass windows, slanting up toward the sky. There were new bedrooms, new beds, and they fell through deep sleeps in thin sheets, Kemy with Bel, and G + B in a triangular room.

EVERY HOT DAWN for three years was announced by cockerels and prayer. On flat roofs across the country, in bell-tipped mosques with the sun at the windows, barefoot worshipers in shrouds of white sank onto their hands and knees and put their heads to the ground. The morning breeze caught the songs and they traveled south toward the ocean, leaving benedictions on breakfast, on cool showers, on scrambled eggs with red peppers and onions and Maggi sauce, the way Festus made it. Hefty Festus who ruled the kitchen in army green shirts and was married to Nanny Delfi in the nurse's uniform. They shared a bungalow and argued behind doors about territories. Nanny Delfi would tell Festus, "You don't put Maggi with eggs, can't you see they are English, mek it plain, sa," and Festus says, "Dela, they love the eggs, stay away from the food. The food pay me—the children and the clean place pay you, okay?" Then Nanny Delfi would pull at his nose and charge off with her pile of towels. She cleaned furiously, under the white sofa, across the mahogany in the study (which had a beanbag, just one), and also human beings. Once a week the twins and Kemy had to stand up in the bath and be scrubbed until they were shiny, until they were almost bleeding. The reflection of Nanny Delfi's clinical frown, with which she met nudity, could be seen on their torsos.

It became inevitable that Ida would join in the arguing, for she was incapable of accepting the concept that she should stay out of the kitchen. What did this mean? Festus kept telling her, "Don't worry, everything is under control," as a polite way of saying keep off my turf, and she didn't like it. She had been brought up in the intestines of kitchen activity, instilled with Nne-Nne's philosophy (passed down through generations of Aruwa ancestry) that a woman knows her family best, loves them best, lives her best, through the kitchen. And whether Ida agreed with this or not, parts of it had stuck, so that she felt most at home sitting near a fridge, or a boiling kettle, or making magnificent smells with new combinations of secrets. Festus would often come back from his afternoon break to find Ida chopping plantain and dropping the pieces into a frying pan of palm oil sizzling next to a pot of rice, and it filled him with fury. He complained about it to Delfi, who told him, "See, didn't I tell you about too much spices, they don like it! You won listen." When Festus eventually confronted Ida by saying simply, "It's my job to cook the food," Ida said, "It's my job too, you see." The only solution was to cook meals together. They argued until they almost agreed about measurements and coconut and chili, about menus and what to have on Thursday, and about the supremacy of yam over cassava in the preparation of eba, which was what was served on the first Christmas Day, with chicken stew, roast potatoes, and vegetables.

"No gravy?" said Aubrey.

"The stew is the gravy," said Ida.

It was a somber meal. There was no tree in the corner and no ribbon around the presents. Halfway through a potato Kemy burst into tears, slammed down her fork and said, "I want to go home. I want to watch *Top of the Pops!*" Aubrey was oddly touched. He pretended to cry and said, "The speech! I'm missing me Queen's speech! Boo-hoo!" which made Kemy laugh. There was surprise Christmas pudding for dessert (Ida had bought three, one for each year) and the Little Ones were allowed sips of brandy to wash it down.

Georgia loved eba, though not too much of it because it was fattening. For the twins' ninth birthday in January there was lots of eba (or mashed potato, as Aubrey had started calling it—but it was better than that because you could dip it in the stew with your fingers). Because they did not yet have any friends in Sekon, apart from one or two of Aubrey's dreary colleagues who lived a block away, the only guests at the party were the staff. Festus, Nanny Delfi and Ida sat on deck chairs in the shade of the orange trees while Aubrey stayed inside because of the heat. Sedrick watched everything from a distance. It was the first party of many. Georgia and Bessi were rara fairies with wands and Kemy an angel with wings made of wire and torn sheets. Bel, whom Nanny Delfi had nicknamed "Mystic Bel" on account of her bewitching green eyes, was God, in tight trousers and a cherry shirt with wide collars. She walked around the garden trying to tell everyone what to do.

"You don't look like God," said Kemy.

"How do you know? God can wear what he wants. Go and get me a Coke."

One of Kemy's wings was falling off, as angels' wings sometimes can, and she sloped across the garden for the Coke. The garden was twice the size of the one in Neasden, and it was alive. Its creatures had the kind of audacity Ham would have found terrifying. Moths were birds. Birds were harlequin bats. The spiders there were bigger than incredible, with muscled legs and visibly volatile eyes, and sometimes, even under Ida's wicked broom, they refused to die. They strutted across the radiant grass with handbags and sunglasses and filthy feet and walked all over the house, taking siestas behind doors and under pillows. Lizards waltzed up the walls, blue lizards with scales, and leaped over people's feet. There were dragonflies whose beating wings you could hear before you saw them, black and yellow ladybirds with eyelashes, tumble-fly who sucked at the blood and left shiny craters in the skin.

And cockroaches. The insect dinosaur.

God waited for her Coke, disdainfully watching Georgia and Bessi granting wishes by tapping people on the nose with their wands. It was at this point, while Bessi was granting Nanny Delfi's nose a five-star holiday in America, that a gigantic flying dinosaur landed just below Bessi's collarbone. It stayed there for a terrible, silent momentless moment. Then it stayed there, glaring up at her with busy tentacles, while Bessi screamed.

Such a beast, thought God, *and so close to the heart.*

Bessi could think of two worst things that could happen. The first was Georgia dying without her. The second was monsters. This was a monster and it was on her chest. Georgia screamed too, and Kemy ran out of the house screaming because she thought the twins were being murdered. She had also just seen a snake crawl out of the washing machine, brass-colored, with brown spots, but she couldn't tell anyone for the noise and the horror. Aubrey stepped out of the lounge with the paper dangling from his hand and said, "What the blast is going on?" Ida and Nanny Delfi shook Bessi by the shoulders to try to get the cockroach off her, but it was clinging, as if the tips of its big legs had been soaked in glue. Festus tried, he had a rougher shake, and still it clung. Bessi was getting a headache and her face was going crimson.

Now Sedrick, who had been standing by the hibiscus bushes at the edge of the garden, approached her. He stubbed out his cigarette on the way and moved very slowly, focusing on the cockroach shimmering in the sun. When he reached her, he bent down so that his nose was almost touching the monster. He could smell little-girl smells, perfumeless, clean sweat. Sedrick raised his hand and aimed toward Bessi's chest. He lifted the cockroach off her and held it in his palm. Its wide brown wings twitched. The children were still screaming. There was a sense that Sedrick and the cockroach were brothers.

And then, as if it was innocent, it flew away.

IN THE BEGINNING it was all too much. The creatures and the longing. The hot Christmas and no roses in the garden. All the strangers. That sad naked man who sometimes walked past the gate in the afternoon and stared into the house (it was the first time they'd seen in real life what a man looked like underneath clothes and it was ugly). Georgia and Bessi missed the loft and wondered about the lodgers. Were the grandmother and the little girl following their instructions? Were they tampering with the beanbags?

At night, in the first weeks, the twins met each other in the middle of homesick dreams and went back together to check. They navigated the indigo skies hand-in-hand cloud-stepping over the Mediterranean toward Neasden, and slipped through the front door, up the two flights of stairs and into their room. Things seemed unruined. The grandmother lay in Bessi's best bed gently snoring and the girl, whose name was Lynn, slept in Georgia's by the window. Lynn dreamed one night that she opened her eyes and saw worried twins in summer dresses (one pink, one blue, with stripes) standing at her bedside watching her. One of them, the taller one, said, *Don't forget the roses.* The dream made Lynn open her eyes, expecting them, but by then they'd gone. They'd left through the window and wandered down deserted Waifer Avenue to the Welsh Harp, strolled along the river and into the clearing where the rope hung. They took turns swinging and didn't fall, and the rope made twisty creaking noises from the weight.

Most times, Georgia slipped away from Bessi to say hello to Gladstone and Bessi kept on swinging. Georgia knocked on the door and Gladstone let her in and gave her hot chocolate. He wrapped a shawl around her and listened while she told him all about Nigeria, the spiders, the cockroach on Bessi's chest, the rain and the rainbows. "It sounds a wonderful adventure, my dear," he said, "but do be careful in the world." Usually she would fall asleep for a few minutes under the spell of Gladstone's voice and then she would wake up flustered, remembering Bessi, and that she was waiting for her. It was time to go, back to the heat, the crickets and the white morning songs.

These trips became less and less frequent. For home had a way of shifting, of changing shape and temperature. Home was homeless. It could exist anywhere, because its only substance was familiarity. If it was broken by long journeys or tornadoes it emerged again, reinvented itself with new decor, new idiosyncrasies of morning, noon and dusk, and old routines. Nanny Delfi singing "Amazing Grace" as they woke up, the minibus that took them to a school with one corridor and back again at lunchtime when the school day ended; Aubrey's glass being set down on a table in the middle of the night; and the long rainy Sundays spent in the upstairs hallway, looking out.

Aubrey left for work in the mornings in much the same way as he did in London, with a briefcase and a tie and Old Spice around his neck. Perhaps because he was not alone in Lagos this time, but a man of experience, with responsibilities and a wife and a family, he behaved in a more confident, sociable manner. His colleague Mr. Reed, and his American wife Mrs. Reed, had invited him and Ida for cocktails at their house on Victoria Island, and in return Aubrey had invited them over for dinner. The dinner had turned into a larger affair, with more guests and slices of pineapple on aluminum platters and even Val Doonican at midnight. Aubrey did not shout as much as he did at Waifer Avenue, and his late-night liquor was less imposing. On mornings after, when the house had slept soundly while he walked around the garden with his glass or sat in the study under lamplight, he would get up early with the heat and be ready by 6 A.M. to face the traffic. Ida, without bags under her eyes, wished him a good day. Troy chauffeured him, over the bridge into the chaos of Lagos Island. And sometimes Bel, feigning sickness to get the day off school, tagged along to keep Troy company, wearing a little denim skirt and a padded bra beneath her vest—and lipstick with lip liner to enhance her pout.

Bel had turned fifteen in August. There she was at the bottom of the marble stairs, a ring of love-heart beads around her wrist, as Troy stood in the doorway with his keys, the morning flapping at his shirt and showing her a small coal snippet of his abdomen. All the way into the center of the city, as they dodged the overcrowded buses and the holes and dead animals in the road, Bel would sit in the back behind him, coughing intermittently, waiting for the moment when her father was dropped off outside Alders' high gates and he disappeared into the world of oil and money, and they were alone, just Isabel Hunter and Troy, in a blond Mercedes, with air-conditioning. She asked him questions. Where do you live, then? (In one of the bungalows, but he also had a place in town.) What do you do on your day off? (Which was Sunday, so they never went anywhere on Sundays.) Have you got a girlfriend? (He had two, the stallion.) How old are you? (Twenty-six.) Can I come with you?

"Where?" he said.

"Anywhere."

He let her sit in the passenger seat and there were times when he'd change gear and his hand would touch her leg. There were other times when he didn't drive straight home but to the edge of the Atlantic, where they walked the dunes on Bar Beach. Bel would sit down on her favorite rock and gaze out at the water, looking mystical and mature, and she hoped he would see her like that. Mystic Bel. He asked her one question: Is this how you spell it? Bel. Yes, that's right—she smiled—that's it. Three bold letters, written in the sand.

When they got back at lunchtime the Little Ones danced in the gravel and Kemy shouted things which were ignored. "Bel fancies Troy! We know, we know, Bel fancies Troy!" Kemy was usually carrying Bumbo, the other dog, Beetle's older brother, whom she'd adopted. He had a permanent cold and a squint and was dying of old age. There were also two cats called Magika and Netty, who liked to mate, and who had just produced four Ham-sized kittens, two of which had been given away to the neighbors. Georgia especially liked the kittens, and let them wriggle about in her hands.

Georgia wondered, when she saw the way Bel looked at Troy, whether they were really truly in love and what that would feel like. It wasn't like being married, because Ida didn't look at Aubrey like that. So was it something like being a twin?

AFTER THE COCKROACH incident, the twins had developed a fascination with Sedrick. They spent a lot of time loitering around his hut, being careful not to get too close in case he had roaches in his hands. The inside of the hut didn't get sunlight, even though it had a small window. It faced away from the sun. Beneath the window there was a shelf holding only a small penknife, for undressing sugarcane.

Sedrick was not in love. Georgia knew. Because he didn't smile very much and never went anywhere apart from to the end of the road to buy three cigarettes. When he was out once, she put a marigold on the shelf next to the knife to see if it made any difference, but it didn't. Being alone inside his hut, even for that moment, made her feel like there was someone behind her who might lock her in.

The twins asked Sedrick questions: how old are you (at least thirty, they bet, but he wouldn't say), have you got a girlfriend (probably not, Georgia knew, but he wouldn't say), did he ever get bored sitting down and if so what did he do when he did, and was it possible to get a disease from holding cockroaches?

"No," said Sedrick, "only if you crush it in your hand—the blood is poisonous."

Had he crushed a cockroach in his hand, did he get sick, what was it like and how long did it take to get better?

"Not me," he said, "but I have seen it, I have seen a man die."

"*Have you?*" Georgia and Bessi said, astounded.

"Yes. And others. In the war."

"I know about the war," said Bessi. "They told us at school. They said that one million people died, isn't it."

"One million," went Sedrick.

While Sedrick was in the hut Georgia and Bessi often ran to open the gate and, being lazy, he didn't mind that. They also sprang out at him sometimes during his walks around the house with Beetle.

"Why don't you wear socks?" Bessi asked him. "You've got dry ankles and we can see them."

Georgia offered him Vaseline. "Nanny Delfi makes us put Vaseline on our feet every day and it makes them not dry."

". . . or we can steal a pair of Daddy's socks?"

Sedrick mumbled something about the heat. He didn't want socks, or Vaseline. He wanted peace, and good views of young thighs, which he savored whenever they appeared.

Among the bungalows, between his and Troy's, there was a small shower room and Bel took a shower there once while the Little Ones were having their bath. Sedrick, dawdling past, peered in through a slit in the door and saw the shimmering backs of Bel's wet sepia thighs and the edge of an early breast. He couldn't tear himself away. He settled there, bent at the door with his mouth open, and didn't hear Ida walking by with Troy's lunch, a bowl of okra soup (slime broth, Aubrey called it, because it looked like snot).

Ida spotted him and, outraged, leaped at him with the soup, turning the bowl upside down on his head so that his face got slimed hotly, with chili and paprika. Onion and tomato mush trickled down his temples. Ida cursed and damned and chased him around the cedar tree, throwing twigs at him until he begged her to stop.

"Stay away from him," she told the twins. "He's a monkey and a dog."

Sometimes Sedrick watched the twins and Kemy doing the Cartwheel Olympics in the garden. Judgments were based on who could do the most in a row, who was the neatest, and who could twist mid-cartwheel and turn it into an Arab spring, which meant a gold medal. They let him be the referee when Bel wasn't there and he decided most of the time that Georgia was the best.

THEY LEFT SEKON only once during the emigration, for an overnight stay in Aruwa. It took a lot of preparation and forewarning and did not happen until 1983. Ida sent a message via Troy, who told his uncle who knew Joseph who told Aka who told Baba that she was finally coming to visit. Baba and Nne-Nne didn't have a phone. Nor did they have a portable television. Ida had not actually spoken to them since 1969, discounting her daily head-conversations with Nne-Nne.

Word spread around Aruwa that the Tokhokhos' runaway daughter was coming, with her white husband and yellow children, and there was much kerfuffle. Many chickens were strangled and a goat was slaughtered. The market was raided for bags of gari and okra, ginger stems and sweet potatoes. The fronts of houses were swept with fan brooms and the singing tree checked its posture.

"Can I take Bumbo?" asked Kemy as the car was being loaded with Brent Cross. "No, you can't," said Bel. "He stinks." The twins giggled. They were ten now, two numbers instead of one. Ida said Bessi was zero and Georgia was one because she was oldest.

It was April. The sun had made coffee of them and against their skin white was blinding. They looked as if they'd been polished. "Are we proper Nigerians now?" Bessi had asked Ida after looking in the mirror at the end of an afternoon in the garden watching guavas grow. Guavas had replaced apples. Hibiscuses had replaced roses. Ida said Bessi could be as Nigerian as she wanted to be. She said, "Half your blood is proper Nigerian, and blood is more than skin." Bessi liked the sound of that. She told Georgia. "Mummy said we can be as Nigerian as we want to be because blood is more than skin. How Nigerian shall we be, then?" This required a beanbag. It often disappeared into the triangular room when decisions came up, most recently, when they should next pretend to be each other at school for a day (result: in three weeks) and whether they should tell Nanny Delfi that Georgia had broken a plate during a midnight feast (result: no). So Bessi fetched the beanbag from the study while Georgia set the scene—a hibiscus in a jar, a light sheet for Bessi. They sat back-to-back, deep in thought. This one took a long time, though not as long as divorce. Eyes closed, lips concentrating, Bessi spoke first: "Not all, so that we can go home in 1984." "Yes," said Georgia. "But a bit very, because that's still a long time, more than one and a half years." Bessi agreed. "We'll have to learn Edo, then," she said.

On the way to Aruwa the twins practiced saying "hello" and "how are you" in Edo. Georgia had a bow in her afro and Bessi didn't; there were thoughts with bows and thoughts without. Everyone was wearing trousers because of the mosquitoes, except for Ida, who had on a wrapper suit and headwrap made out of Nne-Nne's champagne fabric. She was gleaming at the thought of seeing her parents again, and a youthful look had returned to her face. She thought of Cecelia and had the urge to smoke.

Spaces between the signs of life grew wider. Cars disappeared into slow, rusty bicycles and there were cornfields under the hot noon sky. When the car stopped at the edge of Aruwa, the sky disappeared too. It began with two little boys running up to the Mercedes and pressing their faces up against the windows. More faces joined them, and hands. The windows became skin. Palms and lifelines and tongues blocked out the sun and the children were shouting *"Oyibo! Oyibo!"* which meant white, severely undermining how Nigerian they could be, even if they could say "hello" and "how are you."

Troy pushed his way out of the car. Some of the children ran off; others stood back and let them through, led by a boy in a Hawaii shirt with a huge beige smile. Like a sleepy carnival across the warm red dust the Hunters walked into the village, Ida in front, Aubrey holding up the rear, children skipping and gossiping around them. They approached the singing tree. Ida slowed her pace. She walked toward it and stood under the thick green leaves and leaned against the ancient bark. She closed her eyes, unconcerned about being watched. When she drifted away toward the house she began to cry. For Nne-Nne, her face, her mother, was standing there in front of her, in a proud new wrapper, calling out her name. Ida and Nne-Nne hugged for a long time, fourteen years' worth of head-conversations, and Ida almost fell to the ground with gladness.

Baba and Nne-Nne had finally gotten over her escape. Nne-Nne quicker than Baba, who had taken five years in total, including a feud of silence between himself and Aka, an overdose of palm wine and many late-night talks with the ancestors, until eventually he could see the brighter side of his loss. A daughter with a house in England amounted to more in status than a portable television did in entertainment. "Ida live jos by the Queen," he told people. "Yes, on Buckingham Road." He might not have two extra goats, but he had more opportunities for travel (though, it was true, he would probably never go farther than Lagos) and exotic *oyibo* children, golden grandsons in a distant land.

But where were they, these sons? Four girls, he counted, all in trousers! He took Aubrey aside as everyone squeezed into the living room and said, "You mean . . . no sons for Baba?"

Aubrey, in his safari suit, didn't know how to respond to this except by doing what his own father would've done, dragging from it a joke. " 'Fraid not," he said, "four little mites and not an Adam's apple in sight!" Baba was not amused—although he was impressed by the cut of Aubrey's jacket.

The parlor shrank as everyone crowded in. Baba's Singer had been moved into a corner along with his piles of fabric, and the battered radio had been replaced by a larger, newer model, with bright green buttons and a tape deck. The radio was set on a table covered with a plastic tablecloth. The rest of the room was taken up by random chairs, stools and cushions that looked as if they had been borrowed from other people's houses to accommodate the visit. Nne-Nne charged about, patting at surfaces. "Sit down," she kept saying. "Sit down!" The parlor got hotter and hotter as it filled up, and sweat started collecting along collarbones and upper lips. Aubrey ripped off his jacket. Baba studied the stitching. There was meat wafting out from beyond the bead curtain.

The girls, noting that Nne-Nne was not a woman to be disobeyed, sat down on the cushions, Bel on a chair wishing she was with Troy.

They played with their fingers while Nne-Nne and Baba stood back to inspect them. The doorway was left open; it was filling up with staring children.

"Ahh, de twins," said Nne-Nne. "Heh!" She pinched their chins roughly and studied them. "No . . . they are not de same." She held Georgia's face and shook it. "This one *little* fatta." (Georgia was dismayed.) She shook Bessi's face. "This one smalla."

It was times like this that Kemy most wished to be a twin. Wherever they went, they got all the attention. She stared up at the ceiling and it reminded her of the sun-lounge roof at home. She pointed upward and asked in a serious voice, "Is your ceiling made of corgated iron?"

"Corrugated," corrected Bel.

Baba laughed. "We made a new roof, Ida," he said. "Iron much better than reeds for when de rain is very bad." Baba went on to tell everyone how they had lived without a roof, only a sheet of plastic, while the roof was being replaced, and how some of his equipment had been soaked in sudden heavy downpours. Georgia imagined it, lying in bed at night with the stars above you, and the rain falling onto your face. She wondered whether it had rained the night Ida left Aruwa.

Ida had told them all once about when she had left the village. They were alone with her in the kitchen at Waifer Avenue, Bel and Kemy and the twins. She had told them about getting out of bed in the middle of the night and running across the compound. She had described the stars above her as she had waited in the road for Sami to come on the bicycle, and how sad she had felt to be leaving her mother. Georgia pictured it now, Ida creeping out of the house with her bag of things, and the millions of stars outside, waiting for her. She imagined that it would be a very hard thing to do, to run away and leave everything behind and not turn back.

Nne-Nne had her arm around Ida. They were still studying the twins and seemed to be conferring silently, even though Baba had moved on to an animated account of the bad harvests caused by drought a few years before. Bessi was beginning to feel uncomfortable. She hated long-drawn-out comparisons like this.

Then Nne-Nne said, "It is very special to be twins, you kno that? Your motha tell you about them—the stories?"

"*No,*" said Ida, lightly reproaching Nne-Nne. "You scare them!"

"Ah, but come, Ida, mek them tough now, not so!"

"What?" said Bessi.

"Who?" said Georgia.

"Yeah, what?" added Kemy.

Baba had stopped talking. His eyes flashed. He rubbed his hands together. "Dey *kill* dem!"

The twins looked at each other and decided they wanted to go back to Neasden. Kemy slipped her arm through Georgia's.

"Don worry," said Baba. "It's a long time ago." He stood around with his arms folded, wanting sons. Baba was the best storyteller in Aruwa, and he found that his stories were often wasted on girls because they got scared so easily.

Ida unzipped her bags and started taking out the shops—the shampoo and cocoa butter and toys and clothes. There were sighs and excited whispers at the door. "This is for Marion and the children, this is for you, this is for Oncle . . ." When the unpacking was done, Nne-Nne and Ida eloped to the kitchen and came back with plates of mountains. Buttered yam, goat stew, jollof rice with lashings of cayenne pepper that gave Bessi a rash, Kemy a fit of coughing, and Aubrey perspiration, which he dabbed with his handkerchief, sitting flushed in the ditch of an old armchair. Nne-Nne proudly passed around chicken wings and when Bel tried to decline with a "No, thank you," Nne-Nne looked her up and down as if she was a vegetarian and jabbed the plate in her face. "Tek! Eat!" she said. And Bel ate.

They all ate. With inward sighs they ate until their skin seemed thinner and they could barely speak. The only refusal Nne-Nne would accept was Bessi's declaration of her egg allergy, which meant she couldn't eat the crayfish moi-moi. "Honest," she pleaded, Nne-Nne looking suspicious. "Isn't it, Mummy? It makes my mouth sore and my face get bumps and they don't go for two days! Isn't it, Georgie?"

"Yeah," rushed Georgia. "She can't eat egg. Never! Not even scrambled how Festus makes it."

". . . and cheese," said Kemy.

". . . and spinach!" said Georgia. "It makes her teeth itch."

". . . *and* bananas," Bessi added, in case there were any coming. (Kemy and Georgia had recently started a new game of chasing her around the house with banana skins and she was tired of it.)

When they'd finished eating Nne-Nne stared disapprovingly at the food left over on people's plates. She and Ida were sitting together at the table, their thick legs brushing against the tablecloth. They muttered to each other and fanned themselves. From the open door, the many pairs of eyes were still watching.

Kemy had been thinking about what Baba had said earlier about the twins. She wanted to know what it meant, and whether it was a good story or a bad one. Was it a better story, she wondered, than her mother's story about leaving the village on a bicycle?

She spoke up and directed her question toward Baba. "Did someone get killed?" she said.

"Kemy!" Ida said. "Stop that!"

Baba was impressed. He pointed at Kemy and laughed. "This one tough already, you see! I like dis one-o!"

He sat up in his chair next to the sewing machine and said, "You sure you wan to kno?"

Kemy looked at the twins and then at Ida, who said nothing. The twins looked at each other. Bel sighed a might-as-well sigh. The four of them nodded.

"Well!" Baba shuffled in his chair.

A long time ago, he told them, people believed that twins came from witches who lived in the forest.

"Did they have brooms?" asked Kemy.

"Of course!" said Baba.

They flew around and around the treetops on their brooms. They ate birds and made skirts from the feathers. And when they were at their most evil, they gave birth to twins.

"Who were the fathers?" asked Bel.

"The devil," said Baba. "Now listen."

That is what the people believed. Twins were a curse. "The children of *devils*," Baba spat, for he advocated the use of special effects. And they had to be destroyed. So this is what they did. They took the second twin . . .

That's me! thought Bessi.

. . . and *burned it.*

Gasps, four times. Bel glanced at Ida.

Aubrey put in, "But this is a long, long time ago, remember." And Ida said, "It's not true," even though she knew it was. All the stories Baba told were true.

They burned the second twin with the other children of witches, the rest of the cursed. That is, the blind, the crippled, the dumb, the deaf and the sick. And if the father of the twins happened to be a fisherman . . .

"Your father is not a fisherman." Aubrey sighed.

. . . what they did was take that second twin, and *drown* it, "in the riva!" Baba was excited now. The children in the doorway sniggered at the little squirming yellow girls.

Baba carried on, breathing heavily. He told them of a woman who once had two girl twins who were best friends from the very beginning, even before they were inside their mother's womb, when they were spirits. Their names were Onia and Ode. Onia was first. Ode was second—they set her on fire.

When Ode was burned (the father was not in this case a fisherman), Onia got sick and wouldn't eat at all until Ode's ghost entered her body. The ghost came in, and Onia began to eat again from her cursed mother's breast. But Ode could only stay for one year, because that was how long it took for the soul to be ready to leave the earth. After that, there would be no choice.

In that year Onia had many wicked thoughts. She dreamed that when she grew up she would burn down the village and the forest around the village. "Then, after the year was over," said Baba, "Ode left her—forever."

Georgia and Bessi's eyes had gotten as big as Kemy's. Their bellies were full of moths.

"So . . . did she do it?" asked Georgia, because Onia was her.

"Do what?" Baba said, wanting to make sure they were following.

"Did Onia burn down the village and the forest?"

"Of course!" he said. "She became a witch. She destroyed the whole village and the surrounding land, *everything*! And her womb was barren. That was the end of it. So afta that they decided it was not a good idea to separate twins, or kill them. Terrible things can happen, you see!"

Oh, what a load of haddock, thought Aubrey.

The day was beginning to close in now and shadows had gathered in the parlor. Kemy's eyes were huge wet circles and Georgia and Bessi were as still as scarecrows on their cushions. There were vivid scenes in their heads of forests burning and witches in bird-feather skirts and innocent twins being set on fire. Georgia had moved closer to Bessi. She was holding on to her arm as if she might be snatched away at any moment. Ida scolded Baba for scaring the children. "They're not used to these stories," she said. "It frightens them."

Tomorrow there would be more feasts and more visits to Ida's extended family. The thought of it made Aubrey very tired, and he began to doze off. Nne-Nne switched on the lamp and she and Ida huddled together at the table, laughing between themselves. Every so often Nne-Nne pointed at one of the children as if clarifying something. When Aubrey's snoring began to fill the room, their voices lowered to whispers and Ida became very serious.

Realizing that he was going to get no such banter out of Aubrey, and there would be no more storytelling to these gutless girls, Baba stood up after a while and stretched. He grunted something to Nne-Nne, who hardly noticed, and disappeared out into the dark for a nightcap.

It was too hot. It stayed too hot all night. The twins were traumatized and insisted on sleeping together on the floor of the living room holding hands, with Bel for protection in case anyone felt like doing anything to Bessi. They didn't sleep well. Onia and Ode were in the room, one inside the other. And this was the deepest darkness they had ever known, not a light for miles in these long hours, just the noises outside, the bats and the dogs, and that distant sound of fire.

When they woke up the next morning Bel had gone. Georgia peeped out into the morning and saw her walking back toward the house smiling.

She had spent the night in the Mercedes with Troy by a field of tomatoes. She had let him touch her on the breast, pressing it. She had gotten full of breath, and warm and wobbly inside.

EVERY MONTH THERE were power cuts. They lit candles and waited for Sedrick to turn on the generator. And when the power came back they danced. At the house in Sekon, there was enough room for dancing. Across the polished pine of the living room and beneath the dripping chandelier. Bel played records and they made up routines while soul men in white suits sang behind microphones inside the speakers. During the school holidays, when Aubrey was at work, Troy joined in. Bel would sit down and he'd walk up to her and ask, "Do you want to get down?" Bel would stand up beaming and the Little Ones, who were getting bigger, danced around them, singing:

it's only for the sight of you
my eyes open up each day
the rain could fall forever, girl,
if it meant that you would stay
truth is your love's got me flying high
but the ground ain't pretty like you

Twice a year were the parties. Aubrey's swooning cocktail parties with sunset sliding over sequins. The Alders people came and their friends, the Reeds and the Bombatas and Mr. Bolan from the next block and also strangers, who sometimes mistook Ida for a member of staff, so she preferred to stay in the kitchen with Festus and organize the food. The twins and Kemy passed round canapés, wearing Ida's jewelry and Bel's lipstick. And Aubrey drank too much gin and tonic.

During the last party in Nigeria, as heat pressed its belly up against the door, Bel and Troy made buttery love in the bungalow next to the shower room. She was sixteen now and she was allowed. Afterward they lay back and listened vaguely to the shouts and laughter coming from the house. Georgia walked past, looking for the new kittens, but Bel didn't hear her.

Georgia was worried about Bessi, who was sick. It was a Wednesday and perhaps because of this Nanny Delfi had accidentally given her a fishcake with egg in it and Bessi was lying in bed with a face full of lumps. To entertain her, Georgia had kept looking over the landing at the party and reporting back to Bessi what was going on.

"Mrs. Reed is dancing—I think she's drunk." Bessi chuckled from her sickbed.

"That pretty lady is sitting on the sofa and Mr. Bolan keeps looking down her top."

"Mrs. Reed has just spilled her drink all over her. I think Daddy's drunk too."

Bessi fell asleep and Georgia watched her for a while wondering when the lumps would go. She looked out of the window at the night and thought about Ham. She often thought about him at night—it was a time when dead things could come back to say hello, and ask you how you were. When she held the kittens in her hands, it was almost like before Ham died.

Magika sloped into the room.

"Where's the babies?" asked Georgia.

Magika yawned.

Georgia put her moccasins on and a too-big cardigan over her pajamas and crept down the hard stairs. Mrs. Reed was sitting on the end of the white sofa crying. A woman in a sequin dress was dancing to Val Doonican with one hand in the air. Aubrey was sipping gin and talking to a man in an orange shirt. The door was open. She slipped out to join the crickets, and no one noticed.

When the parties happened, Sedrick had to sit in his hut until everyone had gone so that he could lock the gate. He had fresh sugarcane to keep him occupied. His eyes were yellow from watching, his teeth were yellow from sugarcane. As Georgia appeared in the dark, a cockroach crawled up the wall next to him.

Georgia walked around the house and ran her hands along the ivy. She passed Troy's bungalow and found one of the kittens sitting at the entrance to the garden. She lifted it up. It felt warm and heavy.

The garden was beautiful at night. Flowers changed color and the orange trees whispered. The hibiscus shrubs glowed a forest red. Georgia saw the quicklime of a grasshopper taking a giant leap in the grass. Of all the places in the world, apart from the loft and next to Bessi, Georgia felt most at home in a garden. That's where she would live, she thought, if she ever found herself without a loft, because you could never be sure. She would put up a tent made out of something strong and rest there. And in the morning she would open her door to flowers.

There were low lights and voices coming from the house. But Georgia felt that she was very much alone in the garden. It was just her and the warmth in her palm. Until footsteps began to disturb the grass.

She looked around and Sedrick was standing a few paces away from her with a stick of cane.

"What are you doing out here?" he said, half smiling. He leaned to one side and peered at her.

"I'm sitting down," Georgia said, "playing with the kitten. What are you doing?"

Sedrick said: "I'm looking at you. Pretty."

When Ida had called him a monkey and a dog, Georgia and Bessi had laughed. "Mummy said you're a monkey!" they'd joked. "You got *shame*! You're a dog!" Georgia remembered this now.

"Bessi's sick," she said. "She ate egg."

Still holding the kitten, Georgia started getting up. The kitten jumped out of her arms and walked away.

"You want some sugarcane?" Sedrick offered.

Georgia took a piece and said thank you. "I'm going to bed now. Bessi might be awake."

"Want to play cartwheel?" he said. "I bet you can do seven. I'll watch you."

"I can easily do seven," Georgia said. "That's easy anyway." She bit off a piece of cane.

"Do it, then. Do it now for gold," Sedrick told her, standing back.

"Then *you* have to do one after," Georgia said.

"Okay. Do it."

"I bet you can't do one."

Georgia did one cartwheel to start off. Sedrick couldn't do cartwheels. It would be funny telling Bessi and Kemy what he looked like trying to do one.

It was a good garden for cartwheels. She made a perfect shape. She did a neat row of seven all the way to the bushes and got dizzy. Then Sedrick was next to her (she thought it strange how he'd moved so quickly, so quietly—had he done cartwheels?).

Sedrick gave Georgia a rough kiss on the mouth. Georgia said, "Oh, no thank you," and her feet felt as if they'd turned into grass, and grown there, and wouldn't be able to go anywhere until they were pulled out. Sedrick held her by the waist. "Come on, pretty," he said. He smelled of sugarcane gone sour. His wide chest with hair was sticking out of the holes in his vest. Again he shocked her with lips, he knelt down (What is he doing? What *is* it?) and rushed his dry hand up the back of her leg, the early thigh of a girl, the beginning of a place for pleasure.

Earlier that week, they'd had ju-ju men (that's what Nanny Delfi called them) at the gate, with ash rubbed into their torsos, holding knives. They demanded money, otherwise they'd kill everyone. Sedrick had sat in his hut with the door closed while Nanny Delfi and Ida got rid of them by handing over niara through the gate.

Georgia decided now, in this moment, that Sedrick must really be a ju-ju man, not a watchman at all. A ju-ju man. He had seen a man die. He had seen many men die. And she didn't have any money.

"But I don't have any money!" she cried.

Sedrick wasn't listening. He pulled down Georgia's pajamas and was trying to get her foot out of one of the legs so that he could then put her legs into a cartwheel shape. Georgia's skin and underneath her skin was petrified. There were kitteny noises near them in the bushes.

Georgia said desperately, "I can ask Daddy for some money! But you have to stop!"

"Come on, pretty."

Was Bessi dying? They had decided that they would die together. Was it now?

Sedrick pulled Georgia's grassfeet out of the ground and Georgia screamed. In the house, in her sleep, Bessi felt her face throb once.

Sedrick put his hand over Georgia's mouth. It took a lot of coordination. To hold the legs in cartwheel, to cover the mouth, to undo his belt. She was wriggling in all directions.

Yes, this is definitely it, thought Georgia. A wild thought. She saw the headlights. She heard the engine. *Oh, Bessi, be there when I get there, be there when I die!*

In the grass the kitten was writhing. Someone from the end of the scream was coming into the garden. Sedrick heard steps in the grass and started putting himself away. He let her mouth go. The cartwheel collapsed. Georgia pulled up her pajamas with rattling windup wooden hands. Her heart had leaped out of her. She put it back in. The steps were coming closer.

"Hey," said Bel. "Hey, what's going on? Who's that?"

Sedrick pushed himself into the bushes. "Georgia?" said Bel. "Is that you?"

Georgia didn't answer. She felt lines of cockroaches marching up and down her legs. She ran as fast as she could, back to the house. The guests were beginning to leave and she crashed into Mr. Bolan at the door. He glared down at her with red-wine eyes and his tie undone and said, "I hope your mother doesn't know you're not in bed!" Then he laughed very loudly.

Georgia took two marble stairs at a time and entered the shadows into the triangle. Bessi was lying with a sheet over her face. Georgia shouted her name, flew to the bed, and pulled away the sheet. Bessi woke up and Georgia asked her if she was still alive.

"Yes," said Bessi. "Are you? You look funny."

When Bessi had opened her eyes, Georgia had felt a hideous joy.

"Sedrick's a ju-ju man," she panted. "He's a monkey and a dog but most of all he's a ju-ju man. He is!"

Bessi had lumps around her eyes. She looked out at Georgia through the lumps, waiting. She said, "How d'you know that? You look funny."

Georgia tried to think about how she could put the cartwheels and grassfeet and the dark bushes like the evil forest and Sedrick's hands and Sedrick's belt opening into words that were sayable. It was the first time ever, in this land of twoness in oneness, that something had seemed unsayable.

"Has he got a knife?" asked Bessi, who had not completely come out of her dream about going to a flea market with Billy Ocean. When Georgia had asked her if she was still alive, Billy Ocean had been about to put a piece of suya in her mouth. He was waiting now, at the edge of Georgia's face, with the meat hanging from his finger.

"Yes," said Georgia, as if she was somewhere else. "I saw it. In his hut."

"Is he going to kill us?"

"I don't know."

"Well, we should not talk to him anyway," said Bessi, "in case he is."

Georgia felt confused. She couldn't remember something. How exactly, *exactly,* the kitten had felt in her hands while she'd sat in the garden. She couldn't remember it. There seemed, all of a sudden, lots of things in the way.

"Are you all right, Georgie?" said Bessi.

"Yes. I want to go to sleep."

"Let's go to sleep, then."

"Can I sleep with you tonight?"

Bessi moved over. Georgia stiffly lay down. She put her heavy arm around Bessi's waist. She didn't cry, she didn't sleep, and she didn't tell Ida or anyone else about not being in bed.

IN THE FINAL months of emigration two things happened. Kemy saw the snake reappear from underneath the sofa in the living room. She fled to get Festus and Festus knew exactly what to do. He took a knife, a dagger (it was the only thing to use in these situations), held the middle of the snake like a monster handbag, and chopped it in half on the kitchen counter. He chopped the length of it to pieces and the next day Troy ate a piece for breakfast, a marinated, palm-oil-brushed, and high-heat-fried chunk of dead reptile, with the skin still on. Bel was horrified and full of lust.

Sedrick had some too and asked Georgia and Bessi, who no longer spoke to him, if they wanted a bit. Bessi said, "No, go away, monkey," and Georgia couldn't look at him. She had fallen to third place, then dropped out of the Cartwheel Olympics, and when Bessi asked her what was wrong with her Georgia couldn't say it, so she said, "Nothing." Bessi knew it wasn't nothing but she couldn't work out what it was. She said to Georgia, "You can tell me anything you ever want to tell me, you know. Ever," to which Georgia nodded, and looked away.

The other thing that happened was that Georgia's fingers became slippery. She dropped plates and cups and pictures in their frames. A bowl of potatoes on the way to the dining-room table. She dropped a glass in the kitchen and a shard of it landed in the back of her ankle. To stop the bleeding she put her foot in a basin of cold, clear water, and the water immediately changed color to red. "That's Georgia," said Ida. She said it each time something else got broken. "That's Georgia."

Georgia's hands were contagious. The clumsiness spread into Bessi's body, and Kemy's too. Bessi leapfrogged over a chair in the study and cut her chin on the desk, leaving a scar. Kemy slipped at the edge of the upstairs landing and fell down the cruel stairs, splitting her head open. Ida ran around the house shouting "Kemy's dying! my baby, my youngest, Kemy's dying!" and Kemy, who was knocked unconscious, had to have six stitches across her crown. "I almost died," she kept saying when the stitches were taken out. "You're lucky I'm still alive."

On the last Christmas Day, as a farewell gesture, Aubrey invited Festus, Nanny Delfi, Troy and Sedrick to join them at the table for Christmas lunch. There was no Christmas pudding because they'd run out, and Georgia wasn't allowed to carry anything hot or heavy because of her fingers. Nanny Delfi, Festus and Troy sat down. Sedrick wiped his hands on his grubby trousers and approached an empty chair opposite Bessi. Bel instinctively looked at Georgia, whose eyes fell into her lap, and Ida's nostrils flared with disapproval. She turned to Bel, remembering the shower-room peep show, and then back to Sedrick. She said sharply, "Sedrick must watch the gate." Aubrey started to say something but Ida interrupted him. "Go and watch the gate." And Sedrick sank back, away from the table. He went outside and returned to his sunless hut.

Among the breakages and falls, Bel was the only one who didn't get hurt. But she cried all the way home on the plane because of Troy. Georgia was sitting next to her, Bessi by the window looking out at the clouds. Georgia ignored heaven. Instead she concentrated on Bel. She patted her hand and said, "Don't worry, Bel, it's all right. Don't be sad."

On the last Sunday in Nigeria it rained as usual. Georgia and Bessi did what they'd always done in Sekon on Sundays, their faces turned up the way Bel had pictured them. They sat down on the upstairs landing and looked up through the glass wall at the rain coming down. As they watched, Georgia thought how empty the sky looked, like the orange trees in the garden now, sad trees hanging; and not just on Wednesdays, every day.

The rain hit the glass just above Georgia's and Bessi's faces. The slant of it made it feel as if heaven might fall into their mouths. They fell asleep for a few moments underneath the rain.

As they slept they waited for the rainbow. It was one of the best things about Sekon. They knew it would come. While Bessi dozed she imagined herself walking between the green ray and the yellow ray to the gold at the end, holding a snakeskin handbag. Georgia saw herself walking the red, away from the gold, and finding it hard to keep her balance.

They opened their eyes. There it was. The break of rainbow. The rebirth of color.

"Isn't it pretty," said Bessi. "I'm going to miss this bit when we get home."

Georgia had felt the colors and the rain, but she would not miss here. There was something lost. The nowness of things. It was not pretty.

"I don't know what you mean, Bess," she said. "Not quite."

The
Second
Bit

Snowgirls

The snow had come down slowly at first. It had laid itself upon the ground like powder, disappearing into the Welsh Harp waters and tapping silently against the windowpanes of Neasden. And then it had fallen harder. Gusts of black wind slammed the heavy flakes against garden gates and the roofs of cars, against the lamplit pavements and the naked oaks across Gladstone's grounds. The mornings were thickened with white, and the traffic coming in along the A406 moved slowly, taking careful, sleepy turns toward home.

The house was empty when they got there. The lodgers had left the spare keys in an envelope in the porch, and a beer stain in the pattern of a peacock's tail on the living-room ceiling. Shivering from the cold, the Hunters stood beneath the chandelier looking up at the stain. Their faces were dry from the sudden lack of sunshine. Their eyes were glazed from flying.

Georgia slipped away into the garden. When Bessi noticed she'd gone, she followed the open doors out into the sun lounge and saw her standing in the snow. She was wearing Bel's Wellington boots and

Bessi could tell she had that new look on her face, the one that looked at invisible things in the air.

Bessi put on Aubrey's wellies and the snow gave way beneath her footsteps. She stood next to Georgia and said, "Shall we go up to the loft and see?"

"Yes," Georgia said, and faintly smiled.

They helped Aubrey carry up suitcases. His back was hurting again and he said, "Shitting hell, I say," when Georgia's slippery fingers lost a hold of one of the handles. He needed a cup of tea and a sausage and tomato buttie, and to put his feet up after the long journey. While they were struggling up the stairs Kemy asked the twins if she could come up to the loft too. Bessi told her to wait. "We have to check everything's the same."

G + B WAS STILL on the door in chalk but it had faded a little since 1981. So had BESSI BEST BED. And Bessi noticed that above her name someone had written GRANNY'S. She had forgotten what Granny looked like because she'd only seen her in dreams, but she felt extremely angry with her. This was no one else's best bed but hers, who did she think she was? "That granny put her name on top of mine," Bessi told Georgia. "Look. That's rude, isn't it."

Georgia sniffed the beanbags. The strawberry had also faded and she did not know whether all this fading was because of the presence of strangers or the passage of time or something else. But the beanbags had definitely been sat on. She said to Bessi, "They sat on the beanbags too."

"I told Daddy it was a bad idea having lodgers," said Bessi. "You see, look."

The two girls who had lived in Kemy's room, Tina and Alice, had also written their names in green felt tip on the walls, next to Kemy's Michael Jackson poster. Kemy was outraged. She took it as an affront against Michael Jackson himself. She kissed him on the cheek and apologized for letting this happen, then she got Bel to help her move the poster a little to the left to hide the scribbles.

In Bel's room, which was next to Kemy's, the three boys had left behind a funny smell, a mixture of underwear, sweat and bubble gum. Bel had to leave the windows open for three days and three nights. She cried throughout and four days beyond that because she wanted Troy to pick her up in the Mercedes, to see his white shirt flapping in the warm breeze again and to feel that feeling of his thick hands (he had good, clear hands, she'd read them—they said three children, two marriages and seventy years until the end) rubbing up and down her waist and the middle of her back where you couldn't reach if it itched.

Aubrey and Ida's room was virtually unmarred except for the bed, which now had a creak. Apart from that, it had the same yesterday atmosphere, as if the two people who slept in it, the twoness of it, had left. The wardrobes on each side of the room made hollow sounds when they were opened, and the red chair with chipped legs, where Nne-Nne sat sometimes when Aubrey was at work, had been moved away from the bed, closer to the window. Ida moved it back.

The rest of the house had also begun to creak. "They must have had parties," said Kemy, who was looking forward to being ten soon, two digits, which meant people would have to listen to her. "They must have played chase up and down the stairs and in the hallways. See, Daddy, the lodgers did it, I told you it was a mistake, didn't I, having lodgers, they gave us back a creaky house with beer on the ceiling. You should get compension."

"It's compensation and you can't get it for creaks," said Bel.

"There's nowt in a few creaks," Aubrey said. "You'll get used to it."

Well, that's all right for him *to say,* thought everyone.

THERE WAS NEW life under the snow. It was more than apples and roses. It was about foreheads and survival, high school days with boys on one side and girls on another. In the middle of January, Georgia and Bessi turned twelve—old enough to kiss wet-lipped boys over garden gates, young enough to giggle afterward. A new figure entered the loft: Puberty, growling and scowling in a musty corner not far from the beanbags with claws outstretched, dripping bacteria. At night it stood over their beds, hunchbacked and panting damply, waiting for when their bodies would be warm enough for blood and boils, backlashes of sugar (Mr. Kipling's French Fancies on Sundays), and fried food (fish and chips on Thursdays). Georgia could feel it, though when she opened her eyes in the middle of the night she saw nothing but the wisp of a scowl.

They were new girls on old fields. Watley Girls' High School was set on a hill and didn't exist when the Victorians were alive. Back then the area was just wide green fields with golf balls soaring across them. Currently, in the aftermath of the Brent depression, the school had leaking pipes in the toilets and drafts crawling in through peeling windowsills. Watley Boys' High was next door and shared the same entrance. When Georgia and Bessi first walked up the slope past the crowds and gangs, wearing stiff new uniforms and black shoes, still tanned, heads down, there was a hush.

"That's the twins," said Reena to her friends. "I remember them from primary. They went to Niger to live. And now they're back."

Reena had blossomed into a grinning four-foot-eight Pakistani tomboy with a photographic memory. She not only remembered the twins from primary school, she also remembered them from nursery, when they were four, when they were wearing the same-color Puffa jackets with a red stitch inside the collar. She decided, on the basis of a widespread curiosity about their apparent worldliness, twoness, and strangeness, to be their Watley tour guide. She showed them the fence between the boys' and girls' schools that had a hole at the end of it, the yellow-grassed area behind the Portakabins where people who had started smoking smoked ("Not me, though," she told them, "smoking makes you stink") and the battered monument to Charles Watley, who in 1905 had opened the school with the pledge of, it said under the statue, EXTENDING THE ARM OF LEARNEDNESS AND ENLIGHTENMENT TO THE GOOD PEOPLE OF NEASDEN. There were bits of stale bubble gum around the writing and graffiti scribbled up Watley's trousers.

"What was it like in Niger, then?" Reena asked as she led them to the netball courts.

"We didn't go to Niger. We went to Nigeria," said Bessi. "We had servants."

"Wow, did you!"

"And one day I had a *really big* cockroach on my chest, just here. Sedrick, our bodyguard, sort of, picked it up with his hand without any gloves or anything. And cockroaches can *kill* you."

"Wow, that's massive, guy!" said Reena, grinning enormously.

Georgia didn't feel like saying anything. She closed her face. Bessi told Reena about the big white house, the snake and the Cartwheel Olympics. Reena's head was turned completely to Bessi now, and Georgia studied the drawn-on auburn streaks in Reena's black hair.

The three of them were in the same class, blue for Livingstone. At first Georgia and Bessi sat next to each other with Reena next to Georgia, but Reena requested a while afterward that she sit in the middle. She liked being in the middle of the twins (it gave her stature, like a scientist who'd discovered something weird and knew how to communicate with it). Once she was in the middle, Reena often whispered to Bessi during lessons and sometimes they wrote each other notes that Georgia couldn't read because her eyes were starting to blur. She had to rub them and blink very hard to see what was being written on the board and it was getting to the point where she could only read books or do her homework in direct sunlight. This was inconvenient because: (1) Georgia was developing a passion for animal and wildlife books and an interest in theories of evolution (which mostly came in small print); and (2) she liked to hand in her homework on time because it was best to.

It was a growing problem. If she told someone about her eyes, especially an adult, they might—they *would,* she knew it—they'd take her to an optician and the optician would say she had to wear glasses. He'd make a pair up for her and Aubrey would pay for them over the counter, and if she didn't wear them he'd say, "Put your glasses on, they cost good money." So she'd have to. She'd have to sit in class wearing goggles, like her parents, or old-age pensioners, or Fatima, who didn't seem to have any friends. And people would point. They'd say things like "Georgia's not prettier than Bessi now 'cause she's got glasses." The glasses would make her eyes fatter, like the rest of her. People would laugh.

But if she *didn't* tell someone, she might go blind, and if not, she'd definitely get bad marks and maybe even *expelled* for not doing homework.

She hadn't told Bessi. And what made it all the more impossible was the fact that, because of Aubrey, and Wallace before him, Georgia's and Bessi's foreheads were growing at a faster rate than the rest of them, Georgia's backward and upward, Bessi's upward and backward. The Watley crowds had noticed it almost immediately. They got called tefal head, elephant girl, balloon head, and asked questions like "Can I rest my sandwich"—or book, or bag—"on your foreledge a minute?" Reena did not go this far, though she did like to call them "Forehead 1" (Bessi) and "Forehead 2" (Georgia). Georgia knew that Bessi looked at her in class sometimes and thought, *If she had a small forehead things wouldn't be so bad for me,* and Georgia thought the same, only in a different color (her jacket was green, Bessi's was blue and white).

The worst of it was Spam. They always knew when it was coming. Someone would sneak up with one hand ready to aim, most often a member of Big Sian's gang who hated the twins because the boys fancied them (Jonathan Tikka Brown, for example, had recently given Bessi a gift of a felt frog stuffed with beans, and Lee Maxwell had asked Georgia to go out with him, to which she'd said no thank you).

The culprit would then slap a greasy palm over the victim's forehead and shout: "SPAAMMMM!"

For a moment the palm would not depart. Its imprint remained, hot, and tingling. Two years later, the twins would be forced by their situation to adopt a peculiar hairstyle, an afro version of the flick, that scooped and swiveled tuft of hair that reached up from the crest of the forehead, circled, and then kited back down to, in their case, hide the bulge above the eyebrows. Their version was to be constructed thus:

1. Comb the hair with an afro comb, making sure that yesterday's white specks of dried gel are sufficiently banished from the head.
2. Wet the hair and smother with gel.
3. Neatly part an ample section of frontal hair, secure temporarily, and scrape the rest back into a ponytail (keep a towel draped around the neck until just before leaving the house so as not to soil the collar more than is inevitable).
4. Take the parted frontal clump and comb through with more gel.
5. Pull the clump upward, around with a calculated yet sudden twist of the wrist, and then down so that the curly ends brush the left eyebrow.
6. Leave to cement.

The flick would be loyal. It would not wave in the wind or frizz in the heat. And although its gelly residue was not kind to the skin beneath, which often retaliated with small mountains of bacterial rage, the twins would wear the style throughout their adolescence. It repelled Spam slaps. It saved them from themselves.

GEORGIA BLINKED THROUGH the spring. When the sun was out she closed her sore eyes and drew around the fire, taking the heat, hoping to be healed. She did all her homework and all her reading in the garden or the playground and always sat by the window in class.

When Bessi asked her why she'd moved, Georgia said, "I need the light. It helps me listen." Bessi moved next to her, and Reena moved next to Bessi, eventually maneuvering herself back into the middle, between them.

Because of Spam the twins wore hats as often as possible. Woolly hats in snow, headbands in PE, caps in the sun. In home economics hats were compulsory, and there was little reading. For Georgia especially it was the most perfect hour of each week. She and Bessi spent it alone in each other, pondering over mixing bowls, touching sleeves. Georgia was careful to carry everything with two hands because she had broken a plate in one of the first lessons, and although the teacher said it didn't matter, she had been annoyed at herself.

They cooked sponge cakes with inside jam, spicy vegetable pasties, biscuits and figures in gingerbread. It was here, in home economics, that Georgia and Bessi made an important discovery, about oats and honey, about what they meant when they got together and became a flapjack.

Flapjacks were the future. Good, sweet and easy. Take the oats and the honey, margarine or butter, sugar and heat, and mix it to a lumpy, sticky consistency. Flatten the mixture in a baking tray and place in the oven for twenty-five minutes. It was best eaten in the moments between warm and cool, when it was stuck to itself and had not yet been divided. Flapjacks were better than sweets because you could make your own and, a feature which Georgia particularly liked, you could control how fattening they were.

The most essential element of a flapjack was its filling, its personality. Apricot was bitter, nuttier than cherry. Cherry with coconut was richer than cherry alone. Raisins were dreary yet sturdy, and peach and nectarine had not yet been tried. "Peaches are soggy," Georgia mentioned to Bessi as they experimented with strawberry, in their aprons and white chef hats and the big steel ovens all around them. "It might not work."

"We could try it dried," said Bessi, "and maybe with almonds."

Pineapple and cashew worked. Pears didn't. Jam fillings, such as raspberry and black currant, worked very well. It was a feeling of triumph and pure satisfaction to bite into a flapjack whose personality, whose very soul, you had created. But Georgia and Bessi tried not to eat too many of their own creations. They preferred to sample other brands with the money they were earning from starting jobs as papergirls and waking up bewildered at six in the morning.

For as they traveled through flavor, they were realizing that their interest in flapjacks went much further than home economics. This was business.

Georgia suggested it first, in the loft when Kemy had just tasted cinnamon and blueberry during the summer holidays and said it was good, eve. "It's good, Eve" was a line from the film *Being There*, starring Peter Sellers, in which he played a simple gardener whose exposure to plant life had instilled in him a natural aptitude for utopian political philosophy—when he agreed with things he said, "It's good, Eve" to his love interest, Eve, and at the end of the film he walked on water. Georgia liked the film, and she felt a special affinity with the gardener. "It's good, eve," she kept saying. Bessi joined in, and Kemy soon followed.

Today it was hot outside, almost as hot as a morning in Sekon, and in the loft it was hottest. The windows were open and Mr. Kaczala was mowing his lawn in a straw hat.

"I've been thinking," Georgia said.

"What about?" Bessi was leaning out of the window and throwing candy wrappers at Kemy down in the garden. The wrappers got caught in the breeze and floated away.

"About flapjacks."

"Me too."

"I think we should have a company."

"Yeah, me too."

Georgia crossed her legs on her bed. "We could make different flavors and sell them to shops and people."

"Wholesale and retail."

"And make a living."

"Yes," said Bessi, "but *bigger* than that." She turned from the window and looked straight at Georgia. "We could build an *empire*, Georgia!"

Georgia thought for a minute, then said, "As long as we had enough money to live on, that would be enough for me." She started unwrapping a hazelnut flapjack by Traditional Treats. She held it with two hands and took a bite.

"But we could be rich—even famous!" Bessi was saying, pacing up and down. "We could be the Famous Flapjack Twins!"

They laughed. They moved instinctively toward the beanbags, which had finally lost their smell. They sat on them these days much less than they used to. They were finding, as they got older, that some decisions could be made quite simply on their own, without having to sit down.

"Want a bit?" Georgia offered Bessi her flapjack. "It's not bad."

Bessi took a piece, tasted it. "Too stodgy," she said.

"Maybe a bit sweet too."

"Ours will be perfect," Bessi said. "*Ours* will have just the right amounts of everything, not too sweet or heavy—flapjacks should be lighter, I think, in general—no silly flavors that don't sell, something for everyone."

"I agree." Georgia went silent, then said, "So, what shall we call it? Are you ready?"

"Ready."

They closed their eyes to drift through possibles. The lawn mower mowed and the birds outside sang birdsong.

Bessi suggested, after five minutes: "Flap Your Jacks."

"No," they said together.

"Um, what about World of Flapjacks, like World of Furniture?" said Georgia.

"No."

"Jack Your Flaps."

Pause.

"The Twins' Flapjack Company?"

Pause.

"G + B Flapjacks."

"Hmm."

"Or . . . Flaming Flapjacks."

"Lighter Flapjacks."

"Flapjacks from Heaven."

Georgia said, "*I* know! What about what you said, the Flapjack Twins!"

"The *Famous* Flapjack Twins."

"But I don't want to be famous," said Georgia.

"That's all right, I'll be famous for you—you can be the manager and I'll be the face."

Georgia was uncomfortable. "But if you're the face, *I'm* the face too. I don't want to be on telly. I just want to make flapjacks."

"Don't worry," said Bessi, "you won't have to be on telly."

"Good. Okay, then. 'Cause I won't do it."

"All right, all right."

Georgia chewed her flapjack. "I just want to bake them and sell them, that's all."

"I want to make them too and choose flavors."

"We'll do it together," Georgia said. "We're partners."

Bessi smiled to herself. "The Famous Flapjack Twins," she said, marveling.

"It's good, eve," said Georgia.

"It's good, eve," said Bessi.

There was another pause in which they both were thinking very deeply. Bessi rubbed her arms, which had browned in the sun, bringing back Sekon coffee.

Georgia said, with worry in her voice: "So . . . how do you build an empire, then?"

"I don't think it's easy. And you need a car," said Bessi. "But Daddy might help."

"If I'm manager, I'll probably have to be better in math. I'll work harder." Georgia frowned.

THEY WENT BACK to school after summer and concentrated. They experimented with more and more flavors. Georgia battled with her eyes through math and they passed through autumn, the leaves dancing across the river, through the chocolate wind, falling about on Gladstone's lawns. Georgia knocked on his door one night. He was looking older and his dressing gown was fraying but the glint was still there in his smile, the soft light in his eyes. She told him, "Me and Bessi are going to make a flapjack empire."

"Why, that's wonderful," he said. "I knew it would be." She asked him if he was all right. He said, "Yes, dear, I have started sleeping."

"Will you be here next time?" she asked.

"There are no answers, Georgia, only the places," and he closed his eyes in front of her.

There were not many students in the second year at Watley High who knew what sort of work they wanted to do in later life. They had dreams, whims and notions. If they liked science they imagined themselves dressed in white in laboratories, cutting worms in half under microscopes. If they liked music, as Bessi did, they might picture themselves holding microphones, playing guitars in black studded leather, or sitting at a piano in evening wear on the stage of a large, dimly lit concert hall. Others simply wanted to be famous, like Sasha Jane Sloane (1969–1974, yellow for Churchill), who had gotten spotted by a photographer in Waitrose and was now a supermodel.

The future was creeping up behind them and gently tapping, applying a slight, steady pressure. In English, on a frosty day in November, Miss Pinh asked each member of her class to stand up in turn and say what they wanted to be when they grew up.

Georgia stood up, hating all the eyes watching her but feeling proud to know for sure, to not to have to lie. She said: "I want to be a manager and partner of a flapjack company with Bessi."

Someone laughed. Miss Pinh squinted her eyes and said, "That's very good, Georgia," and Georgia sat down.

Reena shot up and said, "A spy," then sat down and it was Bessi's turn.

Bessi stood up. She said: "I want to be the partner and face of the Famous Flapjack Twins"—*She shouldn't have said the name,* thought Georgia, *someone might tell!*—"and after that I want to be a singer, and then I want to meet a nice man and get married and have two children. I'd like to have twins but my mum said I won't because I am one, so I'd like to have a girl first and then a boy."

The class was silent. Big Sian's shoulders were bouncing up and down. A wave of wintry darkness washed into the room.

Georgia was confused. After flapjacks? After flapjacks? What did she mean? There was no After Flapjacks. Not now anyway, not that she could see, not yet. She looked up at Bessi, standing there with her chin up, her back straight, ready for endings. Where was she going?

Bessi sat down. Georgia tried to catch her eye, but Reena whispered something in her ear.

On a piece of paper that night Georgia wrote something down. The thoughts pushed their way out. She used a red pen: *I don't know what I am. But After Flapjacks, if I had to be something, I would work in a flower shop.* She kept her eyes shut when Bessi came to bed, and later, in sleep, she knocked on Gladstone's door. There were dead leaves on the windowsill and the glass was murky.

"Are you there?" she called. "It's cold out."

Gladstone didn't speak. He didn't come to the door. She looked in through the window and saw that the house was empty, apart from a small black cockroach crawling across the floor.

Shortly afterward, Georgia and Bessi were put into separate classes. The staff had discussed it and decided it was time they pursued their individual paths. When the twins insisted they stay together for home economics, Aubrey had to come in for a meeting with the headmistress.

The headmistress said: "Mr. Hunter, it's very important they do not remain too attached to each other. The world outside is a world of separation, they must be prepared."

"Yes," said Aubrey, a little flushed in the cheeks, the headmistress noticed. Georgia and Bessi were waiting outside in the corridor hoping Aubrey wouldn't shout. Last night he had come home late for the first time in a long while, and they had heard him shouting in the middle of the night. He said now, "They're like bread and butter, those two, always cooking together at home and whatnot."

"Flapjacks, by any chance?" said the headmistress.

"Thousands of them," said Aubrey.

Bessi had her ear up against the door. "What's he saying?" whispered Georgia.

"Dunno," said Bessi, "something about the flapjacks."

"But do you not agree, Mr. Hunter, that they would benefit from some independence from each other?"

"Of course," said Aubrey. He leaned toward the headmistress, who was much taller than him. She looked down at him over the desk and thought she smelled a hint of liquor. "I've never been one to sniff at independence," he said. "But when the time is right, when the time is right. And what's an hour in a week of independence? Like bread and butter, they are."

The headmistress asked Aubrey whether, if she might be so bold, he had been drinking in the middle of the day, perhaps a celebration of some sort? Aubrey replied that he never drank during the day, and had never been much of a drinker at that.

As he walked down the corridor toward the exit he held Georgia's and Bessi's hands, one left, one right, very tightly, so tightly that it hurt. Before he walked away he bent down and seemed about to say something. He looked from one twin to the other, then looked away. His voice did not sound like his own when he finally spoke. "Your grandmother's not well," he said. "She's had an accident."

"What accident?" said Georgia. Judith was a hazy pre-Sekon memory, a mesh of white hair and knitting needles that had once or twice appeared in the living room bossing people about. Over the phone, when they had arrived back from Sekon, she had spoken, to each of them in turn, including Ida, and told them to wash their clothes thoroughly to make sure all the flies were gone. "Flies in Africa have diseases," she'd said.

Judith had been knocked over by a bus in central Bakewell on the way to the post office. According to Wallace's forlorn account (his first conversation with Aubrey in years), she had been absentminded lately and had probably walked out into the road without looking, the old pansy. There were damages to her ribs and she'd hit her head badly on the pavement. Aubrey would be leaving the next morning to go and see her in hospital.

"Can we come?" asked Bessi, spotting a perfect opportunity to skip school.

Aubrey said no, that they must stay here with their mother, and Gran would be fine. He wandered off without saying good-bye.

The headmistress allowed Georgia to stay in blue for home economics, but she was moved to red for Nelson for everything else. She sat in the empty space next to a girl called Anna. Anna asked her, "Are you Bessi's twin?" She told her, "You've got pretty eyes, haven't you." They began to share packets of crisps during breaks. Anna had a gerbil at home. Georgia told her about Ham. They discussed gerbil and hamster differences.

It was foreign, living like this, coming across each other in the playground the way others did, as if they were the same as them, the twinless ones. It felt to them like being halved and doubled at the same time. Anna became Georgia's best friend. She was freckled and ginger-crowned and also known as Pigeon-Shit Nose because a pigeon once had swooped overhead and opened its bowels onto the end of her long sharp nose. And Reena and Bessi were already a pair. Reena was getting badder. She began wiping snot on the insides of double-decker bus windows to declare her hardness, and she was sent out of classes for being a nuisance. Twice she'd been caught shoplifting, "once in W. H. Smith," she said, "and once in the newsagent." What happened at Woolworth's that winter, Georgia was convinced, was all Reena's fault. *She started it,* she wrote afterward, *she made us. She's bad.*

T W O   W E E K S   B E F O R E   Christmas, the Neasden branch of Woolies gleamed red, gold and holly green in the gathering dusk. Its hazy candy-wrapped windows blinked like Georgia's secret eyes. Scented crayons, glittered pencil cases, rainbow umbrellas. Chocolate honeycomb, sherbet sachets, pick 'n' mix galore. On weekdays herds of schoolchildren, catapulted by the 3:30 bell from dreary classrooms to the rolling freedom of after-school, hollered and loitered in the playground outside. The boys from Watley Boys' High ogled and asked out the girls from Watley Girls' High. Older brothers and little sisters were reunited. Ties were stuffed into satchels. Teachers were cursed. Crushes were confidentially disclosed.

Among them were Georgia and Bessi, Forehead 2 and Forehead 1, Georgia's backward and upward, Bessi's upward and backward. They were working hard toward Flapjacks and developing a professional attitude. While Georgia raised her hand in 2G to answer "Why did Boudicca lead the revolt against the Romans?" with "Because the Roman army killed her husband and attacked her people," Bessi raised her hand in 2B to answer "Where in Australia did Captain Cook first hoist the British flag?" with "Botany Bay."

They were flanked by Anna and Reena. The twos had become

a four, though it was understood that Anna and Reena were only to-ken best friends, less best than Georgia and Bessi were to each other. This was unspoken and accepted.

The four of them wore identical, roomy white corduroy coats with explosive cream cuffs that they had recently begged their parents to buy from Wembley Market ("It's the style," Bessi told Aubrey, "we need them"). At the school gates, in the playground, in the precinct, the foaming four arrived always as a waddling arctic vision, a vision that would be reluctantly discarded when the winter was over, and washed, wardrobed and yearned for until the next.

Woolies glistened. It beckoned. The security guard at the door peered out at the after-school with a mixture of dread and goodwill. Georgia, Bessi, Anna and Reena approached the double doors. Snow-girls risen from the ground. He bowed as they entered, setting off four scruffy giggles. He watched them scuttle away, past the gurgling prams and nattering mothers toward the stationery section, where the girls, top teeth holding bottom lips, fiddled with pencils of fresh aro-matic lead, sharpeners whose blades flashed under the lemony neon lighting, and smudged their pencil fingerprints onto the latest selec-tion of erasers. He watched them, rocking steadily on his feet and clasping his hands behind his back. More schoolchildren sauntered in and his darting eyes tried to keep track of all ten bouncing lollygag-gers with loud, bickering voices and the after-school racing through their veins. It was not easy. He did not see the foaming four journey-ing toward the candy aisle, where the Twixes beamed in their silken caramel wrappers and nudged the bubble-light Maltesers and the pick 'n' mix sparkled with sugar—the undisputed crown jewels of Woolies Wonderland. The girls huddled together, conferring and rustling for change.

"Twenty-eight pence," Anna held out coins in her palm.

"Thirteen pence," said Bessi.

"What about your paper-route money? I've got fifty pence left from mine," said Georgia.

"I spent it at lunchtime."

They all looked at Reena. As usual she was penniless. Then, without warning, she picked a lime-wrapped mint toffee from one of the pick 'n' mix trays and shoved it in her pocket. Their eyes lit up. They swerved around to see if anyone had seen. It was safe.

"*Reeeena!*" Bessi hissed. "That's *naughty!*"

"Oh, don't be so goody-goody. 'Sonly a sweet," snapped Reena. She lifted a white chocolate milk bottle from another tray and popped it into her mouth, chewing defiantly.

Anna giggled.

Georgia and Bessi said, "It's *stealing!*"

" 'Snot stealing. My brother said anything under one pound's not stealing. It's the law."

They considered this. It sounded feasible. They would ask Bel when they got home.

Fizzy cola bottles twinkled next to rainbow vermicelli. As Reena sucked on her milky prize she arranged her face in a skyward orgasmic grimace. The other three watched her jealously. Milk-livered. Scaredy-cat. Chicken. Reena reigned supreme in the ranks of hardness.

"Dare you," she sucked.

Pigeon-Shit Nose sidled up to the pick 'n' mix. She looked around with beady eyes. She caressed jelly baby bellies with sweaty fingertips. Deep breath. Gather and seize. Remove fisted hand. Look around. Raise hand. Five jelly babies. Open mouth. The babies jumped in. Yippeeeee. Tee-hee. A chomping mouth stuffed with candy babies. Anna's eyes flashed. Reena the pioneer punched her shoulder in revolutionary fashion. They doubled over raucously, cavorting, laughter wrestling with jelly in Anna's triumphant mouth.

"My girl's *bad*, you know!" said Reena.

"You *know* say!" Anna agreed.

The twins bit scaredy-cat lips with chicken teeth. They touched eyes. Shrinking.

Georgia nudged Bessi. "Let's go," she said. But Bessi didn't move.

"Goody-goody twinnie twins!" Reena taunted.

"*Shaaame!*" lashed Anna, sentencing them forever to further humiliation. As if Spam was not enough.

Two aisles away the security guard, sufficiently assured that the other lollygaggers were up to no more mischief than replacing studied, unaffordable goods incorrectly, heard the hooting of the forgotten four. He walked to the end of the confectionery aisle. He peeped down it, seeing nothing but the loitering snowgirls, two guffawing, two silent and shuffling their feet. No hands pocketing sweets. Not then.

He watched.

Bessi knew what they had to do. "Come on, Georgia," she said. "We've got to do it."

In a hasty telepathy of embarrassment they decided that something sugared, something superior to jelly babies or milk bottles, yet something less than one pound, had to be *taken*.

Woolies didn't sell flapjacks, so they chose the Twix. Not one, but two. A twin bar each for the soon-to-be *bad* girls.

Georgia and Bessi sidled up to their biscuit-centered prey. Facing each other, they checked for candy police, sliding their eyes nervously. It was safe. A clammy left hand and a clammy right hand wiped white corduroy. One last terrified check. One sudden image of their parents. Butterflies tickled their intestines with frenetic wings. Deep breath, one each. Place hand on Twix. Open fingers. Softly lift. Seize. Remove fist. Check for police. Fill pocket, one each. Touch eyes, gleeful, guilty. *'Snot stealing*.

Then why was the security guard charging toward them without his smile? And why were their best friends slinking away from them? Why did their hearts rattle and reel? Terror snowballed. They whirled around and saw candy policeman, kind eyes replaced by ice, the mouth now pursed and lined with punishment.

"Right, girls, come with me," he said.

No *buts*. No *'snot stealings*. Just hold hands and follow him to a very tall candy policewoman with disgusted mercury eyes and a

Woolies manager badge—Mrs. E. F. Winters. Two Twixes are re-
trieved. Two twelve-year-old souls quake. Anna and Reena back away,
saving themselves, out the double doors to freedom.

Georgia and Bessi's sentence was worse than imprisonment. The
most perplexing, most frightening, most intimate kind of exposure.

Mrs. E. F. Winters ordered: "I want you to go home now and tell
your parents what you have done and that you have been caught doing it."

Tell their *parents*? Aubrey's wrath. Ida's disappointment. To two
other shoplifters, Anna and Reena for example, who had proved their
hardness, this would have been a lucky sentence. A let-off. *They* would
have agreed instantly, promised to inform their parents, strolled away,
and "forgotten" to keep the promise. But for Georgia and Bessi, whose
quivering memories dipped into five years ago when Bel had stolen
socks from C & A and Ida had chased Bel around the dining-room
table, over and over, and then sat on her when she had flopped onto
the sofa, surrendering—*sat* on her—and Aubrey had made her stand
in the cupboard under the stairs for a whole afternoon with no dinner
afterward, the punishment was devastating.

Their stammers staccato'd in time with each other.

"I p-promise."

"I-I promise."

And together now. "We p-ro-miss."

Mrs. E. F. Winters watched the two brown snowgirls waddle away,
hands interlocked, heads earthbound, and out the double doors.

White corduroy returned to the falling snow.

ON THE WAY home through the dusk that had become night the
twins shed tears. Bessi's arm looped through Georgia's, their hands
squeezing each other in Georgia's pocket, they assessed their choices.
They walked back up the steep narrow alley. There were cracks in the
ground and when it rained they looked like silver veins; or in the

mornings, when the twins were the first to tread it with their papers, fat orange slugs still slept there wetly, making them dodge. Tonight the alley was snowing. *Everything is white,* Georgia thought softly through her anguish. *When the white is over, the cracks will show.*

At the top of the alley, she saw again a small black cockroach, scuttling across the snow. It grew before her eyes to the size of a rat. It turned its dirty head and looked at her and she looked at it back.

"What are you looking at?" said Bessi.

I'm looking at you, pretty, he said.

Georgia slipped once or twice on sketches of ice.

Bessi said, "What shall we tell them? Daddy's gonna kill us."

Georgia thought of the most obvious thing. "Let's say there's a cockroach in our room. Then we can tell them upstairs, in private, maybe just Mummy on her own."

"You don't get cockroaches here."

Yes, you do, thought Georgia. She looked at Bessi sideways. Her eyes were stinging.

Bessi said, "A spider."

Georgia nodded.

They would keep their promise. They would tell. But after further discussion it was agreed that they would not tell Aubrey and Ida, because Aubrey would rant at them for stealing while their blessed Gran was still not right, and there was no telling what Ida might do. They would tell Bel, which was almost telling their parents, except Bel did not have the authority or the bulk to sit on them. They would keep their promise to Mrs. E. F. Winters.

They walked up the driveway and in through the back door of home. Kemy was drawing a woman in a red dress at the kitchen table. She looked up when they came in.

"Where've *you* been? Mummy's annoyed."

Bessi was the first. "Only at the library with Anna and Reena."

Georgia followed. "We were *working.*"

"*I'm* working."

"No you're not," said Bessi, "you're crayoning. That's not working."

"I *yam*! It's homework. I'm going to be a dressmaker!"

"Where's Bel?" asked Georgia.

"In the sitting room watching telly. Daddy's home early."

It was delivered as a warning. The twins shuddered. Kemy carried on drawing, with added sobriety, determined to prove to Bessi that she too had important things to do.

They hung their coats in the hallway and crept into the sitting room. Aubrey's eyes were attached like a magnet to the TV. Snooker highlights. The kiss and crack of red and yellow balls and a white one colliding. Bursts of applause. Bel was sitting on the sofa with her legs tucked beneath her. She looked bored. Safer than Aubrey. The twins touched eyes. Deep breath. Hello.

"Oh, *there* you are. Where were you?" asked Bel, not quite angry.

"Library."

"Working."

Aubrey did not adjust his vision. "You should've phoned, your mummy's been worried. Why didn't you phone?"

"Forgot."

"Sorry."

Aubrey glazed back wearily into snooker land. Bessi dived in.

"Bel, can you come upstairs for a minute? There's a spider in our room."

"Yeah. A *really big* one," Georgia confirmed.

Bel looked them over.

"You just came in. How do you know?"

"We went upstairs first. It's still there. It was there this morning as well. It's even got hairy legs," said Bessi.

"Hairy? I don't think so. I hate spiders. Why don't you ask Dad?"

"Nooo! We want *you* to come."

Bel huffed. "It's probably gone now anyway. I have to help Mum with dinner."

The twins looked at each other and squirmed. They had not

envisaged that Bel might respond with such complexity, such lethargy. They could not insist. It would arouse suspicion. But they had to tell.

And then it occurred to Bessi: Perhaps they didn't have to tell. Perhaps this was their chance at being *bad*.

"It doesn't matter, then," she said. "We'll sort it out."

Georgia was confused. Bessi pulled her hand as she walked out of the room, her eyes on fire. "That's it!" she hissed as they climbed the stairs to the loft. "We did it!"

They marched to school the next morning and Bessi told Anna and Reena they'd gotten away with it, shrugging as if she hadn't been terrified. "It was nothing," she said. "They couldn't touch us."

Anna and Reena were impressed. "Bad girls," they said.

For a time the cool gray eyes of Mrs. E. F. Winters haunted them in the stillness of night. But the snow melted. The cracks in the ground showed through. Summer blushed, and the eyes faded away.

"Bessi," said Georgia as they lay in the dark the night of Woolies, without a spider in their room.

"Yeah." Bessi waited.

Georgia wanted to tell her about the cockroaches, about what happened. She wanted to say, *One night in Sekon . . . that night.* She wanted to say, *Sedrick, that night, he.* But she felt them crawling toward her, up the bedspread.

"What?" said Bessi.

"My eyes don't work properly," said Georgia.

Bessi was silent.

"I think I need glasses."

"Me too," said Bessi.

6

Mr. Hyde

The film *Dr. Jekyll and Mr. Hyde* was nothing like *Dallas*. There were no shoulder pads or Bobby Ewings in tuxedos. Mr. Hyde's makeup made him look like a potato, and his metamorphosis screams sounded false. Nevertheless, it was the concept of the film that brought Georgia, Bessi and Kemy downstairs to the sofa when it came on telly, to watch and wait for that moment when the nice doctor, the kind, selfless, beloved doctor, drank his mysterious blue potion and then seethed and bulged into the debased Mr. Hyde. His chemical alter ego. Because it was just chemicals, they believed, that sometimes turned Aubrey into a monster. They imagined that this was how it happened: Aubrey drank the syrup-tone whiskey—a glass, and another glass. It moved down toward his heart. There was a fierce and helpless roar in the dead of the night, the splitting and reddening of skin, the immediate acceleration of hair growth and the sudden expansion of body muscle. And the nice doctor was no more. He lay sleeping somewhere in a syrup haze and would arrive back the morning after Mr. Hyde's moonlight massacre, a little groggy, a touch confused and in absolute denial of his own indecency.

Bel no longer watched it. She was nineteen now with a boyfriend called Jason, who had a car, bought her earrings and hadn't gone to college. He was four years older than her and worked in the box office at the Cricklewood Odeon. Jason had a gold tooth like Troy, which was the first thing Bel had noticed about him as he pushed toward her a free ticket to see *Back to the Future,* and brushed her little finger with his thumb. Waifer Avenue thumped when he came to pick her up in the Jeep with black windows. It thumped in chairs and in the carpet. "Tell that boy to turn his music down!" Aubrey shouted. "How he can afford a car like that anyway I don't know."

Neither Georgia nor Bessi had gotten around yet to asking Aubrey's advice on empire building because he hadn't been in a good mood for a long time. (They had, however, been busy conducting flapjack surveys, so far in Willesden and Kilburn. This involved going into possible flapjack outlets—newsagents, supermarkets, cash-'n'-carries—making a note of brands and flavors, and carefully looking out for local pedestrians eating flapjacks. They had also deduced that the average cost of producing one flapjack would be eighteen pence.)

Since Judith's accident, Aubrey had been spending more time in the sun lounge or walking about with a glass in his hand, and there were no cocktail parties to make it seem festive. There was just him, in the middle of the night, with the fridge humming and the new creaks. His mother hadn't recognized him when he'd visited her in the hospital. He had sat with his face very close to her bandaged head and she had opened one eye and looked at him. "Dorset's too far but I'll need the green one first," she'd whispered. She had then fallen back to sleep and not woken again for seventeen days. A month later Aubrey had spent a week with her at the house in Bakewell, which now smelled of must and dirty socks. Wallace wheezed in cigarette smoke and told Aubrey, "She never came back from where she went," while Judith sat by the window, thin and white, smiling occasionally and forgetting Aubrey's name. The whole thing gave him a lost feeling, like a teenager who had left home for the first time.

Georgia asked Bel what was wrong with him. Aubrey didn't talk to anyone about his mother, except brief reports that she was "on the mend" or "more or less back to normal," but they all knew it must be more serious than that because she didn't phone anymore. "Why doesn't he tell us about Gran?" Georgia asked. "Is it a secret? Is she going to die or something?" Bel told Georgia that she didn't know, but she did know that their father was a repressed male animal, and this meant that he didn't know how to talk about his feelings. "Is it?" said Georgia. She liked sitting on Bel's bed, next to the windowsill where she burned her incense sticks. Today it was Purple Musk from Shepherd's Bush. "How did he get to be a repressed animal?"

Bel stopped with her mascara. She searched past herself in the mirror. "He didn't answer his demons," she said. "And now they're eating him up."

"Oh," said Georgia. She felt prickly. "Will it get better, Bel?"

"People can change," Bel said. "Something incredible could happen. It's all in the stars. Don't look so worried, darling, be thirteen. Here, want some gloss?"

These days Bel liked to wear apricot lipstick with a brush of gloss across the top and the earrings Jason bought her, two and a half pairs at a time because altogether she had five piercings in her ears. Golden violins and planets in hoops dangled about her neck. Her hair was enormous, black and curly, and oiled with rosemary to make it grow. Bel was studying to be a chemical-free hairdresser—"no relaxing, no bleach, just plaits, afro treats, twists and henna"—and Kemy and the twins were her practice models. She could often be seen with one of them sitting with their head between her knees while she plaited their hair into zigzag cornrows or pineapple shoots, or sprayed the twins' afros to make them shiny. Bel knew all the gels and oils to use and all the ways to get beautiful. She wore Ida's shawls and glitzy high heels that she complained about afterward, in a heap at the bottom of the stairs when the boy who hadn't gone to college dropped her off. Aubrey waited up. He swayed in the hall. He told her she looked like a gypsy and that ruffian's got a cheek bringing you back this late. Bel kept silent and waited until he'd finished, which took about forty-five minutes because there was a lot to cover (Jason's loud music, lack of further education and probable investments in dubious enterprises, Bel's ungratefulness for Aubrey's fathering, Ida's failure as a mother and wife, Britain's failure with public transport particularly the London Underground, the increase in speed bumps in Willesden, and the fact that he had been working for almost thirty years and he was bloody tired).

"Good night, Dad," said Bel when it was over. "Try and get some sleep."

Aubrey looked up the stairs after her with fuzzy vision. Down in a hovel inside himself it struck him she was beautiful, they all were getting beautiful, like Jacqueline Flynn all those years ago in Bakewell with her red hair and perfume, little women, with pretty green and brown eyes.

To watch *Dr. Jekyll and Mr. Hyde* and anything at all on TV, Georgia and Bessi now had to wear their National Health Service glasses. They were farsighted. They could see all the way to the A406 and Wembley Stadium across the rooftops, but not words or television. At Watley they were being called the Goggle-Eye Spam Twins and secretly they blamed each other. Twins often develop bad eyesight, the optician had told them, and there wasn't much to be done about it. "It's because you're special," Bel said. "It's good to be special. Don't forget, you're lucky to have each other. Now don't forget."

Dr. Jekyll screamed and rolled his eyes and gritted his teeth in his laboratory. Syringes and test tubes got knocked over. Mirrors smashed. The floor got covered in poison. And the nice doctor was no more.

MR. HYDE AND Ida did not get on well. In fact, Dr. Jekyll and Ida did not get on, and Georgia and Bessi had come to accept that being married meant not getting on and not getting divorced. Ida had re-treated back into her dressing gown as the Sekon sun had faded. For her, home was not homeless; it was one place, one heat, one tree. She made herself a bubble and it was called Nigeria-without-Aubrey. Her children were allowed inside, Bel on her right, Kemy always on her lap, where the lastborn never left, and the twins a little way off, in a bubble of their own. At dinner, Ida sometimes said "pass the pepper" in Edo, and Aubrey would stab something on his plate; or in the early mornings, she said, "At home now, they're singing." She held Edo lessons in Bel's room on Saturdays, because language was loyalty, and Ida was not pleased when Aubrey told her to stop. "We're in England now," he said. "The girls don't need Nigerian here. They'll forget it soon enough." The lessons became secret and eventually the twins dropped out because of flapjack commitments, Kemy dropped out because the twins had, and Ida only spoke Edo to Nne-Nne now, mostly upstairs alone in the evenings.

And very occasionally, to Bel. Ida was not a woman who approved of swearing, or of using the names of the gods in vain. But on a blustery October afternoon in 1986 when Bel took her by surprise, she could not help herself.

She said, *"Ovia!"* which in translation was not dissimilar to "Jesus Christ almighty" or "God have mercy."

Bel had asked everyone to sit down in the living room. She had a grave look on her face and Georgia wanted to ask her if she was all right. The cricket was on. Aubrey clutched the remote control.

"Turn off the TV, Dad," said Bel.

"There's only one wicket left, dammit!"

Bel sat still in the armchair closest to the door and waited. Autumn leaves were flying at the bay window outside and the telephone wires were trembling in the wind.

"Will you turn it off, please, Dad?" said Bel. "I'm pregnant."

That's when Ida swore at her. She got up, losing a slipper, staggered over to Bel and tried to sit on her. Bel jumped up just in time, having been half expecting this after the incident with the C&A socks. When your children disappoint you, you sit on them—that was how it went. Nne-Nne herself had sat on Ida many times and Cecelia had sat on Baba before that.

So Ida fell into the empty chair and the cricket match stayed on because Aubrey's fingers were too shocked to turn it off. "Bloody hell," he muttered. "Bloody hellfire, what the devil—the lout." Kemy and the twins pushed their shoulders closer together on the sofa with their arms clenched in their laps and looked from Aubrey to Ida to Bel, who was standing in the dining room in tears, looking ready to run.

"It's that boy, isn't it?" said Aubrey. "With that ridiculous car."

"Jason," said Bel.

Aubrey started muttering again about Jason being a lout.

"He's not a lout!" cried Bel. "Don't call him that."

"He's a lout and a bloody lout! Have you told him, then? Does he know? We'll see whether he's a lout."

"I *did* tell him and he's not a bloody lout, Dad!"

Ida was slowly shaking her head, looking down through the carpet. "You see," she was saying. "You throw your life away, like me. See what happen? You are just a child."

Bel was the only one who heard her. "I'm almost *twenty*. God!" she said.

"Yeah," Kemy put in suddenly. "She's old enough to be a mum. I know this girl at school, her sister's only eighteen and she had one last year! A boy. And she's fine. She's alive and doing well and her mum helps her take care of the baby."

Aubrey shot a look at Kemy, who was wondering whether she should have kept quiet.

He turned off the TV. It was quiet thunder. He stood up. He said the words.

"I'm going out."

Please don't, thought the house.

He didn't say good-bye. They heard him get his coat. The front door slammed. They all looked up at the beer stain on the ceiling.

"Sorry," said Kemy.

"It's not your fault," said Ida.

WHEN AUBREY SAID "I'm going out" there was always lots of cleaning to do and things to prepare. They had a few hours to make perfection, contentment and supreme obedience. The vacuum, dusters, brushes and polish were laid out on the kitchen table. They checked the chores list, which Aubrey had established last year when Kemy turned ten. They got confused about whose turn it was to do what because today was Thursday and the cleaning was usually done on Saturdays. Bel sniffed and said, "Just do what you would've done on Saturday." So Kemy got the stairs, both flights with the pan and brush. Georgia, living room. Bessi, dining room. And Bel got the rest. The area around the front door shuddered. Dusk was gathering itself. They sped to their stations and began.

Ida took out onions from her plastic bags and started cooking. She didn't expect that Aubrey would bring home fish and chips tonight even though that was the Thursday dinner. Nne-Nne sat down on a stool by the sink and rubbed her knees. My bones are getting worse, she told Ida. I'm getting tired. Then Nne-Nne started on a story about Cecelia. She chuckled. Hmm! You kno what she did? When she was sixteen, before she ran away, a boy from Inone tried to kiss her body in the night by the shrine when she was giving worship. So Cecelia, she lifted her leg and kicked the boy in his stomach. Nne-Nne slapped her thigh. Yes, she was strong, Ida. She jumped up high and beat that worthless boy until he begged her no more, and the next day she reported him to the elders. After that, she started to carry a knife in her skirt. The knife went with her to Lagos. She was tougher than you, Ida!

The house was beginning to smell of polish and air freshener and the sandalwood joss sticks that Bel was burning in all the rooms to cast out bad fate. Kemy was making banging noises against the stairs with the brush. Georgia had the vacuum. She was moving armchairs and the sofa to suck out the dirt from under them and check for cockroaches. In the dining room Bessi was singing the Eurythmics song about the angel. It was a reason to sing, that there was still space in the air, lightness, the smell of onions, that in this moment the house was clean and loose and free.

It was six o'clock. He might be anywhere but most probably at Alfred's in Neasden precinct talking to Jim at the bar. Jim was the plumber who sometimes fixed the boiler. Aubrey was knocking back syrup to wash the day, and telling Jim about how you worked for thirty years of your life and what for, eh? For a broken boiler, that's what. Jim laughed. And the missus, though, lovely, your missus, he said, a real African queen that one! Aubrey's head was starting to dance. A waltz. He took its arm and let it lead. Into the empty glass he disappeared—and from the murky bottom, Mr. Hyde was rising.

Georgia left the living room and went upstairs. She looked back once at the front door. From the top of the stairs the mask with the straw hair stared down at her with no eyes. It was dark now. She heard someone crying.

She pushed open the bathroom door and sat down next to Bel on the edge of the bath. They were wearing aprons with old stains on them. Georgia put her arm around her sister and looked at the heater.

"I don't know what to do," said Bel.

Georgia sat quiet. Unless you were extremely important, like Gladstone or God, there was nothing to say when someone didn't know what to do.

Bel carried on between sobs. "Jason said he wouldn't run off, he's not like that. He's not a lout."

"No," said Georgia. "Not if he says he'll look after you anyway."

"A baby," said Bel to the white walls.

"A baby."

"Do you think I'd be a bad mother?" asked Bel.

Georgia thought about it. She pressed her lips together. "You'd be a good mother to a poor little thing like a child."

Bel looked at Georgia and wondered, as she often had.

"You could call it Bel, or Bill, or Bob. Or Bumbo."

"He said we could get married," said Bel.

"Did he?"

"But I don't know if I want to marry him."

"You don't have to," said Georgia. "Then you won't have to get divorced either."

"Who's getting divorced?"

Georgia shrugged. "Lots of people. Reena's parents did."

"That's other people."

Georgia turned to her. "Do you know what I think, Bel?" she said. "I think you can do anything you want to do, because you're Mystic Bel . . . Be mystic."

Bel laughed and Georgia smiled down at the heater. They heard Bessi singing from downstairs.

"You won't leave, though, will you?" asked Georgia.

"I don't know."

Bel paused and looked inside Georgia at the thing that wasn't right. A fear, a panic, a way of looking out.

"Georgia," she said. "Are you all right, love?"

"Yes," said Georgia.

Bel took her hand. "So. I'm Mystic Bel, like you say. And you have a secret."

Georgia kept her eyes low and searched invisibles.

"Do you ever miss Sekon?" Bel asked. "I do sometimes. Kemy says she misses Nanny Delfi."

"No," said Georgia firmly.

Bel moved closer to Georgia and lowered her voice. "I heard you scream that night, you know, when I found you in the garden? I couldn't see properly but I know something happened there, Georgia . . . I wasn't sure, whether Sedrick might have . . . he just always seemed cruel to me." She waited for Georgia to say something, but she stayed silent, rubbing her toes together. "I've been waiting for you to come to me, love, because I couldn't be sure. Why don't you tell me now?" Bel traced a line on Georgia's palm with her fingertip. "This line here means there's something in your heart, and you should say what it is because if you don't you'll always be sad. Like Mum, except at least she's got somewhere to go and get happy."

"I've got somewhere," said Georgia stiffly. "I've got a place to go."

"Where?"

"Bessi. Bessi and me."

"What about when Bessi isn't there?"

"She'll always be there. She's the best bit of me. We're half each."

"Georgia . . . tell me. Did he touch you?"

Georgia stood up suddenly and saw her face in the mirror. A pitiful thing, not pretty, a dark old thing. The worst bit. She sat back down and her eyes got slippery.

"Come here," said Bel.

All over Bel's apron, through the gravy stains and tea, she spilled herself.

She tumbled through cartwheels and heard the roaches marching. Mr. Bolan had such a loud voice. Don't tell your mother you haven't been in bed! he shouted.

"Don't tell anyone, Bel!" Georgia said.

"Not Bessi?"

"Not Bessi."

They sat still. The house was still.

"Bessi is where bad things never happen," said Georgia.

PERFECTION, CONTENTMENT AND supreme obedience were waiting for Aubrey. All the mirrors had been polished, along with the tabletops, sideboards, door handles, shelves and Aubrey's desk, with every piece of paper replaced exactly as it had been found. At 7:30, Ida, Bessi and Kemy watched television with the sound down low so that there would be enough time, because when Mr. Hyde came home, when his keys jangled outside the door, the evacuation procedure had to be quicker than quick. They'd have to: straighten the cushions on the sofa where they'd been sitting, make sure the tassels at the bottom were dangling properly, check for pens, bits of paper and anything else that could be on the floor, put the kettle on for his tea, get his dinner on the plate, turn off the television, put the remote control on the left arm of his chair and run upstairs to bed with tissues to shove into their ears to block out sound.

The house waited, and everything in it.

The waiting began to buzz.

At half-past nine he had not come. This night will be a night, Ida said to Nne-Nne. He is late. Nne-Nne was shaking her head. Big mistake, she said, marrying that man. He took you all this way away from home and for what? Where are your happy times here, Ida? He took you away from yourself.

Ida turned up the heat on the cooker.

"Come," she shouted. "Let's eat."

She slammed out plates and dropped rice on them, chicken stew on top, vegetables on the side, among them spinach (Ida had forgotten that Bessi was allergic, despite the list on the wall called *Bessi Can't Eat . . .*). Kemy checked the twins' plates to see if they had more than her. Georgia kept her red eyes lowered so that no one would see.

They ate in the dining room inside the waiting and the buzzing and the tightening air. Runner beans ran down throats. Chicken was sucked of its salts. Bessi pushed her spinach to the side of her plate and Ida used more cayenne pepper than usual. No one said a word. They ate quickly yet savored everything as if it were the end of food.

There was no time for cherry bakewells or peeling pears or warming up ice cream. Bel washed up swiftly, Georgia dried, Kemy and Bessi put away.

Before they left, Ida took Bel's arm. She said, "Don't worry, it's okay for me, we sort it out. I'm sorry."

The exodus began. Skyward and away, the marching feet. Kemy tripped up on the stairs. "Oh, let me sleep with you!" she asked the twins. "Please. It's better in the loft!"

"And you too, Bel," Georgia said. "He'll want to get you most. Let's all sleep in the loft."

Bel and Kemy sped up with their duvets and dressing gowns. Teeth chattered as they were cleaned and clothes were thrown in corners. Ida closed her bedroom door and put on her hairnet. The house lay down and prayed for peace.

WHERE DO THEY wander, the angry ones? The moors would have him if Neasden had moors. But there are the hills, and there is a storm tonight, and moonlight. Mr. Hyde is blowing in the wind. He roars and shakes his fist at the sky. It begins to rain. His dance carries him through the empty streets in the rain and his hair is getting wet. Mr. Hyde staggers up the alley where the moon has leaked into the cracks in the ground. He looks down and sees silver, electricity, around his feet, the silver men rocking and swinging and flying, and he thinks, faintly, *Ah, there you are, ah, there it is, don't spare the horses! Is the dinner ready, missus? It's cold out here.* He wanders past Waifer Avenue because sometimes Mr. Hyde forgets the man he came from. He is made up of the worst parts of that man—they often forget each other.

SLIPS OF RAIN rushed down the face of the moon. In her sleep, Georgia pushed away the covers. She opened the window so that the moon was naked, and watched it. *Full and bright you are*, she dreamed, *what a face*. She pulled herself up with groggy arms and clutched the windowsill. She stepped over it, sat down on the sill and didn't feel the cold air around her ankles where the nightgown ended. Georgia dangled on the edge of the house, on the edge of sleep, and dreamed in colors of Sekon, how the kitten felt that night, because in sleep she could remember. It felt as soft as a beginning, it felt simple, it felt like light in her hands. The best time, the best journeys are sleep, under a cover in the dark, and safe from the dark; we are free to roam back to our own first lights and find the ones we have lost, the un-ruined, the ones we dream of becoming again.

Georgia sat very still as the rain wet her legs. Behind her, Kemy and Bel were asleep on the floor, snatching rest. Bel was dreaming of a girl on the edge of a house. And Bessi tossed in her sleep. She dreamed of the sound of keys, and then she opened her eyes.

Was it a figure there in the window, or was she still sleeping, with her eyes open, like Georgia did sometimes? Like that time Bel came out of the toilet in the middle of the night and found Georgia standing there on the landing, just standing and watching nothing in the air, asleep. Bessi closed and opened her eyes again to check. Yes, it might be Georgia, on the windowsill. Yes, she's going to fall and hurt herself.

Bessi's heart beat suddenly hard and fast. She had to keep quiet, she knew. Bel had explained once that if you wake someone doing awake things in their sleep you could kill them, the shock could give them a heart attack. So, quietly now, Bessi threw back the covers and sprang toward the window. Inside herself, shocked, she was calling Georgia, Georgia in the window! Stay there!

She gripped the back of Georgia's nightgown and pulled as gently as she could. Georgia fell back onto the bed with her legs in the air, and woke up. Bessi was allowed to speak. "What are you doing, what were you doing, you scared me to death, you could've fallen, what were you doing, Georgia!" Bel woke up and saw the window open and

Georgia disheveled on the bed. She went to see her eyes, and there were bits of moon there, and she knew that Georgia had been somewhere far. "Be careful there," she said quietly. Then Kemy sat up saying, "What? What? Is he back? It's freezing in here."

Georgia looked about her. "I was sitting down," she said. "I was just . . . looking out."

What she didn't say: *The night, the silence, something that lives inside them, it called me, it wants me, and I answered.*

Three floors down, a set of keys danced in the lock.

The front door opened. The front door slammed shut.

"It's starting," said Bel.

For a moment they were statues just out of sleep. They stopped breathing. Ida alone in her room stared at Nne-Nne. It was that instant of nothing, of death, the silence down in the soil, before what you imagined you couldn't bear.

Bel swung back to life. "Okay," she said, "into bed, don't make a sound, be asleep. Have you got tissues?"

"I haven't," said Kemy.

Bel grabbed the toilet roll out of the bathroom and gave a piece to Kemy. She kissed Georgia on the cheek. They lay back down rolling tissue balls and stuffed them into their ears. Kemy took the extra precaution of covering her head with her pillow and securing it around her ears with her forearms. Now she could hear only the silence of cotton.

He was wet and standing in his wet clothes and the mirror could see him but he didn't look. He opened the front door and slammed it again, harder, so that the house shook. That'll do it. Mr. Hyde took off his coat, creaked into the kitchen and put Jack Daniel's on the table. Smooth brown shoulders and a long warm neck. He sat down and poured himself a glass. The glass knocked the wood, the legs of a chair scraped the floor, the wind-chime bells rang out as he wandered into the sun lounge—it's a symphony of discontent. They could hear it, the creaks, the terrible music, through tissue balls and double-deckers of pillow. There he sat, by the dishwasher with Jack, and out in the dark he saw a figure among the trees. She reached out her hands and said, I'm going now, my best boy. We must face these things with fortitude. And in the wind and the rain the apple trees moaned.

Where's the dinner? Where's the girl? Mr. Hyde was hot in the throat and hot in the heart but cold in how to get there. The bells rang. He walked up and down the hall. It was time for shouting. "Isabel!" he said. "*Bel!*"

He marched for more Jack and gulped and shouted, "*Get down here, Bel!*"

"Be asleep," said Bel in the loft. "Be asleep!"

He pumped his fists. He was pink all over, lobster pink, boiled in the cheeks, beetroot lips, sticky fists. Bel didn't come. In bed, Ida tossed toward the window. Nne-Nne's eyes and Nne-Nne's cheekbones flashed in the dark. Be tough, Ida!

Mr. Hyde began to mount the stairs. The middle stairs creaked most and the top two had a deeper sound—the house knew exactly where he was. The door to Bel's room was closed. Mr. Hyde opened it and barged in. He swayed in the empty dark. The fury and the terror got bigger. He burst into Kemy's room and there was just moonlight there, in a pool on the bed where Kemy should be. "Fucking God almighty, where the devil are they!" he said, squeezing his fists. Ida braced herself. Mr. Hyde charged out onto the landing and swung around and mounted the stairs to the loft. Ida jumped out of bed and put on the magic dressing gown. He bellowed, "*Bel! Are you up there? You get down here!*"

The tissue wasn't working at all now. Georgia and Kemy had run into Bessi's Best Bed because it was farthest from the door, which definitely made it best tonight, and they'd wrapped themselves around each other and they trembled. There was no key. They'd been asking for keys but Aubrey kept saying no, they didn't need keys, they were too young for keys. Bel had stopped saying "be asleep." She was on her feet in her long silk dressing gown in the middle of the room, ready for him, her temper beginning to thump. "If he tries anything, if he tries, oh, shit!" Mr. Hyde banged the door with his fist.

The light out in the landing was on and it rushed under the door. Bel thumped the door back. This did not seem to Georgia or Bessi the best idea but Bel was hot tonight, volatile, like the spiders in Sekon, like Ida when she was pushed too far.

Ida shook the world now. She ran out into the landing in her hairnet and gown and looked up at Mr. Hyde. He had that look of shrinkage, a livid pink devil with a shrunken neck.

"Get away from there with your trouble," she said. Nne-Nne was behind her, the cheekbones sharp.

Mr. Hyde scowled. He stamped down toward her and wobbled his damp finger in her face. Jack Daniel's flanked him like a stinking bodyguard. "I'm talking to Bel," he said, "I've been walking in the rain and I'm tired, I'm hungry, I've been working for thirty years. You get out of my way, woman!" He started back up the stairs.

Ida grabbed his arm.

"Try to mek trouble with her, I will lose my tempa!"

When Ida lost her temper, she was capable of killing. She was might and she was thunder, the first that God ever made.

"*Leave* dem!" she said.

His face was the other face. Her heart was the wild thing underneath. There was no place to meet or talk or simmer. Inside Mr. Hyde, Aubrey wanted to cry out. What he wanted was to take his wife in his arms and tell her he was sorry for it all, and that he needed comfort. He wanted to be a good strong man for those he loved. But he couldn't get out.

Mr. Hyde ripped his arm away. "*Bugger!*" he shouted. Ida followed him up the stairs and got his arm back but Mr. Hyde's body was made of iron. He broke free. And when she got him back again, four stairs down from the loft, she slapped him hard across the cheek. Mr. Hyde slapped her back.

"Monkey," Ida yelled, "you dog!"

They had put on their dressing gowns, the children. Ida and Mr. Hyde fought on the stairs, which was not a lot of space for fighting. They rolled down the stairs to the first-floor landing. Mr. Hyde roared. Georgia and Bessi locked hands. Kemy was afraid, her eyes in circles. Now it was time. Bel opened the door and the four of them burst out of the loft and swept down into the thunder, their gowns billowing out behind them.

Bel and Kemy, oldest and youngest, pulled at Mr. Hyde's arms. Georgia and Bessi took Ida but she couldn't be held. She had used her nails for scratching and her legs for kicking. Mr. Hyde shouted over the struggle, "I want to fucking hell dammit talk to Bel!" who was behind him, there on his arm wrenching it back. He spun around and gripped her by the neck and shoved her to the floor. Bel banged her head against the bathroom door. Kemy screamed.

It could be the sound of the youngest screaming. Or it could be the sight of the oldest hurt, that makes a woman lose completely the order of things, the sense of past and future and what if, what would happen if. Ida and Nne-Nne and Cecelia's ghost went downstairs to the kitchen. It did not take long, as long as it takes fire to spread. They arrived back. Bel looked up, her head dazed, and saw them. "Mum," she said. Ida was holding the Sunday mutton carver, the largest blade in the house, and Nne-Nne was behind her all in red. They were going straight for Mr. Hyde, where his heart was. Cut him, said Nne-Nne.

Ida raised the knife. A strange croak flew out of her mouth. The tracks on her cheeks blackened. Kemy fled. Next door the Kaczalas opened their eyes to little girls screaming in the night. The knife came down. It slashed Mr. Hyde down the arm and lifted again.

"Stop it, Mum! Look!" cried Bel.

The blood ran through Mr. Hyde's shirt and he didn't seem to notice. His hair was standing up. His dentures fell out. "She makes things . . . so very, very difficult . . . for me," he said.

The knife was coming back down. As it got closer, Ida saw the blood seeping out of Aubrey. There were open cuts on his face from her nails. Her girls were wailing. She heard Aubrey her husband whisper, in his blood, in her blood, in the blood of their children, I'm sorry.

The blade came down, and fell away.

IN THE HUSH, a panting, whimpering hush, Kemy said, "You wouldn't, Mummy, you wouldn't have done it, would you?" She was curled up three stairs down from the loft, visible through the triangular hole in the banister.

The man on the floor stood up. He looked up at Kemy through the triangle. He was not quite Mr. Hyde and not quite Aubrey. He walked past Ida and went down into the bottom of the house. In the kitchen, he sat down and stared at the fridge. He held a pen and not a drink in his hand.

Bel had stood up and was holding Georgia close to her. She wished she could have hidden her away from this night. And she wished she could stay.

"You're going, aren't you," said Georgia.

"Yes," said Bel.

(Aubrey wrote, *Your father's tired, your father doesn't know what to do all the time,* on a piece of paper and left it on the kitchen table.)

She called Jason, packed some things and put on an orange dress that smelled of rosemary, with green high heels the color of her eyes.

Just before dawn, Ida went downstairs. Aubrey was asleep in his chair. The photograph of his parents was lying on the floor next to him. Ida woke him up and bandaged his arm. They didn't look at each other.

"Bel is going," she said, "I will take her room."

Ginger

The apple trees were ghosts. They reached up their arms, they swayed and yawned on Wednesdays, but no one heard. The grass around them grew wilder, and in the shack at the back of the garden the spiders forgot how incredible they were. During the great London storm of 1987 the terrible wind blew away part of the fence. A year later Mr. Kaczala mended it. Georgia became a vegetarian, Bessi discovered the truth about the parson's nose, Diana and Charles had arguments in the evenings. And in Kilburn, a child was born.

Bel had moved into Jason's flat and she took in her chemical-free-hairdressing clients at home. She'd produced business cards to advertise her services and she handed them out, one hand on the pram, the other outstretched, on Kilburn High Road, where she bought all her shoes. For a small extra fee, and if the child, a boy, was sleeping, she also read palms.

She came to Waifer Avenue twice a week with Jay in the pram, while Aubrey was at work. She and Ida whispered to the child about mystery, how thunder and lightning were a mother and son, and the sun and the moon a man and his wife. Nne-Nne sang him old songs from the singing tree and he had the permanent look on his face of being startled. He would never get to meet his other great-grandmother, because Judith had finally slipped away in her sleep the night before he was born.

Of his three aunties, Jay liked Kemy the best. She lifted him up and gave him plane rides. She kissed him and took him for perilous walks through the misty wild of the apple trees. It was there that Kemy would stop, and think about Michael Jackson.

Very soon,

Michael Jackson

was coming to Wembley.

"Do you understand, Jay?" Kemy said while the little boy bounced about in the grass. "He's coming. At this moment, he is on tour, getting ready."

Georgia looked out of the loft window. She blew out smoke. Bessi, Anna and Reena were in the bathroom behind the saloon door. They were talking about sex. She had come away for a minute on her own.

She heard Reena say, "You're supposed to breathe heavily and make noises, so they know you're enjoying it." Then Anna: "It's better if you moan too. Trevor likes it when I moan. It gets him all excited." She heard Bessi laugh and Reena say, "Yuck, that's nasty."

Georgia saw Kemy with Jay in the trees. She could tell what Kemy was thinking about because she had a daze about her, even from all that way up. The sun glittered out over the evergreen tree. Georgia closed her eyes. "Are you going downstairs, Georgia?" called Bessi. "If you are, could you get some tea?"

She left and went downstairs to the kitchen.

The twins had arrived at breasts and cigarettes. They did not have cleavage, like Bel had when she was fifteen. They needed Wonderbras to get cleavage and would not be able to afford them until after the Empire, so they did without. Georgia wasn't much bothered, and she couldn't understand why Bessi went on about it, or why she felt she had to wear lipstick and eyeliner wherever she went, like Reena, who smudged a black smile beneath her eyes every morning. "It's all right for you," Bessi said to Georgia sometimes with a touch of jealousy in her voice, "you don't need it. You're a rose, aren't you, like Bel says, and you don't even realize it."

Georgia prepared the tea. She put out biscuits and told herself, *Just a half, to dip in tea, not a whole one.* She slipped outside to quickly water the roses. There were two bushes now. She'd planted another one, in yellow. They were growing together, young and fierce and old and weathered, the stems and thorns pointing in different directions.

She came back in with Kemy and Jay, who was sleepy. He stumbled around in the kitchen, then lay down on the floor and closed his eyes. "He's falling asleep!" said Georgia. "Just like that!" She imagined the inside of Jay's head a soft light place of gentle weather.

"You taking that upstairs?" Kemy said, looking at the tray.

"Yeh," said Georgia. "You coming?"

Kemy took Jay into the living room, where Bel was doing Ida's hair, and followed Georgia up the stairs. As they approached the loft, the others were still laughing. Bessi's laugh had gotten louder recently, Georgia had noticed.

Mostly now, the twins came to decisions without each other. And this summer, as the apple trees swayed and Bessi didn't hear them, she'd made one of her most important decisions yet: Bessi had decided, with her eyes shut for some time, that she would be bold. She would be strong and bold forever. She would fear nothing, not Mr. Hyde or Big Sian or the gigantic world, and she would laugh a lot, even when she didn't feel like laughing. Because if you wanted to be anyone in this world, she'd realized, you had to be more and less than what you were.

Georgia didn't agree. She'd said, "No, Bessi," over their cigarette (they smoked between them and never had one each because it meant they'd be whole smokers—this way they were only half smokers). "To be," said Georgia, thinking about it, "you have to . . . just be. Yes, that's what I think. Like Jay." Bessi shook her head. She held out her fingers

for the cigarette and said, "Give us a bit, you've had more than me."
"No I haven't," said Georgia. "Yes, you have," said Bessi.

Georgia and Kemy walked into the smoke. Georgia lit joss sticks
Bel had given her. Kemy coughed and waved her hand. "You shouldn't
smoke, it's nasty," she said. "Yeah, it stinks, dunnit," said Reena.

They all settled in the bathroom with tea, biscuits and the skylight
raised. Georgia sat back down in the bath next to Bessi with her legs
over the edge. "Give us a bit." She held out her fingers.

Anna was still talking about Trevor. She had told them the story
several times. They listened to it again. Georgia's and Bessi's minds re-
volved around the story. It had stems and long arms and they traveled
out beyond it to what the story might be for them.

Anna had first slept with Trevor against the wall of his parents'
garage. They were standing up with their tops off. "Trevor's got gold
hair on his chest and he loves ginger," she told them. "He said he loved
me because of my hair. He said, 'You're a gorgeous ginger girl,' and he
kissed me on my cheek, here, on my neck, here—and then on the
boob. That's when I sighed, like this."

Anna breathed in and out deeply. They watched, mesmerized, as
her chest rose and fell. Bessi imagined a tall man standing behind
her with his arms around her waist. Georgia focused on not seeing
Sedrick, but another figure, waiting to hold her and kiss her slowly.
Kemy thought about Michael Jackson and felt shy. Anna went on:
" 'Ginger girl ginger girl,' he said, all the way through. It was, well,
sexy, and it didn't hurt a bit, like they say it does. It was lovely. Afterward, every night, I let it happen again and again and again in my
head. It never goes away."

Georgia sipped her tea. *Sex is ginger,* she thought.

And don't forget to sigh, thought Bessi.

DEAN AND ERROL were brothers. Bessi saw them first, two boys
leering out from the top deck of a double-decker 182. The twins didn't

know it, but Dean and Errol were lords of the double-deckers and their sport was to sit on the backseats and hunt. Watley Girls' High, they had heard, was teeming with virgins. More so than St. Peter's or Copland or anywhere else in Brent. So when the 182 sped past the Watley gates at 3:30 P.M., Dean and Errol would twist in their seats and crane their necks and singe the thick smeared windows with looking. Their eyes were quick. In that one gusty sweep of top-deck travel they worked like radars through the mulling crowds, separating the dogs from the babes. And if there were babes sweet and lush enough, they took immediate action and jumped off the bus at the next stop. With seduction in their stare and a secret swirl below their waists, they would aim and strut, and then fire, when they were close enough to smell her hair or see the quality of her skin, with a tried and tested chat-up line. They said, "What's yer name?" or "What's yer number?" Or currently, "Are you going to the Michael Jackson concert?"

Georgia and Bessi were spotted, that July, during Watley's summer school when no work was done, when instead girls and boys were relieved of the boredom of the hot streets by unisex-game tournaments set up in the playground. They got sweaty in short pleated skirts with numbers on their chests. Bessi was a renowned netball shooter. She closed one eye, aimed and fired and the net flashed as the ball slipped through. Georgia preferred the running, up and down the court making a breeze, calories dripping off her.

This Friday the world was melting. The sycamore trees along Oxgate Road drooped beneath the sun. The insides of cars were sticky and the outsides mirrors. Georgia and Bessi were fresh from the shower and had spent half an hour getting their flicks right. Bessi had applied her makeup. Their glasses were tucked up in their cases, out of sight. They smelled of cocoa butter and Slick & Sheen hair gel. Dean and Errol registered their fine light skin and beguiling twoness from the 182 and jumped off.

Bessi's eyes had risen as the bus raced past and she had seen Dean's round black head swivel and his eyes leap for her. She had liked his face. It was soft and it was strange, dusted chocolate, not fine exactly but finer than Jonathan's, who still followed her around and gave her things—a Blankety-Blank pen, a Rubik's Cube on a key ring—which she always threw away.

She had seen Dean and Errol leave their seats and bounce toward the stairs, and, quietly, she had hoped. Because boys who were not from Watley were not to be sniffed at. They were maximum cool. To be asked out by a non-Watley meant the kind of kudos that could work wonders for a Goggle-Eye Spam Twin.

Bessi stood casually next to Georgia. Despite Spam, she liked standing next to her twin, and Georgia did too. It made them feel proud.

Bessi adjusted her flick. She could see them coming now.

As Dean and Errol strutted closer, Dean kept his eyes firmly on Bessi. Under his breath he said to his brother: "She's fit, innit?"

"Which one?" said Errol. "They look the same to me."

"Nah, man, that one on the left, she's sweeter, man. Taller too."

"She ain't taller. The other one is."

"What? You blind!"

"Tch! Whatever. They both all right, innit."

"Yeah, anyway, shut up na'man."

The brothers swaggered up. One thumb hooked over his back pocket, accentuating the rhythmic limp in his stride, Dean goggled Bessi. The main reason he felt he had to make it clear to Errol that he wanted her was that she was the one who'd seen them on the bus and she would be the easiest to chirpse. It was not easy being a man. Dean was not a bad looker, he was even handsome in certain lights and shades, but rejection happened in the chirpsing game no matter how fit you were and it was a difficult thing to stomach. Errol, on the other hand, had no real preference, he really could not see any difference— pretty lips, gelly flicks, fit bods and sandy skin (and sand was better than coal—a light brown black girl on your arm was good for a man's street cred, it meant you could get a white girl if you wanted to but you'd decided to keep it real and stay with the race).

Bessi nudged Georgia, who had noticed they were being approached but was pretending that she hadn't. She looked at the sky. She looked at the lamppost in the street. She checked her flick. She glanced at Errol, the one who wasn't watching Bessi, the taller one with the bigger head.

"They're non-Watleys," whispered Bessi.

"Oh," said Georgia, feeling nervous, feeling unpretty. "Well, I don't care." But somewhere she was thinking, *Ginger, what is the ginger in sex? Is it like caramel?* Errol was caramel, and rough-looking, but rough in a heat-tossed, muscly way. Both the boys were wearing vests. Errol's was green, gold and black, the color of the Jamaican flag; Dean's was red. They had muscles, both of them, like in the adverts. Georgia's stomach started swirling. They were here.

Dean stood before Bessi with thumb in back pocket. He swept a gaze from her face, down over her belly top and Sasperilla jeans and back up again, and began.

"What ya sayin," he said, with the sun in his eyes.

Bessi looked at Georgia and then past Dean's ear, stumped. It was an odd question. The Watley boys said it too, and she never knew what to say. It was not a How are you? and nothing as specific as a What's yer name? and it seemed unfair, because it obliged her, not him, to offer a subject for conversation. She took an anxious breath, and shrugged and nodded at the same time.

Then Dean said: "What's yer name?"

Now that was easy. "Bessi," said Bessi.

"Nice." Dean nodded. "You going to the Michael Jackson concert?"

Errol, in the meantime, had been standing opposite Georgia, smiling softly and rubbing his chin, convinced this action made him look sexy. Each time Georgia's faraway eyes wandered up to his he caught them and held them a few seconds, until they scurried back down to the ground. Errol looked down at her pink denim skirt with the buttons down the front. He wondered about behind the buttons. She was thinking, *What should I say, should I say something, what?*

Errol said at last, "Are you two twins?"

Reena had appeared. She smirked and butted in with, "Naaaaah! *'Course* they're twins, can't you see?" for which she received a cold stare of disapproval from Georgia and Bessi.

"Shut up, Reena," Bessi said.

"Well, I'm going down precinct anyway," Reena called, walking away, and the four were left to themselves.

Georgia was desperate to say something in case Errol thought she was dumb. "We *are* twins," she rushed. "I'm Georgia. I'm older. We're identical." She hated being the Quiet One—it made situations like this so much more awkward for her, there were roles to break out of.

"You don't look identical," said Errol.

He's thinking I'm fatter, thought Georgia, *or he's looking at my ears, isn't he looking at my ears?* "I'm forty-five minutes older," she said, as if it might explain something.

"Yeah, man, I'm older too," Errol said. "We're brothers."

"You don't look like brothers," Bessi put in, comparing Dean's dustiness to something sweaty about Errol; they were completely different colors, and Errol had a flat, soggy-looking nose.

"We're half brothers," said Dean.

"Oh," said Georgia. She looked back at the lamppost in the street. Everyone had gone quiet. "What school d'you go to?" she asked Errol quickly.

"We're finished with that, man. School's rubbish. Slavery, man."

Bessi was excited. She nudged Georgia. Non-Watleys and well-'ard school-leavers too! She spread a vast smile in front of Dean and he took her to one side, holding her elbow. Georgia was left alone with Errol, who still made no effort at thinking of things to talk about. The only thing she could find to say now was, "Are you going to the Michael Jackson concert?"

"Bro's tryin'a get tickets," said Errol. "We might. Why, you wanna go?"

"Wouldn't mind."

Georgia checked to see what Bessi and Dean were doing. Bessi was writing something down on a piece of paper. She gave it to Dean and he looked her up and down again. The two of them walked back toward her and Errol.

"Dean might be able to get us tickets for Michael Jackson. He's got contacts in the *music* industry," Bessi said, looking overjoyed. "Good, innit!"

"Yeah," said Georgia. Errol had not yet asked her for her number.

He took a little red book out of his back pocket. He started opening it. Then he looked up, confused, and said, "Oh, what's yer name?"

"Georgia," said Georgia.

He opened it on *J*. "Can I have yer digits?" he said.

"All right." Georgia took the book and got a pen out of her bag. She turned from *J* to *G* and thought, *Can't he spell?* She wrote down the number, which was, of course, the same as Bessi's, seeing as they shared a bedroom, and Errol could easily have gotten it from Dean, because they lived in the same house too. But it was very important, this, writing down her number in Errol's book, because she was one person and Bessi was another. They had different handwriting.

All the digits delivered (with minimal coaxing, the boys noted), Dean and Errol walked Georgia and Bessi down to the precinct to hang out under the breezy leaves and the promise of non-Watley kisses. The twins looked on proudly as the same old Watley boys chirpsed bored Watley girls, standing as close as possible to their exotic fanciers from Wembley. "We can hear all the concerts from our place," Dean told them, "the bass an' everything. It's just down the road."

"Yeah, we can hear it too from our house, but it's probably quieter," said Bessi, "and we have to stand outside."

Errol said to Georgia, "You're the quiet one, innit. She's the loud one."

Georgia tutted under her breath. "I'm loud sometimes," she said, thinking *So bloody what if I'm quiet—what's the thing about it?*

KEMY WAS LEARNING to walk on the moon. During her seven years of Michael Jackson worship she'd done everything a number one fan must do. The poster she'd had since she was five, the one of him in a black suit leaning against a wall with his hands in his lovely pockets, was tatty now, brown at the edges, and it was rolled up under the bed. She'd replaced it with the *Thriller* poster, Michael in a red leather jacket with a werewolf behind him, clutching his shoulders. When she was eight, she'd written him a letter asking him to come over for apple pie and then take her to the Wimpy in Willesden for a burger ("I like cheese and bacon," she'd written, "but the twins don't—they don't like pork because Ham's pork and that's the name of our hamster. He died. Do you like pork?"). So far Michael hadn't replied but Kemy didn't mind, she understood he was very busy and that he probably never would write back.

She was going to that concert. Even if she had to go with Aubrey. She wanted Bel and Jason to take her (the twins were too young, they had no money, they were not much better off than her) and Bel had said they would—but they might not have time in the end, what with being parents. But she was going. Oh yes. She was going to moonwalk outside the arena in the queue and inside too, in the aisle. For her practice sessions she referred to the instructions provided in her book, *Michael Jackson: The Rules of a Number 1 Fan:*

1. Find a smooth surface suitable for dancing. [Kemy used the kitchen lino.]
2. Stand with your feet close together, the left foot slightly ahead.
3. Lift the right heel as if you were taking a step.
4. Lower the right heel, lean on the right foot and drag back the left

foot to where the toes are level with the right heel. [This is where Kemy gets confused.]

5. Lift the left heel and drag back the right foot. Repeat and practice.

She almost had it. She was one step away from the moon. Kemy was getting on Ida's nerves because she was always under her feet in the kitchen. She was there now, when the twins got home with flushed cheeks.

"You're tanned," Kemy shouted over "Beat It." "Were you at the precinct?"

"Yeah," said Bessi. "It's so hot." She couldn't keep it in. She knew Kemy would go wild with jealousy. She turned off the music and said it all in one breath: "We met these guys, Dean and Errol, they've left school, and Dean's got contacts in the *music* industry and he's gonna get us *free tickets*—"

"He might . . ." said Georgia.

"—for Michael Jackson!"

Kemy stopped her moonwalk. She stood very still and swallowed. Her eyes got much bigger than they had ever been. She said: "What about me? Can he get me a ticket too?"

Kemy and Bessi had had many arguments recently over Michael. Kemy praised everything he did, every song. But Bessi, who now read music magazines, did not approve of the "direction" Michael had taken with his latest album, *Bad*. "*Thriller* was much better," she argued. "It had a much better concept." (She'd read that in *Smash Hits*.) "But he's brilliant," insisted Kemy. "He's a genius and he can do anything he likes. So shut up!"

Bessi was laughing. Kemy still hadn't moved. Her next movement depended on whether Bessi could get her into Wembley. Only her mouth moved. *Please,* it said. And the eyes shifted from twin to twin.

"I'll see what I can do," said Bessi, raising her chin and then sauntering up to the loft.

Over the next two weeks the Hunter telephone was congested. When Bessi was not talking to Dean, Georgia was talking to Errol. The phone rang so much that Aubrey said, "Bugger that thing!" whenever it did. Mr. Hyde made an appearance (though milder now since Ida's knife), asking who they were talking to, and left a note on the kitchen table: *I pay the bills in this house and unless you want to leave you will do things my way. You are not to disgrace yourselves.*

The phone was usually answered by Kemy. She always got there first, in case it was Dean. She asked, "Who's calling, please?" and if it was Dean she said, "Hello, this is Kemy. I like Michael Jackson very much." Dean usually said nothing and waited for her to get Bessi. "Well, good-bye," she would say. "I'll go and get Bessi for you . . . bye, then."

"Your sis is desperate, innit!" Dean would start off. And Bessi would remind him to try to get Kemy a ticket too. Georgia also reminded Errol to remind Dean. Errol was better over the phone, she discovered.

The conversation got belly-prickling. The four of them, in twos, they talked of parents and siblings, Nigeria and Jamaica and the last time they went there (though on this topic, Georgia preferred to listen). They talked of DJs and raves and the best tunes and the first and last lips that touched theirs, the voices becoming softer, the space around them quieter, and the memory of faces closer to beauty and perfection with each passing day. Georgia and Bessi fell in love with the ends of telephone lines. They updated each other on new and vital bits of information—Dean had a driver's license, Errol said Georgia had a sexy voice, Dean knew LL Cool J's second cousin. In their dreams they let their telephone lovers kiss their collarbones and lay their hands beneath bra tops, the warm fingers resting there, and sliding down to find the waist.

It was not sex they dreamed of. It was touch. The tenderness and the inflammation of touch. Georgia wrote it in her notebook: *I would*

*like to hug him in the dark, and it will be warm and safe. I will tell him
to make it slow.*

In the days approaching the concert Kemy bugged Bessi about tickets up to six times a day. Bessi told her Dean said he'd get them. But Kemy needed a sure thing. "He's talking rubbish," she said. "He's not getting them." She called Bel in a fever and Bel checked with Jason, who said yes. "I've got a ticket!" Kemy shouted. "I'm going I'm going I'm going!" She moonwalked. She shimmied. "I'm going to see Michael Jackson!"

On the last day, Dean broke the news to Bessi over the phone that the promoter he knew hadn't come through with the tickets and he wouldn't be able to take her. "But," he said, "you could come cotch at our place"—their mother's—"and listen from there, it's only down the road, remember. Come na'man. Bring Georgia. We'll play some tunes. An' I might be able to get tickets for when he's playing next month."

They used Michael Jackson, Anna and Reena as their alibi. Aubrey said, from the armchair, with a little Jack in his tea, "Make sure you're back by twelve." And Ida said, eating her warmed-up ice cream upstairs in Bel's room, "Don't talk to boys," which was currently the most common thing she said apart from "Have some Vicks."

IT WAS THE year of fishtail skirts and electric blue and Georgia was wearing both, the hem swishing around her calves like a flashy mermaid. They were walking along Forty Lane toward Wembley, around them the lights, strobes of red, a whiz of pink, white standing still on lampposts. Bessi was wearing a tight red dress. She was saying to Georgia, "Michael Jackson is a perfect example of someone who's taken as much space as they want in the world. I mean, he wakes up in the morning, the world is at his feet, and he made it so. Anyone can do it."

"Not just anyone," said Georgia. "I don't think it's as simple as that. Some people couldn't survive with the world at their feet."

"I could," said Bessi.

"I couldn't." She hurried forward. "Is my skirt stuck to my tights at the back?"

"No."

Their jackets were thin black Petticoat Lane leather, birthday presents from Aubrey the year before. Georgia's was longer, past her hips. She kept pulling it down at the back.

It had taken them two and a half hours to get ready. In the loft there was only one full-length mirror.

"Tell me honestly," Georgia had said to Bessi, looking over her shoulder at her reflection. "Do I look fat? I do, don't I? I look massive. Don't I look like a truck on the way to Tesco?"

Bessi laughed. "*No,* silly! You look lovely. That blue's *gorgeous.*" She was trying to inch her way into the mirror. The two of them got caught at once, and the bad things doubled. The thighs, the bums. *Just look at those legs,* they thought. *Athlete's legs.* Oh, why had God given them such bulges—thighs, bums, foreheads? It wasn't fair. Georgia had skipped lunch in preparation for the evening. Bessi felt bloated from the chicken sandwich she'd eaten. "What about me?" she said. "I look like a whale!"

"No, you don't. Maybe I should take off the tights." Georgia started taking off her tights.

"Your legs will get sweaty."

Georgia put them back on because her legs looked funny sticking out of the bottom of the skirt like that. She changed her skirt. She ignored her growling stomach. She changed her top. Bessi tried on different shoes. They gelled the hair. They arranged the flicks.

"What are you going to do if Dean tries to sleep with you?" asked Georgia before they left. "Are you going to?"

"Are you?"

"Don't know. Are you?"

"I might, if it feels right," said Bessi. They were sitting in front of the mirror, smoothing eyebrows, checking, one face next to another face. Almost the same face.

Georgia said, "I might, if it feels safe."

"You look nice," said Bessi.

They left. Perfumed and flustered, they stepped out into summer.

British Telecom was responsible for the images in their heads. Through the crowds at Wembley Park they searched for two flawless Romeos and couldn't find them. Instead they found Dean and Errol, leaning against a fence. It took a few moments to recognize them. BT had concocted piercing eyes, dazzling smiles, good teeth. Georgia re-tuned to Errol's soggy nose and the sweat on him. And Bessi noticed Dean's pink whites of eyes, and that he had a discernible scar on his bottom lip. Neither of them had the best teeth.

But the twins were not altogether deterred. They were still non-Watleys. Dean could get them in to see Michael, not tonight but maybe in August. He knew Cool J's (second) cousin. And also, there might still be tenderness.

"What ya sayin," said Dean.

What does he mean? thought Bessi. *What the bloody hell does that mean?*

She said, "Fine." (Was that the right answer?)

"Wha' gwan," said Errol.

Georgia said, "Yes."

She smiled. He gave her a strange look. (*You're the quiet one, innit.*) They fell into pairs. Boy, girl, boy, girl. There were lots of people wearing black leather jackets with silver zips in salute to Michael. Boys had grown their hair for the event, and had it relaxed. They were surrounded by Jheri curls and Michael's songs blasting out from car windows. Wembley, a place where in the afternoons old women used prams as shopping carts, had become the center of the world. They didn't see Kemy. She was in there somewhere, probably near the front (she'd insisted Bel pick her up at four o'clock and let her queue out-side). Dressed all in black, she'd gelled her hair and made her lips bright red, and put on shoes with flat soles for moonwalking.

They walked away from the crowd, shouting over the noise and not hearing one another. Dean said, "The final shows will be better," and Bessi thought he said, "The guy knows they'll be better." "What guy?" she shouted. "What?" yelled Dean. Georgia didn't like shouting and she didn't like crowds. It was too much effort to dodge the people and not bump against Errol and shout at the same time. Whenever Errol said something she nodded as if she'd heard him.

When they arrived at the front door Georgia and Bessi felt dirty. Was two weeks long enough to know a guy before going to his house, indeed, his mother's house? Is this what slags did? Were *they* slags? They touched eyes. Errol beckoned with his big head as they stood on the doormat. "Ya coming in?" he said. The low ceiling made his head look bigger.

"Take a seat," Dean said. He glanced at his brother. Errol moved to-ward the kitchen. Errol in a green shirt, Dean in an orange polo, com-plementary colors, gold chains around their necks.

Georgia and Bessi sat down on a cream fake-leather sofa. Bessi crossed her legs and leaned back on one arm, careful not to touch the sofa with her hair. Georgia sank back, and remembered just in time about the gel. Was it dry yet? She sat forward again in case it wasn't. She thought: *Bessi looks sexy, crossing her legs like that. She looks confi-dent. How does she do that?*

Dean was in the corner searching through tapes. "You like rare groove, innit, Bessi?"

"I thought we were gonna listen to the concert."

"Yeh, man, we will, he's not on yet, though. He won't be on till nine, you know."

"Oh, okay—got any Roy Ayers, then?"

"Plenty, man," said Dean.

And Roy arrived like smoke. With musky strokes of piano and

a voice inflamed with tenderness he wafted into the air, over the cactus plant and glass coffee table, under the lights, crept across the crimson carpet to tug at the twins' nerves with beats of silk. Melody melted them. Georgia touched her hair and saw it was dry. She leaned back and Bessi leaned back. *It's good, eve,* they thought.

Errol came out of the kitchen with a bottle of Pink Lady. "Or d'you want Thunderbird?" he said. "We've got some if you want some. Which d'you like best?"

"Pink Lady," Georgia said.

They were given glasses and the ivory liquid tumbled in. It tasted sweet. The sweetness clutched Georgia's throat. She drank some more. Bessi drank some more. They peeped at each other over bulbs of glass.

THE STAIRCASE WAS a spiral up to the unknown. It posed threats and promised a kind of wonder. Bessi followed Dean up triangles, her legs turned to syrup, one last slurry smile at Georgia, a kind of good-bye (*Farewell, sis, you look worried, don't worry*). She followed him, swivels in her brain, beneath her feet, let him lay her down on sheets, let the darkness engulf her, the music send her. He led her into his room to the wide bed, an orange glow from a lamp creeping toward the covers. It lit her skin. He swept his eyes over her shoulders, her stomach, her breasts, and down her legs, avoided her eyes and kissed her. Bessi looked into the touching. He kissed her deeper. She was sweating. His tongue moved into her mouth and she wondered whether to trust it. She wondered whether Georgia trusted it, supine in electric blue on the sofa with Roy Ayers behind her, the blue fishtails traveling up her legs now, his hands over her chest, lips at her neck. *Don't worry, sis.*

Trust me, he said. Come on (pretty), he said, lay back, relax. The dimmer lights were dimmed. On the coffee table, two glasses, a final sip of lady. The lady danced and Georgia sinks back. She tells herself,

I am in a bright field on a big blue day letting him take off my top. Yes, he leads me to the daffodils and takes off my clothes and I tell him *be slow love, be very slow*. He kisses me with his caramel mouth and I let myself fall. This is it, my swirling stomach, the butterflies, this is ginger. And then he says, What's this? On your stomach? It's a scar, she tells him. From what? he says. From being born, she tells him, and eating dust. What? he says, and looks at her strangely again, and then he carries on. He avoids her eyes and avoids her scar. It doesn't matter, she thinks, and looks into touch.

Fingers trailed thighs and the edges of breast. Lips shadowed nipple and sucked inward. They arched and stretched. The caramel and chocolate palms, moist now, sliding along sand torsos, pressing on hips narrow with doubt and trembling with the possibility of opening, of what it would mean, how the world might change. It was a chance, just a chance the fingers searched for, firmly, everywhere, and Bessi felt her legs yawn outward, slowly, obeying. Dean lay down on top of her. And then another music started. The Wembley crowd was roaring. Michael stepped onstage in black leather and zips and Kemy had love and passion all over her face. He sang. Kemy cried. And Bessi held her breath and tried to sigh.

But the pain. The blood. On the sofa. Is there blood? His mother. What will she say? What if she walked in right now and saw Errol on top of a girl she's never met with her big legs open on her sofa? Roy Ayers has gone. I can hear Michael singing and people screaming (*Kemy, I wish I was there with you, I wish I was still new and young like you*). I can hear, very faint, a kitten in the bushes and there's heat all around me but how I feel cold. Can't he stop? Won't you stop? It hurts. She tries to push him away and he carries on, moving inside her, planets between them. He races through her.

And left her far behind, sailing away with something of hers, something he was not worthy of and she could never get back. Bessi watched his face exploding above her, the mouth open, victorious. She lay there and waited for him to pull himself together. "I came out in time, innit," he gasped, and collapsed on top of her. He'd squirted and seeped all over her stomach. Sticky. Gross. He was panting like a dog. And there in the corner of the room, in the orange shadow, Mr. Hyde was watching.

What's up? said Errol. What d'you mean? said Georgia, staring at the cockroach crawling up the wall. Didn't you like it? he said. Yes, she said. You could've fooled me, you hardly moved, you go on like you're dead. Thanks, she said. She gets her clothes and puts everything back on and sits on the sofa with a dreadful smile. Oh! she thinks, the sofa! A tissue, a cloth, she says, quick Errol, blood! He's getting annoyed. Nah worry, man, there's nothing there. What's *up* with you? And she asks him, Where's your bathroom?

GEORGIA WASHED HER hands at the white sink and concentrated hard on the water. She used soap and rinsed. She used soap again and rinsed. Then she rubbed water on her legs, arms and neck. She wet that face, the thing in the mirror, it needed cleaning. She rubbed it in her hands for fifteen minutes and then wiped herself dry with a towel, all the way down to her ankles. There, all clean. She wiped her hands again. There there, all clean.

When Georgia came out of the bathroom, Bessi was standing at the bottom of the stairs with her hair messy and her dress crooked. Dean and Errol were standing by the sofa. They were all staring at her. Bessi looked shocked. Georgia held her hand over her stomach, above the scar.

"Georgie." Bessi walked toward her. "What's wrong?"

"I don't feel well," said Georgia. "Can we go home now?"

Georgia had a craze in her face. The hem of her skirt was all wet. Bessi was alarmed. "Yes," she said, "we'll go now. Come on."

Bessi turned to Errol and her eyes said, *What did you do? You didn't hurt her, did you?* And out loud Errol said, "What's up with your sister, man? She acting kinda strange. She always like this?"

Georgia didn't hear all of what he said but she heard the "strange" bit and the "she always like that?" *Not always,* she thought, *not always.* "Can we go now?" she said.

"I'll phone you," Dean said to Bessi as they left.

Errol tried to take Georgia's hand and say something, but she wandered out into the street.

It was night. There were traffic noises and Michael noises. Bessi put her arm through Georgia's arm. "Tell me what it is, Georgie," she said. "Talk to me, tell me."

But it felt so much better now, out in the cool open air, just the two of them. Georgia said, "I'm all right, I promise. I feel better."

"But what happened, with Errol?"

They walked, Bessi with inward feet, Georgia with outward feet.

"It hurt," said Georgia.

"Yes. It did."

Georgia said: "Bess, I have . . . shadows . . . in my head."

"What shadows?"

She stopped. She looked into her other face, the happy innocent one, and thought, *I will not bring her darkness, stay there.*

She walked on. "It's nothing," she said. "I'm just a bit blue, I'll be all right."

When they got home Mr. Hyde was in the kitchen. He stood up and started starting something.

"Where've you been?" he said.

But Georgia was not in the mood for any shouting. She walked up to Mr. Hyde and said very clearly, her voice shrill, "I'm going to bed, Dad. I'm going to have a bath and then I'm going to bed. Good night."

Bessi followed her upstairs. She ran a bath for her in the downstairs bathroom, they held each other tightly, and Bessi placed her thumb in between Georgia's eyebrows to smooth away the frown. "One day soon," she said, "we'll go away together just you and me, and everything will be lovely." Then Georgia locked herself in the bathroom, and stayed there for two hours.

When Kemy got home she ran straight up to the loft. She told Bessi all about Michael, about how he'd whirled and strutted and taken her to the moon. "He was *bad*," she said, her hair wild from sweat, her lipstick gone and her moon slippers smudged with dirt.

ERROL PHONED ONCE, a few days later, when Georgia was about to have a bath. The tiny bubbles were bursting as they spoke. He asked her wha' gwaned and whether she wanted to get together. Georgia said no thank you no. Errol was relieved. She put down the phone and went to take her seat in the water.

Bessi stayed with Dean for three months and left him at Halloween. He tried to stop her. He pulled her onto his lap and twisted her arm and she escaped.

They dressed up that Halloween. Reena had the house to herself and invited everyone over. She said they had to be scary. Anna came over to Waifer Avenue and they got dressed together in the loft. Bessi put on black tights and a black leotard with white bones pinned on top, a skeleton with a gorged face, which she covered in plastic scabs. Kemy chose Dracula. She powdered her face and drew a vampire hairline and two rows of eyebrows. She drenched her lips in red and gave herself paper fangs. Anna wrapped herself in bandages so that only her eyes and nostrils were free and said she was a mummy.

Georgia was a ghost. She cut a hole in an old white sheet and put it over her head. She smothered her face and her afro in powder. That was all it needed.

At dusk, the four of them walked along the A406 to Reena's house. They carried sparklers and listened to the Halloween bombs going off. They laughed a lot and made noises appropriate to their costumes. Reena, who was a werewolf, howled and threw open her door. "Come in, horrors!" she boomed.

In her tiny bedroom they ate chips and got drunk. Kemy whipped out her *Forever, Michael* album. They danced up and down the stairs and got hot and then they lay down. Michael sang a slow song. "Listen," Kemy said. They let him sing:

one day in your life
you'll remember a place
someone touching your face
you'll come back and you'll look around

They lay there, sprawled over one another, and wiped their eyes.

Flapjacks

Bessi spread out the map of the world on the floor of the loft. The map was old and curling at the edges from being imagined over. Her fingers moved across the sea. She spotted herself, alone, sitting in a Spanish bar and sipping a long cool drink. *The whole world*—she marveled—*look at it.*

The time had come for the Empire. Over the four years since its conception the twins' flapjack research had become substantial, and was kept in a folder under the alcove. Georgia had been especially diligent about keeping the empty flapjack wrappers, labels and notes in neat piles so that when the time came a plan of action could be easily constructed.

First of all, she suggested, they had to perfect their recipes and confirm their range of flavors.

"Yes," said Bessi, "then once we start selling we can branch out a bit."

"One thing at a time, though," Georgia said.

They spent the holidays before the start of Watley sixth form preparing themselves. Labels were typed bearing the name *The Famous Flapjack Twins,* and freshly baked sample flapjacks were wrapped in plastic wrap (the most cost-effective packaging according to the notes). These were passed out to Watley pupils as complimentary tastes, and well received, then batches of the real thing were sold at lunchtimes from a table at the back of the canteen. One flapjack cost forty-five pence. They became a popular dessert and midafternoon snack, the top flavors being apple-almond and cinnamon-and-blueberry.

Georgia was satisfied with local trading. It was all just about enough for her to sustain a sense of purpose—the baking and wrapping and labeling, pulling out of the oven fresh flapjack trays with new souls, along with the perpetual fostering of the roses and the lives she was discovering in her history books. She was especially interested in Disraeli, Benjamin, 1804–1881, who was Britain's first and only Jewish prime minister, and Gladstone's archrival.

Bessi was not so content. Within a year she became eager to branch out beyond Watley and even beyond Neasden. Neither of them could drive, so they'd have to do it without a car. "We need a business card," she said, "like Bel with her hairdressing. We need to spread the word." They bought colored cards with their profits and Reena helped them arrange the information on her computer. The sheets were printed out and then cut up into slightly crooked business cards:

The Famous Flapjack Twins

Freshly baked golden flapjacks
Flavours you have never tasted before!
Good honest value

Call 01 450 0267 for delivery

"Now," said Bessi. "To the city." She did her lips and her eyes. Georgia did the ends of her twists. At first they put on the same white tops, and Bessi had to change.

Georgia put two nectarines in her bag and they waited for the tube at Neasden Station, a double-edged, open-air platform on the Jubilee line, formerly the Fleet line, and changed to Jubilee in 1977 when the Queen went silver. Stanmore lazed at one end, at the far north, quiet avenues and debonair houses, and the miles and miles of track reached southward through Wembley, past Neasden, into shabby Willesden Green, where the second zone began. The houses sucked in their stomachs and the traffic got louder, shops and walkers multiplied, and the stop between St. John's Wood and Baker Street was a long chugging black tunnel into the madness of zone one. Here life was speed, lights and sterling. Green spaces fell away. Tourists stood baffled on street corners with maps dangling at their sides and beggars sat against the walls of department stores looking out for guilt. The smog snarled above it all, oozing poison. The blossoms were out. It was a damp spring day.

As the tube raged through tunnels Georgia and Bessi saw themselves in the world of the black windows, fuzzy girls in bright tops, their lives getting quicker. They got off at Charing Cross and walked through Trafalgar Square to Piccadilly Circus. Pedestrians yelped beneath the towering walls of lights clutching bags of shopping and trying to overtake. Double-deckers smirked and puffed out fumes which people stepped into, women with bare legs in thick bracelets of smoke. The noise was thunder, the same as it had been when Georgia was lost at the Leicester Square fair, underneath the orange polka-dot horse with wings. For hours it seemed she had crouched there, looking out at the cold endless spin from a merry-go-round, and she had felt certain that she was much safer where she was, under the belly of a fantasy beast, that it was kinder than the beast out there.

As they crossed Shaftesbury Avenue Georgia slipped her arm through Bessi's. A bulky man with a pale frowning face pushed past her. They stationed themselves next to the Trocadero.

Bessi took a few of the cards out of her pocket. Georgia got hers ready. "So . . . we just, hand them out, then," said Bessi. They stuck out their hands with the yellow cards in their fingers. People ignored them. Bessi stepped forward, feeling slightly ridiculous, and began pushing them into passing hands. Georgia picked up momentum too. "Flapjacks?" she said, though no one could hear. "Good, sweet flapjacks?" They worked until they got tired and hungry and leaned back against the wall.

"Want a nectarine?" said Georgia.

"Go on then," said Bessi.

Flapjacks were for business. Nectarines were for pleasure. These were sweet. Perfect balls of juicy sunset sliding down their weary throats.

"The fruit is good," said Georgia.

"The fruit is fine," said Bessi.

The circus spun into evening. It began to make Georgia feel giddy, the voices and the flashing and the gaudy heave of a thousand nights out. There did not seem enough room for everything. "Let's go home," she said to Bessi. "I've had enough. I need a bath."

"You go," Bessi said. She was watching a woman standing alone by the fountain looking around her, as if she did not know where she was. "I feel like staying out for a while."

"What for?"

"Nothing. Just." There was a hint of defiance in Bessi's tone.

She watched Georgia walk away through the crowds with her shoulders narrow. She watched the top of her head disappear down the steps. And she began to walk.

Just as if she was lost, she wandered through the streets and the back roads looking in shop windows and restaurants. She walked into a café wearing an imaginary Spanish dress with a wide skirt and sat at the counter alone. Georgia was somewhere else. Bessi asked the waiter for anything in a long glass. She sipped it, slowly, glancing at people walking in and out, a waitress wiping tables, the girl in the mirror with the plaits. It was just her.

This is what oneness must feel like, she thought.

THE FLAPJACK CALLS did not come as much as they expected. In June they received three inquiries. One from a man with a small voice: Bessi picked up the phone and he said, "Are you famous, then?" Bessi said, "What?" And the man said, "Famous Flapjack Twins— that's what I'm asking, are you famous?" Another was from an old woman who lived in Hertfordshire. Kemy answered this one and the woman asked whether she could speak to one of the Famous Flapjack Twins. "They're not in," Kemy said. The woman told Kemy a long story of how she herself had been making flapjacks since she was a girl (she'd even had a recipe published in the local newspaper), and the other day her daughter, who visited her twice a month with her husband Jeff, had given her this delightful little yellow card and she'd decided she'd give it a try because she always liked to keep abreast of new flapjacks. After several attempts Kemy managed to tell the woman that she wasn't sure whether the twins delivered outside of London because they couldn't drive yet, but she'd tell them to call her back.

The other caller was a gruff-sounding man whom Georgia spoke to. "Yes, this is the right number," she said. The man lowered his voice. It seemed he was in a phone booth. "I've seen your card . . . flapjacks, eh, nice touch! Hope that's not all you do!" Georgia immediately put down the phone.

That was all, apart from the Hertfordshire woman, who kept ringing back and insisting the twins come and have tea with her and bring their recipe so that they could compare. To stop her calling, Georgia prepared a package for her containing four different flavors and a photocopy of their recipe. "She's probably lonely," she said to Kemy.

The twins went out again and got rid of more cards, this time in Kilburn and Cricklewood, and at the entrance to Brent Cross until a security guard asked them to leave. Orders trickled in. They got a request for twenty flapjacks for a kids' party in Dollis Hill. "This is it!" said Bessi. "It's starting!" But after that nothing again for weeks. Aubrey advised them that this was normal for a new business. "It takes time for things to get going," he said. "You've got to be persistent, that's the thing, you've got to crack on."

But Bessi was getting restless. The beginning of eighteen and all there was to look forward to was exams and failing flapjacks. What would it be like, she wondered, to be lost entirely? To awake in another place, not home, to be stripped of everything until all that was left was your mind and body and the future? "To the twins," said Aubrey for their birthday toast. "To the twins," went the chorus. And Bessi added something of her own. "To being old enough," she said.

As Aubrey advised, Georgia remained persistent and kept the stall going at lunchtimes. "I told you," she said, "it's better to just keep it local for now, while we're new." She succeeded in dragging Bessi to Hertfordshire with her to see Edith (that was her name) who, when she had received her package, had gotten so excited by the originality of flavor, the cinnamon-and-blueberry especially, that she felt she just *had* to meet them. She'd kept calling. She said she'd given Beccy (that was her daughter) and Jeff (her husband, you know Jeff) a try of the choc-and-nut and they'd mentioned they might even order a few themselves! Kemy decided she was a stalker. She went with them to Hertfordshire on the overground for strength in numbers.

On the journey, Georgia dozed and woke and looked out of the window, and later she wrote it down. *There were fields and small houses out on the edge. I saw a girl standing on the train tracks. She was wearing a dress and boots, and waving at me. I waved back.*

Edith was tiny, with pink hair. She opened the door and said, "Ooo, aren't you all a lovely color!" and sat them down in her bungalow to show them pictures of Beccy and the children, and give them tea and Edith's Flapjacks (she'd decided to name her own brand, the twins had inspired her), which Georgia felt were perhaps too stodgy, too

much margarine, and less sugar. *What do you think, Bessi?* her eyes
said. Bessi shrugged and looked away.

In her best bed, Bessi kept having the same dream. That her clothes
didn't fit properly. She was sitting on the floor in the loft and her
jeans got tighter and tighter and started to split. Her legs got longer,
her knees expanded, her foot crashed through the roof, the window
shattered.

One morning while Georgia was downstairs Bessi took out the
world and spread it on the floor once more. Nations bulged. Oceans
waited. She walked up along the coast of Brazil and dived into the
Caribbean Sea. She advanced toward the edge of Senegal, across
Ghana, and back into Nigeria for a little while, to see how it was, to
have a piece of suya, and then onward to the Atlantic coast, into the
blue, to find an island, a place she'd never been, and sip a long cool
drink.

Georgia came upstairs with Gladstone and Disraeli. She'd taped
her revision notes with Kemy's help—Kemy read the questions,
Georgia read the answers—and listened to it on her Walkman while
she was washing up. *Unlike Disraeli, Gladstone had little interest in
foreign affairs. He approached decisions with caution. He was willing to
work in consul with the great powers to preserve peace. He had a Euro-
pean outlook. He was noninterventionist yet his morality compelled in-
tervention in certain cases, for example, the Bulgarian massacres. His
reasonable policies, however, sometimes seemed weak and spineless . . .*
She turned off the tape when she saw Bessi sitting on the floor with
her head hanging over the map as if she wanted to become a part of
everything else.

"What are you doing?"

Bessi looked up and grinned like someone who had just realized
that the world belonged to them. "I'm going away."

This is how it would be, Georgia knew. Bessi walks away, she turns
back once and waves, the sea takes her off, a black hand reaches for
Georgia. It is dreadful and silent.

"You can't go away. We've got exams."

"Not now. After the exams."

"But how long for?" Georgia asked, getting angry.

"I don't know. I've only just decided."

Bessi got up and sat on her bed. Georgia stood at the other end of the room, picking at her nail. Between them on the floor the world stayed open.

"Don't you ever get the feeling that life is too small?" Bessi said. "Like, there are parts of you in different places, and you have to go and find them?"

Georgia didn't reply.

"That's what I've been thinking lately anyway. I have to go away, and soon, to see stuff."

"What stuff? Where?"

Bessi's voice sounded underwater.

"Okay, I haven't decided *exactly* yet, but I want to go somewhere in the Caribbean, to an island that's hot. I could get a job or something or do voluntary work. Lots of people do after A levels. You can get placements where you stay with a family . . ."

"Yes, I know you can," said Georgia. "I'm not stupid."

"Well," said Bessi. She looked at the map, then back at Georgia. "Do you mind?" It annoyed her that she felt she had to ask for permission.

"You can't just go off on your own all that way!" Georgia snapped. "You said we'd go away together one day, remember? You're only little, what if something happened to you?"

"Like what?"

Georgia heard water lapping against the side of a boat. The boat drifted across the lake. She wanted to lie back and dip her fingers in the water. Quietly she said, "Anything could happen, you don't know. It's—dangerous."

"It's *exciting!*"

"What about the flapjacks?"

"The flapjacks aren't working," Bessi said. "It's silly."

"Silly?"

"Georgia. The Empire isn't going to work."

Georgia threw her face toward the window and glared out at the clouds. She wanted to say, *Don't go, how dare you? Don't go.* While a part of her said, *Let her go.* She fought with herself. She panicked.

"It'll be good for us," Bessi was saying. "Don't you think it's time, to find out who we are when we're on our own? We can go away together another time."

"I am on my own when I am with you," said Georgia.

Bessi walked across the room toward her. She took her hand and said, "Georgie, we are Hunters. We hunt. I want to go hunting. Let me go."

There was a pause. Birdsong, outside.

"Then go," said Georgia.

She slept deeply that night. A glittering sheet of water, a boat crossing to the other side where the mountain started, rising upward in jagged green toward the end. She lay back in the boat and saw the mist at the top of the mountain, silver light, a color into which things might disappear. Seagulls cast flight shadows on the surface of the lake. The water stroked her fingers. It said, tenderly, *Lie back now and rest, dear, lie down here and rest.*

BESSI GOT FIZZY. While Georgia slaved over her books she got a part-time job and did her research. She found a place in the Windward Islands where she could volunteer and Aubrey, also fizzy, helped her pay for it. Six months, she decided, that would do nicely.

Ida tried to stop her. "Why not tek your sista?" she said. "I don't understand. Why do you have to go all that way alone?" But Nne-Nne was quick to remind Ida that she herself had done much worse, running off at fifteen not eighteen to wherever in the middle of the night. Nne-Nne leaned back in her red chair and laughed. We have another Cecelia again, she said. Ida, the Bessi is exactly your own daughta! Heh!

Nne-Nne was right. "Mum," said Bessi. "I'm going on my own, and you can't stop me."

You see? Nne-Nne sniggered. You see it?

Ida remembered the night, that night. The moths at her ankles, the skinny moon, devils on the stars and the sound of the bicycle wheels along the road. Beneath the fear there had been a feeling of flight, of glorious possibility, and there was nothing else like the way that had felt, nothing since. In Bessi's thirst for adventure, Ida was reminded of the rift between what she once was and what she had become. It left her restless, with a feeling that her children, that the world, were walking past her. She had a sudden and immediate urge to go outside.

She gave Bessi six months' worth of Vicks. "When you hurt yourself or when you can't sleep, rub it in," she said, "whereva it hurts."

Bessi did her plaits. It took her seven hours with Georgia doing the ends and Bel doing the partings. Bel was opening her own hairdresser in a basement in Kilburn and Jay was four years old now, with zigzag cornrows and smart shirts from Jason. He had not lost the startled expression on his face and this was due to his mother and her mother and her ghost mother and the things they told him. The week before, Jay had asked Bel, "Is Nne-Nne a real gran?" Bel had explained it like this: "Sometimes people get lonely and sometimes they get scared of things. To help them, they think of something that will make them feel better, like a special person, and this special person, Jay, if they think about it for a very long time, starts to be real. If you imagine it hard enough, it becomes a real thing. Do you understand?"

Jay didn't understand all of it but he told his mother yes.

Bel let him help with Bessi's plaits. He had to pass her the beads to put at the ends. He said, "Here 'tis, Bel," and she said, "Good Jay, now wait for the next one."

The night before Bessi's going, the twins stood at the window and looked out at the evergreen tree. Aubrey walked up through the garden. His hair had arrived at smoke and it glowed whitely with his cigarette. Kemy knocked on the door (that was still a rule).

"Can I come in?" she called. She wanted to be a part of the good-bye.

"Come back in a minute," said Bessi.

The footsteps sank downstairs.

They did not speak.

Bessi put her arm around Georgia. "Will you be all right?"

"Yes," whispered Georgia, then louder, "I'll be fine."

"See out there?" Bessi pointed to the tree.

"Yeah," said Georgia.

"I'm taking it with me. And you as well. So if you ever want to dream together—meet me by the evergreen tree."

"Oh Bessi, you have to take care, please be careful!"

Face-to-face, touching eyes and touching hands, they became the only ones again, like before they got here, before the headlights. Georgia kissed Bessi softly on the lips.

"Nectarine?" she said.

They shared it, alternate bites.

"It's good, eve," they said.

Kemy knocked on the door again. "Can I come in now?"

She stood between them at the window looking out. She held a hand each and imagined one of them missing. "It's weird, isn't it?" she said.

The whole family drove Bessi the hunter to Heathrow. It was a daylight drive. When they arrived, Aubrey grabbed a cart and savored the moment; and it occurred to Bel, who was used to slowing down to wait for Ida, that her mother was walking faster than usual. They all followed Bessi as far as they could.

She left. She vanished.

This is how it went, as Georgia knew it would: They had arched their backs and opened their arms and embraced for a very long time. Bessi had whispered, "I love you, okay? Don't forget." And Georgia watched her walk away, through the glass, into the dark. Something reached for her, overhead, behind her, while Bessi turned back once and waved.

9

Selected Letters

Dear Georgia,

Here I am. In a little blue house on a hill. Mrs. John lives here on her own and I've got her son's old room, which is separated from the parlor, that's the living room, by a curtain. It's got two big wardrobes full of old stuff and the bed creaks—can you hear it? I'm sitting on it now drinking a glass of ginger ale and talking to you. Everything's strange and different. Fancy this, me being halfway across the world and you being there. It feels odd.

The village is tiny. There's one road all the way through it with brightly colored houses on each side. At the bottom of the road then a few steps down the main highway, there's a beach with black sand, because of the volcanoes. Black sand, imagine. I take off my shoes and sit down on the black and blue shore and let my feet get wet. And all over this place the plants are a lush green, the leaves and flowers are swollen with it, I'll dry some orchids for you and bring them back.

Most of all it's hot, I mean hot, like Sekon, maybe hotter. Everyone in the village stares at me wherever I go as if I had an orange head with squares on it. It reminds me of Aruwa. The children whisper as I walk past sweating through my vest. Mrs. Monk, who lives around the corner from Mrs. John, sits on her porch and says, "Walk so fast, something burning?" So I've slowed down but they still stare. It makes me want to go home and be around people who understand the inside of me.

I don't start working at the school until next week, so for now I'm sleeping, sweating and eating a lot. Mrs. John thinks I'm a rhinoceros. She gives me tons of rice and peas, and chicken, she even tried to give me the bum but I wasn't having that. I've told her I can't eat eggs or spinach and I don't like bananas. She's fine with the eggs and spinach, but she doesn't get the bananas bit. Her son Mervin is a banana farmer. In fact, most of the men in Trinity are banana farmers because it's a banana village. There's a plantation not far away up the mountain where they all go in the mornings with their knives. Mrs. John keeps putting sliced bananas on the table at breakfast. She sits down and watches me not eat them, then she says to me, "Why not try the banana, it's good for you?" And she's arranged for Mervin to take me up to the plantation because she thinks it will cure me. I don't want to go, I don't want to go, if I must go I'll have to hold my breath to hide from the smell.

They have good nectarines here, the biggest and juiciest I've ever seen, they look like oranges. I've been eating them a lot because my flapjacks are running out. How are you flapjack-wise? How are you everything-wise and what's it like in the loft without me? How are the others? Tell Kemy she's a silly cow.

Georgia, what I love best is the music in the air. All day long it plays at me from the open doors and I feel like dancing. It's mostly reggae, lovers, some ragga, lots of Dennis Brown, Lucky Dube, Gregory Isaacs, and my favorite, a song called "Cottage in Negril" by Tyrone Taylor. So I'm getting lots of singing practice, and tomorrow night I'm going dancing at the Trinity disco with Ainsley, a guy I met on the beach. He and his sister took me for a walk in the palm-tree forest and I sang "Cottage in Negril." They said I have a good voice.

It's dark now. It gets dark at seven and only takes about ten minutes, just falls down like a blanket on top of us. Mrs. John's put out some more food, so I better be going (I'm getting fat). Write me back soon, okay, I hope you're looking after yourself and eating properly. Love you, sweet.

Bessi

Thursday 9/12/91

Dearest Bessi,

Life is bananas, isn't it. You go all that way away and come face-to-face with the devil. Tell that Mrs. John you have an incurable psychological allergy and there's no telling what could happen if you ate one. Tell her she's playing with fire.

I am so glad you're safe and sound and I have a picture of where you are because I've been fretting about it, the thousands of miles of water, you out there in the abyss. I get worry attacks every so often and think, Oh my God, Bessi (oh oh oh) oh dear, I hope she's all right, oh dear! But there you are, in the blue house, and don't worry about the staring, I understand completely that feeling of being different—they will melt to you very soon, because people do. And please don't swim out too far from the black shore.

I'm sitting on the mat in the garden because I think these are the last days of the sun. It's warm enough for shorts and orange juice with ice. I've just watered the roses, they're looking fine, and I've been thinking about starting an allotment next to them, not a proper one, just a small patch for fruit and veg. It came to me in a flash of lettuce leaves after a conversation with Bel (I was a bit low, I think it's that gloomy autumn light creeping into the weather) and she said why not grow something? So I might.

But, Bessi, there's other news, from Nigeria. We got a letter from Uncle Joseph the day after you phoned and Mum said to write you and tell you. Baba died a couple of weeks ago. Joseph said his heart had been getting worse for a while and they were expecting it. Mum's really upset. She keeps crying and saying she should've gone home more often, that when your parents die you are like an orphan. She says you should be here with us. Her and Bel are going to Nigeria next week for the funeral in Aruwa and it looks like they're going to stay there for at least a fortnight. It's going to be strange around here with just me, Kemy and Dad.

Apart from that not much else except applying for jobs that I'm not sure I want to do and thinking more about university and which one where what when why and it's turned into a bit of a crisis actually. Dad keeps asking what my plans are and I think I'll probably do history but I haven't decided where yet and he says, 'Well, you better decide soon.' So I've been thinking about all this, the future, everything, crowds of it, and the autumn coming, and last Wednesday I was filling in an application form and my hand just stopped writing in the middle of Waifer. It wouldn't move, it was spooky, I felt myself tumbling, like I'd fallen off a tightrope, so I put the pen down (do you like my pen by the way? it's a present from Bel) and signals went off in my head, like fire drills (the pen I'm using now is different from *that* pen, though—I've thrown that one away in case it was an evil pen) and I couldn't do anything else for the rest of the day except watch telly, then I broke a mug while I was drying up and Mum said, "That's Georgia," and I wanted to hit her.

I'm fine now, so don't worry. Bel and Jay came over and spent a few days and we went for a long walk in Gladstone Park. That's when Bel suggested growing things again and I thought about the lettuces. It got to dusk as we were walking (don't you love that color, dusk? what color is it there?) then later Jay fell asleep on the sofa and Bel massaged my temples because I had a headache. Jay is so cute, I would love to be in his head for a day or a year. Hang on a minute, I'm just going to get a Viennese whirl—

I bet you think I've got a butter shortcake biscuit with a cream and jam center in my hand, don't you? Well, you are mistaken, because I haven't, it's a fag. That's the latest Hunter joke you need to know about. It started when I said to Kemy, "Shall we have a roly-poly," then she said "Swiss roll" and I said "Viennese whirl" and so on and so on. I was laughing all over the loft and Kemy went to make me some tea and I missed you because you're the only one who understands how hysterical everything is. I've finished my chocolate gâteau now.

Kemy wants to say hello so I'll be off. Write back as soon as you can and don't worry about the evil pen and all that, I'm sure I'll be clearer about things in a couple of weeks. I love you very much. And the loft? How is it without you? It's cooler at night and a little barren during the day.

Yours ever,

Georgia xx

Hi Bessi,

You're a sillier cow. Just a quick one to say I'm applying for a job at Safeway and not missing you at all. I got my GCSE results. I got an A for art. And I'm going out on Friday evening with a guy called Lace but I'm not telling Dad. Have you met any possible boyfriends yet?

Georgia told me to tell you she's decided to grow strawberries first then lettuces. I hope this allotment idea doesn't mean we're going to have to start eating dodgy tomatoes and things. She also said to tell you that flapjack-wise she's fine (whatever that means).

So take care, bye,
Love Kemy

October 13, 1991
Trinity Village

Georgia sweet,

Thank you for the flapjack. I miss you loads but it's good, eve, because I'm having the time of my life and I wouldn't change it for anything. Yesterday I jumped off a very tall rock into the ocean. I was a rocket and I shot to the bottom of the sea. It's a white-sand beach near town and you have to get a bus there—I've told you about the buses, haven't I, how it's like suicide taking one, but I'm used to it now. When it gets to my stop I shout STOP THE BUS quite easily. My voice is getting louder.

Across from the beach there's an island and I swam to it. The sea got prickly halfway across, little sea creatures biting my skin. But it was worth it because reaching the other side was like winning, just me and my body getting me there. I met a boy on the island. His name is Pedro and he had swum there too. He is superdishy he is and we spent hours there talking as if we were the only two people in the world. He's eighteen, he works for his dad or something, and he has a good chest. I gave him Mrs. John's number and he phoned me the next day (Mrs. John gave me that "aren't you going to eat the banana?" look) and invited me out dancing, and I said yes. So you can tell Kemy I finally have a possible boyfriend.

But Georgia, how now. It sounds like the job interviews were getting you down. You shouldn't feel bad for wanting to walk out, I'm sure most people feel like that, and at least you stuck it out and got there in the end. Congratulations, then, you're in insurance—and in Bond Street too! You probably would've started by now, so how is it? School is going well, the kids call me Miss Bessi. We're taking them on a trip on Thursday to the Twin Piton mountains, which are two mountains who are twins, Gros Piton and Petit Piton.

They took me last Tuesday, to the bananas. Mrs. John said no more excuses and they came for me at dawn in Mervin's truck with knives. They drove up the mountain and they led me into the green banana prison and I held my breath. Then Mervin and his mate chopped one in half, and *peeled* it. Mervin said, "Try it." Georgia, they made me, they said Mrs. John said I must try it, so I ate and it was horrid smelly banana filth. I was surrounded by bananas dangling and the smell got me overwhelmed and I was sick all over the chopping board and Mervin's mate *laughed* at me. I told them, I have an incurable psychological allergy, like you said, but they just kept on laughing. It was the worst experience of my life.

That night I dreamed we were at the evergreen tree sitting down. We were watching birds and I think we saw an owl but it was a bit dark so we weren't sure. I woke up missing you and I wanted to get on a plane and come home to pluck you away with me. It's frightening sometimes, being out in the world among strangers and bananas.

I'm glad Baba had a good farewell and that Mum could be there for it. They know how to throw a party in Aruwa, don't they—it seems right, somehow, that he was buried by the vegetable plot. It means he's still a part of things, especially with Mum getting his walking stick too. Please give her a kiss from me.

Let's go to the evergreen again soon. Eat well, be happy, just be. And beware of evil pens.

Lots of love, Bessi

> Monday 11/11/91
> Lint Insurance, Bond Street

It's me.

I'm at work next to the filing cabinet and I've been thinking about happiness. Does it mean bouncing about and smiling a lot or is that charge in the heart and wanting to cry? Does it stay always? I wanted to ask you this last night at the evergreen but I couldn't find you—you must have been busy, or in some other dream.

Because I'm beginning to think happiness is a sensation, or a visitation, not a way of being. It goes up and down up and down it goes and sometimes there are bruises. I'm not sure how much longer I can get on the tube every day and come here. There's too much noise and I feel as if my life takes place in boxes full of faces watching me, and the faces are not kind like yours, Bessi. The city is a beast and it is inhabited by beasts. I would like to be where you are now in the lush green and the music.

I'm sorry, it's not a good day. Mr. Hyde was on the prowl again last night waiting up for Kemy. She was out with Lace all night and she got back at eight o'clock this morning and they started arguing (she should've phoned, it was selfish of her) and Mr. Hyde looked half-dead and there was red around his eyes. I don't like that color, red. Tania's not in to-day, with her slowly blinking eyes looking at me from the other side of the filing cabinet, so the office is particularly dull, and all I want to do is go home and turn the soil in the garden. Tania bought me a book called *Green Fingers for a Greener Mind* and it shows you how to grow herbs from hanging baskets, which I'm going to try. Everyone here says me and Tania are joined at the hip. I think they all think I'm weird, apart from her.

It was wonderful to hear your voice on Saturday and I felt stupid for sobbing like that, I was just a little overwhelmed because I haven't seen you in so long and it doesn't seem right. Life is less alive without you, so hurry up and come home, will you. The loft is very still.

Guess what, Mum has started taking cookery classes at Willesden College. She goes once a week, on her own on the 297. And Kemy's got some news, which Mum isn't happy about, so I'll send this when she adds her note. I've decided to apply to Middlesex for next year—do you know what you're doing yet?

Try and get to the evergreen again soon, and beware the bananas.

Yours,

Georgia xx

Hi Bessi,
I've decided to grow dreadlocks like Lace. That is my news. Good innit. Merry Christmas in advance.

Love Kemy

December 13, 1991
Trinity

Dear Georgia,

Sorry I'm late writing back. I've been hectic with the kids' concert and your letter didn't get here until the 28th. You don't have to apologize for telling me if you feel bad. I want you to come to me for anything you need. Is work any better now? Is Mr. Hyde still about? I worry about you all, we have to get out. I'm not sure about Middlesex, though. I haven't even thought about university at all, except that I might skip it altogether. You don't need to have a degree to be a singer, you just need to sing and meet the right people. Anyway, right now, tomorrow is not my concern. Not when I have stood at the edge of a volcano.

Georgia, I must tell you. Me and Pedro—I think I may be in love, he is the most gorgeous thing on earth, I've enclosed a photo to prove it, look . . . see, isn't he?—we took a truck up to Lud Point and then walked up the mountain. It got colder and colder the farther we got, and the wind picked up. The ground turned to dark gray and there was lots of dust. It looked like we were just walking toward a mist because that was all I could see ahead of me. I kept saying to Pedro, "Where's the edge? Will we fall?" But once we were inside the mist, it disappeared. I looked down. And what I saw was rainbows down there, in a huge scoop of earth shaped like a mountain upside down. It paralyzed me. It was quiet and I couldn't speak. I imagined walking down the rainbows like we used to in Sekon by the window. I wish you could've seen it. The most beautiful thing. We sat there for ages in the mist, and Pedro had his arms around me, and that was happiness.

It was dark when we got back to Trinity. Pedro walked me up to Mrs. John's and the stars affected me. I mean, I looked up, and there were thousands of them. It was difficult to see the darkness behind. The volcano and the mist, perhaps it was magic, because Georgia, I was like an angel. I was silver. Do you remember that story Baba told us in Aruwa, about the twins? I don't know why I thought of it at that moment, walking up through Trinity in silver, but it all came back to me, the forest and the witches and the fire. I was ten years old again. We were sleeping. We could hear fire.

The things. These are the things I came to this island for. To blow my mind with what I didn't know. I did not know who volcanoes were until I got here. Imagine it, sweet. The mist, the wind, the mountain upside down.

When I grow up, I want to be a volcano.

Love and a hug,

Bessi

January 8, 1992

Dear Bessi,

I'm sure you enjoyed Christmas on the island and I don't mean to spoil your fun but I think it might be time for you to come home now. I'm very worried about Georgia. At Christmas she practically locked herself away in the loft and hardly ate a thing. She drifted out into the garden on Boxing Day and just stared at her allotment, and when I went out to see if she was all right she said, "We're nineteen soon, I'm going to be nineteen without her." It was freezing out there. Nothing's growing yet in the soil, it was all cracked and icy, but she just stood there, staring. She's too quiet, there's a dark, lost look in her eyes. You should come home, Bessi, she needs you. She's not like you, with your wings and your ease. So please, come home and comfort your twin.

Safe journey,

Bel

The
Third
Bit

What Is It?

It was not always easy, buying milk. Before the milk (or the tomato purée, or the newspaper) could be bought, there were decisions to be made and questions to be answered. Up above her head was the decision to be made as to whether or not it was possible, at this moment, to actually do it, what with all that it meant. And making this decision required, first of all, an assessment of her current state of mind. Blue would suggest it was mildly feasible. Lilac even more so. Yellow was a good place, but she was not often yellow when it was difficult to buy milk or tomato purée or a new pen. Orange meant it could be dangerous; something terrible could happen on the way down the hall, or worse, in the street—it had happened before, the panic, the meanness in a face floating by—that would send her running back without the milk. And if she was red, an unforgiving place of chains and confusion, it was out of the question absolutely, milk, onions, a walk in the street, everything.

That was the first thing. And once she had established the color of life on that particular day in relation to buying milk, she then spotted the next question which asked her how exactly she intended to go about it, and this was a very large question. She could faintly see the words written in the air in red letters, up above her head. *How WILL IT BE DONE?* The question gave birth before her eyes to other questions with nervous voices who asked her such things as whether she should brush her teeth first or change her clothes first and what she was going to wear anyway, where she'd put her wallet, where she'd put her keys, whether she needed to buy anything else apart from milk, and if so did she have enough money and would she need to go to the bank?

But the bank was a whole other set of questions.

Often it was easier not to buy the milk and have an apple instead, which was actually much better for her than fattening cereals. But if she did brave it, if she managed it, the appropriate clothes (a pair of denim dungarees, a Christmas-present sweater from Bel), no terrors in the drafty hall, out the front door and along the street to the minimart at the end, she found more problems. The minimart was out of semiskimmed. The milk aisle was crawling with human beings. She would have to squeeze past and one of them might know her from college and want to engage in lighthearted chat of the kind that took place in the student union bar around low sticky tables. There was a time and a place and a color for lighthearted chat, and it was not in the minimart next to the milk on an orange day, unless it was Bessi, unless it was Bessi she was talking to, about Tyrone Taylor or when they'd go to Brighton to see the sea, or whether broccoli was edible when it was yellow, or how funny Jay was when he'd tried to spell *whunderful* like that, unless it was Bessi, unless Bessi came and pulled her out.

And yet, other days, on yellow days, it was nothing, buying milk. It was a skip to the corner with forty pence and back again with a carton in her hand.

The carton goes in the fridge, the muesli has a partner, there is breakfast. Life is simple.

Georgia's room in the flat in Tottenham had one small window. It looked out north instead of south, which meant that she was on the wrong side of the sun. Her flatmates, Cynthia and Jo, had taken the best rooms, where the windows were innocent. Even in the spring, Georgia's window, which she had stripped naked on moving in, remained weak and possessive with its light. On yellow days without questions it could give her sun. On red and orange days it got shifty and found an old gray cloak to wear.

It showed her the upside-down sofa in the jungle of the backyard. And when she opened it there crept in a subtle smell of petrol and chicken patties which drifted on the Seven Sisters air. More than anything else, there was noise. Georgia opened her window and she heard the arguments and the shouts coming from West Green Road, the shudder of concrete beneath the roaring high-street traffic, the children next door screaming, the dogs and drills and motorbikes. The noise was followed by headaches, and so she closed the window.

Next to it, on the bookcase, was its equalizer: dried St. Lucia orchids from Bessi, in a sandy bell-shaped vase. And a photograph: *Bessi in Trinity, with sunglasses.*

She had come back last year the darkest coffee ever with a new walk and foreign memories. Georgia, leaning over the railing with Kemy, had seen her glide out of arrivals in a strange green hat close to the skull, a serene expectant smile, and things were best again. The world was the right way up. Holes were filled. There was nothing anymore to dread. Bessi put down her bags and they stepped into a mighty hello. "Hi, sweet," Bessi had whispered into her hair, "I'm back."

The room was half the size of the loft and the bed was not far off the floor. There were two cockroaches, she knew this, she had seen them once, small ones, stamping about under the desk while she was studying. She had closed her eyes and had the following conversation:

Now, we talked about this, didn't we?

Yes. We did.

We said, if this leaving home thing is going to work, there have to be drills.

Yes. Drills.

Cockroach drills, bad-dream drills. And what was the cockroach drill?

A cockroach is a flat-bodied insect that mainly inhabits tropical environments. They thrive on dirt and darkness rather than cleanliness and light.

Yes. That's it.

Robinsons, page 209.

Very good. Good girl.

And since then, nothing. They left her alone with her history books. She was interested in how the past had made us and she remembered what Gladstone had told her many years ago, that everything had already happened. "Do you know?" she said to Cynthia and Jo at the kitchen table where they came across one another in the evenings. "Today is past's future, and today is also the future's past. We have already happened."

"You could have a point in that, George," said Jo, who compulsively abbreviated people's names and had recently shaved her head. "That's what déjà vu is, could be."

"She's wise, isn't she," said Cynthia, who always said very little.

History was a way of watching from outside. She looked at people in the past in the same way she looked at people in the present, as belonging to someplace beyond her own moment. She looked at them, like photographs.

Along with the emergency drills, there were preventative methods, pacifiers and pick-me-up activities for fighting red and orange days. When the great black hand was sensed lurking near her, she should stop still and take ten deep invigorating breaths from the base of the stomach. As you are breathing, according to Carol Fielding's *Your Breath, Your Life,* imagine a white light shining above you; with each inbreath you are filled with this healing light. If you wake from a bad dream, Carol also offered, in the chapter "Leaving Anxiety Behind," lie back down in the sheets with arms open at your sides and relax every muscle in turn, down through the body, ending at the feet, breathing in, breathing out. Another book, *The Essential Guide to Aromatherapy,* advised that chamomile, lavender and rose essential oils were excellent for restoring a sense of calm. All these things contributed not only to a healthy mind, but a healthy body too, obviously improving circulation and respiratory journeys, while also opening the mind to the idea of holistic, alternative self-care, said Carol.

She was talking about DIY happiness (was that what Bessi had meant in her letter?). Good health was happiness. The right foods, the right combinations of vitamins and minerals and proteins sliding down into the body was a good, cleaning feeling of happiness. To wash it down each day with four pints (as advised in *The Detox Bible*) of fresh mountain water was a kind of minor DIY baptism, the restoration of the self to a state of purity. And exercise was the dealer of natural highs. Twenty minutes' jogging, a few laps of a pool, an hour of aerobics could evoke such euphoria and a sense of well-being that if it didn't, Carol would eat her hat. Of course, exercise was also useful for not getting too fat, and Georgia wanted never ever to be a big bumbling blob, which was what she became when she got past eight stone. The aim was lightness, to glide, to slice through water, to take up very little space. At seven and a half stone the world was full of the possibility of yellow days. During three-day fruit-and-water detoxes she savored the sensation of shrinking. As she sat at her desk, she felt that there was less of her sitting there, and this was a good feeling, a DIY happy feeling. Breathe in, breathe out.

On the way back from the airport, Georgia had also noticed that Bessi had new eyes. They were tougher. They had seen volcanoes and they wanted more.

"You've lost weight," she'd said.

"Have I?" said Georgia, flattered.

"She's been on another diet," said Kemy, who'd tried it too, out of interest, but had thought it unreasonable not to be able to have custard creams.

Back then, Georgia's holistic alternative self-care literature took up only a small space on the loft bookshelf. Bessi stepped back in and the loft returned to (beanbagless, strawberryless, but nevertheless) magic. She told Georgia the black sand memories, how she'd ridden standing up on the backs of trucks down the winding road to town, watched an open-air gospel concert and people twitching with the hand of God, and out of the tiny plane windows seen islands like big black bears asleep on the sea. She said, "It's so beautiful there and so warm. I wish I could take us all back there to live. London's an ugly place, isn't it."

"Oh yes," said Georgia, amazed that Bessi had only just noticed, that it had taken the comparative effect of six months in the tropics to see what a cold and trapped and dirty mesh of poisonous streets it was. Commuting to the Lint offices in Bond Street on the tube every day had confirmed this. She had developed a ritual.

Before she left, she told herself: *You will count to five now and when you have finished you are dead until you get home tonight. One. Two. Three. Four. Five.*

Simply, she wanted to lie down somewhere green, where she could hear the birds, the sea, and the kindness of the sky. She wanted to learn how to wander through time, and even to shed it.

Bessi had returned to a fierce winter. Her teeth chattered at dinner and she wore two cardigans, one on top of the other. She scratched rashes sprouting on her arms and mourned the loss of vitamin D. St. Lucia coffee shrank backward from her skin. Trinity, and Pedro, and Pedro's chest were the heaven she'd lost (even though, if she was honest, she *had* gotten rather bored toward the end and she *was* relieved to get away from the bananas). "In Trinity, the oranges are green, you know, not orange," she said. "In Trinity, there was music everywhere, it's so quiet here!" and "In Trinity, Mrs. John doesn't use washing-up liquid, you don't need it, she just uses a brush."

Kemy said it was a classic case of the holiday blues.

"But it was *more* than a holiday!" Bessi whined. "It was a whole other *life*."

"Well, anyway," said Kemy. "You'll get over it. So, d'you like my locks, then?"

Kemy's locks had not yet reached the level of mat and solidity that constituted dreadlocks. Bel had explained to her that the softness of her hair meant it might take years to get there. For now, to Ida's disgust, uneven clumps of hair wired together by daily applied beeswax hung noncommittally from Kemy's head. She had ditched her Michael Jackson poster—though she would always hold a place for him in her heart—for Maxi Priest, and she and Lace had had sex to marijuana and the *You're Safe* album in her room while Aubrey was at work, Ida at her Brazilian cookery class, Georgia out walking in Gladstone Park, and it was assumed by all that Kemy was in her room studying. She had confessed to Georgia a few days later, and added, "Lace is my nyabingi prince."

Bessi sniffed at Kemy's hair. "It smells funny," she said, "and they look dusty. You should've seen some of the locks in—"

"—Trinity, yeh yeh yeh," said Kemy.

The spring seemed to cheer Bessi up. The Neasden sycamores swelled into blossom pink clouds reminiscent of flapjack-Edith's hair. While Georgia tended to the allotment that was actually a vegetable patch and, as always, the roses, Bessi started singing again. She sang Randy Crawford's "Streetlight" and Kenny Thomas's "Thinking About Your Love" in the bath and in the garden and up and down the stairs, in her newly louder voice, as if she hoped someone might spot her, like Sasha Jane Sloane had been spotted in Waitrose. She wrote a song devoted to Pedro called "Lucia Lover" that went like this:

My Lucia love is yesterday
until the ocean parts
Lucia boy I'll walk away
from home back to your heart

lovely Lucia Lucia love
oh lovely Lucia Lucia love

and she performed it for Georgia and Kemy in the loft, using her fist as a microphone, her brow taut with passion. Georgia said she thought the chorus needed some work, and Kemy said it wasn't bad but sometimes she went flat and she might have to do better than that to get on *Top of the Pops*. Apart from this, Bessi showed no other signs of career building.

Aubrey told her: "You'd better start thinking about what's next, hadn't you? The horse won't budge without a kicking."

Ida said: "Why not go with your sista? To Muddlesex?"

Kemy said: "Don't go, Bessi! Don't leave me here with Mr. Hyde in the nights!"

And Georgia said: "But I'm not going anywhere. I'm going to commute."

At least, that was the idea until she got there—without Bessi, because Bessi, after leafing through the Muddlesex prospectus, had decided that university was a lot of haddock if you wanted to be in music, and that getting a job as a waitress in an all-night diner in Soho was a much, much better way of getting spotted.

The corridors had blue doors and loud echoes and the rooms had blue chairs. The crowds of students made her feel lost and nervous, and Georgia tended to rush in and out of classes to avoid them. Eventually, she began to recognize certain faces. One morning on the tube, Cynthia stepped into her carriage. Georgia remembered her from the common room, and Cynthia smiled and sat down and didn't say anything. She had very pale, almost translucent skin, and they quietly shared the journey. Georgia had a lot of respect for people who could be quiet, who could creep gently through the world.

She began to think of leaving, like Bessi had left for Trinity. It would be strong and daring of her, wouldn't it, to be the one to leave for good, to do it first. At Christmas, three weeks after it was announced that

Charles and Diana had decided to separate, Georgia concluded that probably, if she could do it, if it felt safe (and she *could* do it, of course she could), then she might, after all, go.

Charles and Diana were very sad about it all. The Queen was disappointed. It had been an "annus horribilis" for the family, she said with a tight mouth in her speech by the Christmas tree at Sandringham. Ida, suffering from a cold, watched the speech from her rocker and Aubrey listened with his eyes shut from the chocolate armchair.

Georgia told Bel what she'd been thinking about. They sat together on the edge of the bath.

"Why not?" Bel said. "Leaving home was the best thing I ever did, and you're old enough now. It'll be good for you."

"It will, won't it?"

"Yes, of course." Bel had plastic reindeers hanging from her earrings from Jay's Christmas cracker. She put her hand on Georgia's wrist and added, "But just you, on your own—without her."

"I know, Bel," Georgia mumbled.

And it *had* been a dreadful Christmas. Ida's cold had made her bad-tempered, and it meant that Georgia was next in line to cook the turkey (Bessi never prepared poultry because of the parson's nose, and Kemy couldn't cook). With Georgia being a vegetarian, her turkey failed to be the turkey of kings and queens, and Ida nagged at her for being "silly about food." To add to this, two days before Christmas Eve Aubrey had caught Kemy and the twins smoking weed in the loft (Kemy was the pusher, Georgia and Bessi only dabbled). He'd sniffed a funny smell and knocked on the door, opened it, and there they were, the Little Ones, sitting on the floor with an unusually shaped cigarette jumping out of Bessi's hand onto the carpet, the funky smoke curling around the room. Mr. Hyde exploded later that night. "I'VE BEEN WORKING FOR THIRTY-FIVE YEARS AND THIS IS THE THANKS, *THIS*, THE LOUSY ROTTEN MUTTS!" On Christmas morning he was still fast asleep in his armchair, and no one had known whether to wake him and forget about Christmas or leave him and forget about Christmas. Lunch was an extremely late, soggy meal of tasteless turkey, and vegetables cooked by Kemy, through which something sepulchral and silent, not quite Mr. Hyde but only just Aubrey, in a cardigan, had kept a tight leash on any possibility of festive merriment or good cheer.

At the end of the day, Georgia and Bessi went up to the loft for a Baileys and a Viennese whirl. Georgia said: "Bessi. I really, really, *really* want to get out of here."

And Bessi said: "I know what you mean, sweet. Me too."

They sipped Baileys. They looked ahead of themselves.

Georgia was ready. "I'm moving to Tottenham with Cynthia."

Bessi scratched her arm and nodded, too quickly. "It makes sense," she said.

"Why don't you move in with us?" Georgia found herself saying (*If she says no,* she thought, *I'm going anyway—there will be drills*).

Bessi thought about it. "Give us a bit." She held out her fingers. Georgia passed her the chocolate gâteau.

They drifted through possibles. Bessi smoked. Georgia waited. Then Bessi started shaking her head.

"No . . . no, it wouldn't be good. It's too far, I'd get bored, and we can't leave Kemy on her own."

Georgia took three deep breaths, as Carol advised in chapter seven, "Emergencies!"

"Bessi," she said. "I'm getting out."

Oh, but it's full of good-byes, Georgia wrote, packed and ready, sitting alone on her bed—it would always be her bed, it had taken her to Gladstone, the moon, St. Lucia and the evergreen, it was a boundless bed. She stood up and looked out. They were down by the apple trees in their anoraks and Bessi was waiting for thumps. I think Ham's d'stressed, said Georgia. Is he in the bathroom? said Bessi. You don't have to have a bath, said Georgia. What shall we do? They came into the loft and sat down in the strawberry corners. Georgia watched them and wanted to decide with them, but there was nowhere for her to sit.

She traced the chalk ghost of 26a on the door. The twins stayed where they were. They did not look up when she left the room.

Bessi cried at the good-bye. She was working four nights a week and hadn't been spotted yet.

"Don't forget to water the roses and the lettuces," Georgia reminded her.

She arrived in Seven Sisters and stripped her evergreenless, sunsetless window. She lit a joss stick as Bel had instructed her, to clean away the person before, and placed Bessi's orchids carefully on the bookcase. When Bessi came to visit, sometimes accompanied by Kemy, they sat together on the bed and the room became brighter. Neither Georgia nor Cynthia had many visitors to the flat. The people who came were mostly Jo's friends, who gathered in her room listening to music and shrieking with laughter. Occasionally, Cynthia's brother Toby would come, always late at night. From Cynthia's room, which was next to Georgia's, she would hear low voices and the intermittent sound of a guitar playing.

As time went on the rumble of the Tottenham traffic spread into Georgia's head. It was as if it was always there, and the people were always pushing, and the cars were always sneering at her, and the men on West Green Road were always shouting. There were few hills. It was London in a way that Neasden was not London. It had no river and none of the right ghosts, no alleyways with silver streaks, and no lofts for kingdoms of two.

In Downhills Park she found three willow trees standing in a triangle. They made a silent green house where the white daylight picked through the roof like so many stars. There were dead brown leaves on the floor. She stood inside, while birds passed overhead, and a thin woman slumped on a bench outside hummed to herself and stared at the ground.

The first appearance of red was in a lecture when Georgia put her hand up to ask a question that she forgot when she put her hand up. What was the—? How do you—? There appeared words, faintly, the real questions, up above her head. And how, exactly, they asked, will you go about this? Is it a question that they, the others, will find worthy? And what *was* the question? *What is it?*

She sat there with her hand in the air and couldn't put it down. The eyes of the other students waited. Questions lurched off the ceiling and squabbled. She lifted the other arm and used it to bring down the arm in the air. She got up and left and went straight home. And lay down.

It became difficult, some days, to buy milk.

Music

Digger's of Soho was next door to a club called Spicey Riley's. Between the early morning hours of three and six, steamy clubbers staggered out of Spicey Riley's and into Digger's for chips, club sandwiches, pizzas and tortilla wraps, which were Digger's specialty. Many of them were still hallucinating, tripping along roads of ecstasy or acid. There were nights when someone might jump up onto their chair, in sequins and a belly top, and start shouting at the dancing video screens along the wall above them. More than once, people had walked into the mirror wall, thinking Digger's was twice itself.

By the time the Spicey Riley's influx started, Bessi was sleepy. An important part of her did not yet understand this business of being awake all night. This part of her fantasized about sumptuous duvets and the loft in lamplight. Yet the other part of her, that wanted desperately *not* to be serving chips and espressos in a Digger's apron in the middle of the night, and getting the tube home in the morning with the nurses and security guards while the garbagemen lugged stinking bags of rubbish off the Soho streets, but to be making records (or something that involved traveling a lot and eating out a lot and wearing superdishy clothes), sent her to the toilets to reapply her lip gloss and back out into the music and the mirrors with the smile of a winner. Because you just never knew who could walk in. Sasha Jane Sloane probably had no idea she was being spotted but I'll bet, Bessi thought, she'd had on her lipstick, and without that she wouldn't be where she was today. And Bessi had heard from Digger himself, the man in the T-shirt with DIGGER on the front who spent a lot of time sitting down, that Spicey Riley's was frequented by certain members of the music industry.

She walked, with a bounce and a tray, up and down the metallic aisle, preferring to think of it as a catwalk (or something). When the customers waved or shouted or pointed for more this or more that, she responded with a dazzle as late as 5 A.M. She kept an eye on the door for the spotter. Early in her third month there, a man with big shoulders and a shimmering turquoise shirt had walked in with two glamorous-looking women. As Bessi took their order, smiling brilliantly, she noticed the man studying her and she was convinced it was him (spotters were usually hims, she assumed). She waltzed off and told the cook to hurry and the barman to hurry, and as she sped back with the tray she felt the spotter's eyes, all over her, measuring, imagining. Can't you see me? Bessi said with her hips, with her teeth. Can't you see me up there, like Mary J. Blige?

The spotter paid the bill. As Bessi leaned in to take the money, the man put his hand on her waist and whispered in her ear.

"What?" Bessi shouted. "I didn't hear. What?"

The man moved his hand down over her hip, which Bessi was not at all sure about. "I *said*," he drawled, "do you wanna come back with us, my beauty?"

Oh. It's not him, thought Bessi.

She stood up, snatched away the money and said, "No thank *you*."

"The filthy dog!" she told Georgia over the phone when she'd woken up the next day at 4 P.M. Breakfast was at four. Dinner was at eleven. There was no lunch. She lived in nightworld and her face was going sallow.

Georgia told her to be careful of men like that. "Don't go home in the mornings until it's light," she said. "Why don't you work in the day instead?"

"They're not open during the day."

"I mean work somewhere that is."

"Oh *no*, Georgie! The whole *point* is that people get spotted more often in the night, in clubs and bars and stuff. So it's better. You have to make sacrifices if you want to conquer the world, you know."

Georgia grunted. Conquering the world was ridiculous.

"Did I tell you?" Bessi was getting excited. "Digger said *music* industry bods go to the club next door, Spicey Riley's, producers and artists and journalist sort of people. We should go there sometime and see."

"I suppose."

Bessi had a sudden thought. The two of them, looking super. The dishy twins. Now there's a spotter's dream.

"Georgia," she said. "Have you ever imagined yourself on telly?"

"No. Never," said Georgia.

Bessi continued practicing her singing at home and being dazzling at Digger's. With her tips she bought a pair of hazel contact lenses to jazz up her eyes. She asked Kemy whether they suited her and Kemy said "Hazel smazel, what's wrong with brown?" It crept into five months and seven months and summer came and went, Kemy's dreadlocks got solid, Georgia became a second-year. There were several more indecent proposals and Bessi got less dazzling. She became a whole smoker; she sampled acid with a fellow waitress and saw a polar bear walking up Regent Street in the early morning. It began to occur to her that there was a very slight possibility that it might not happen at Digger's, that, in fact, nothing might happen at Digger's, ever. And shortly after Bessi had this revelation, she got into an argument with another "spotter" and slapped him across the face as he went for her thigh. Digger was not happy about this. He told her that the customer was always right no matter what because the customer paid her wages, not so? And if she wanted to stay a lucky Digger's girl then she'd better treat the Digger's clientele with a little more appreciation. "You play the game, eh, and they tip you more!"

Bessi crawled to Tottenham in the wind and the rain. She sat in the kitchen while Georgia made mushrooms on toast with not a lot of oil. Georgia had given her Bel's Christmas pullover to wear. It was a beige color, with red flowers and a wide collar, and it made Bessi look pale and small. She wrapped her hands around her mug of tea and closed her eyes. The kitchen was a womb. Georgia was cheerful today, she noticed. She told Bessi that she was starting to like living there and that Cynthia's brother Toby had promised to teach her to play the guitar. They ate their food and then went to Georgia's room. The safety of it and the danger outside, or the fact that she missed hearing Georgia breathing at night, or that Trinity was yesterday and Digger's was today, or that the future might ruin her, or simply because she was tired and uncertain, Bessi sat down on Georgia's bed and began to cry.

"Oh, Bess," said Georgia, patting her. "Don't cry!"

"I'm not crying," said Bessi.

"What is it?"

"Everything!"

Georgia rubbed her shoulder and hugged her. "You need to get out of that place, you know. Just leave. You can get a job somewhere else—you can do anything you want."

"Can I?"

"Of course you can. Anything."

"But, Georgie, I want to be . . . I want to be . . . *more*."

"I know."

"And it's so *hard*."

"It is hard. It's not easy," said Georgia.

"And I'm so tired and I haven't even started yet and I'm just a waitress at Digger's—"

"You are not a waitress at Digger's. You are Bessi. That is a lot to be."

Bessi started to feel better. She laid her head on her sister's shoulder.

"Lie down with me, Georgie. You're such a good listener."

They lay back. The gray window watched them. Bessi fell asleep for a few minutes and woke again, in the silent afternoon. She remembered all that time and space ago, two furry creatures with petrified eyes, staring into the headlights, the engine surging, the lights threatening blindness.

"Are you awake?" she said.

"Yes," Georgia answered.

After a pause, Bessi said: "I think, sometimes, that we weren't made for this world."

Georgia stroked her. She remembered it too. "I know, darling. That's what I've been trying to tell you, all this time."

HE DID NOT phone very often, and when he did he asked for Cynthia. She had come to recognize his voice: melodic, sleepy, with a question mark at the end of sentences. When Cynthia was out they talked for long periods, as if they knew each other well. Georgia would sit in the hallway, moving one foot in and out of her slipper, her studying forgotten. As he talked, she pictured him that morning in September, when she had walked past Cynthia's room and glimpsed him standing by the window, his thin torso alight in a blast of sun.

At the start of the new term Jo had ordered Cynthia and Georgia to the union bar to celebrate her birthday. Cynthia, who hated pubs, had agreed to go only because Toby sometimes played there. "I like watching my brother make a fool of himself," she said. They sat at the sticky tables amid loud messy discussions and the guzzling of beer. Georgia sipped her wine, making vague attempts at lighthearted chat and watching Jo getting drunk. She was about to go home when the entertainment started, two shaggy boys with long hair playing guitars, one of them Toby, with his bootlaces undone.

"Jimi Hendrix," announced Toby, "will never die. He lives in a hut in Friston Forest in Eastbourne, where he taught me this song."

There were lazy laughs in the audience. Conversations resumed. Toby glanced at his bandmate and hoisted his guitar. They played "Belly Button Window'" hesitantly at first, then louder. Toby flicked his hair off his face. Georgia watched his fingers walking across the strings like ballerinas on their toes. She thought of Hendrix in his hut with Toby and couldn't help smiling. People shouted over the music, Jo was cackling with one of her friends; and Georgia had the thought that human beings were nonsense. She said to Cynthia, "He's not that bad. He's quite good, actually."

Afterward he came over to their table and Cynthia said, "Georgia's your only fan, you'd better buy her a drink." They sat close to each other. She turned and caught him watching her. Her eyes were drawn to his mouth, a gentle mouth that looked as if it had been left there, as an afterthought.

Toby was a final-year student in the sociology department. Four afternoons a week he worked in a factory inserting batteries into the backs of clocks. Music, he told Georgia over the phone, was all about timing and symmetry, but music had to be created outside of time, which was why the factory was good training—he could practice losing himself in the clocks while being surrounded by them. Toby believed that music should have nothing to do with making money; it was about being pure. He rehearsed in the evenings with Carl, his bandmate, in a room above a pub, and always finished late, sometimes going to Cynthia's for the night because it was closer.

She began to listen for him, the tapping at the front door as she slumbered, the approach of his footsteps into the next room. At 1 A.M., the autumn warmer than usual, he knocked on her door. He was standing in the corridor with his guitar, wearing a shirt that was far too big for him. Georgia noticed the sharpness of his shoulder blades. "I thought you were awake," he whispered. "A lesson on the guitar?" He taught her a simple melody consisting of five notes. It was a terribly sad song, Georgia thought, but beautiful. Afterward they made tea, Toby stirring plenty of sugar into both mugs. He looked childlike, drowning in his shirt in the lamplight, and he talked about Cynthia as if she were older than him instead of younger. Friston Forest, he told Georgia, had been their favorite place when they were growing up.

Just before he left, Toby lingered at the door. He said, "Not many people have symmetrical faces, but you have, exactly the same on each side, like the clocks." He became shy, as if he'd failed to say what he had wanted to say. They stood in the approaching dawn, unsure of what to do with their hands apart from touch in some way, yet knowing that a touch too early could ruin a whole world of touching.

"Thank you for the lesson," she said.

"We'll do it again."

The days turned to yellow. Toby invited Georgia to watch him rehearse and he spent more nights talking with her in her room. He believed in Hendrix like Georgia believed in Gladstone. "I was fourteen. I found him in the hut and the first thing he said to me was, 'Toby, friends and talk are overrated.'" They went walking in the dark. One night they climbed over the wall into the park and she took him to the willow house, where she had only ever gone alone. They stood in the cold November leaves. It was easy. While he kissed her, he held the back of her head in his palm as if it were a baby's head. She felt that nothing would ever hurt now, and that she might, after all, have the capacity for non-DIY happiness, the type of happiness that came by itself and could not be learned from sources like Carol.

Cynthia asked her, "What have you done to my brother?"

They decided that they would take the train to Brighton to see the sea. Toby wore a red woolen hat down over his ears and Georgia a white coat with silver buckles. They walked down the long hill toward the blue at the end. It was Sunday, the streets were empty. Avenues sloped off the main road peacefully and Georgia peered up them. She imagined living in one of the pastel houses with Toby, a loft beneath the roof for when Bessi came to stay.

On the pebbles, as the waves crashed against the shore, they sat down by the old West Pier and ate doughnuts. The West Pier was the ghost of the main pier, the one with the amusement park and lights and psychedelic shops. The West Pier was a shadow on the water. Its legs were crooked and the railings rusty, or broken off into the bottom of the sea. Georgia said, "I bet there's ghosts here."

She started a second doughnut and didn't worry about what Carol or the detox bible would say. With Toby—who was a man of sugar, with sugar all over his lips now—food was an adventure and there was no danger in it: in toasted halloumi cheese and warmed-up chocolate cake, or fresh salmon bagels from the Bruce Grove Bakery in the middle of the night with mango juice.

Georgia asked him, "Do you like the city?"

"Not much," said Toby. "It's fun sometimes, but I think it's all madness and choking."

Georgia laughed. Her laugh was getting louder. "It is like that, isn't it." She thought for a while, then said, "I wish I lived somewhere like this, somewhere calm with a West Pier. I'd be a lot happier if I could walk down the road and sit on the beach and think."

"What would you think about?"

"Bessi says I think too much, and I get so sad sometimes—so I'd think about nothing."

"It's hard to think about nothing. I've tried it. You end up thinking about everything and getting stressed out. It's best to just think of one thing. A good thing."

He put his arm around her shoulder. "Sadness comes and goes like seasons. Look at the sea," he said. "Think about that."

They said nothing for a long time. Georgia watched. The sun put diamonds on the waves. Toward dusk, there was a change in color. It astonished her. Toby had fallen asleep with his head back against the wall. On the train home he slept some more, while behind them pebbles melted into concrete, and pastel buildings toppled into the sea.

Georgia wrote in her notebook, so that she would not forget: *Peace of mind, give me the calm to notice that there is a point along the ocean's horizon where the watery blue changes to a deeper complexion of blueness. When I cannot think of nothing, I must get away and come and find the sea.*

It was a day that mustn't end so Toby didn't go home. They lay down next to each other in Georgia's room and touched eyes. His gentle mouth; his thin, childish body. The ghosts in the room were only good ghosts who had traveled with them from the West Pier. They told him to be slow. They told her to be calm. *He lays me down, it's far from here, and I am not afraid.* Her breath was running away from her toward him and it was very hot; they shared sweat and tongues and legs and Georgia felt that flesh was not enough, she wanted to go beyond flesh. *Take me to the water, to the edge, to the edge, lift my clothes, push the covers away,* and Toby sank inside. They fit together. It was twoness, it was silence, they had left themselves behind.

In the hours toward dawn he woke up three times. Each time, he stroked a part of her. Her head. Her leg. Down the side of her waist. "I want to take you away," he murmured. And fell back to sleep.

WAIFER AVENUE WAS becoming a quieter place. Bessi was at Digger's most nights, and when she came home she slept all day. Kemy had started college in Camberwell—where Lace happened to live—and she spent more and more of her time in south London. Her intentions of becoming a dressmaker had not changed; she was, in fact, harboring thoughts of an empire. At college she had begun to experiment with fabric manipulation. She dipped silk into the juice of onion skins, tied it in knots, and watched it turn to caramel. She was also using mango skins and beetroot, which were stunning against the light.

Ida went out more too, occasionally to church, sometimes to see Bel and Jay in Kilburn, and regularly to her classes in Willesden, to which she had added math and pottery. She had not yet been as far as Tottenham, but she phoned Georgia often to make sure she was eating properly and studying hard.

A few weeks before Christmas, eager to avoid a repeat of last year's hostilities, Kemy made a quick exit from Waifer Avenue. Lace had asked her to be his nyabingi queen and she couldn't refuse. She took everything with her, the posters under the bed, the clothes she didn't wear anymore, every single thing to do with Michael Jackson, and the photograph of her, Georgia and Bessi in front of the garden fence.

"I'm the last one here," Bessi moaned. "I never thought I'd be the last to leave."

"You'll be all right, Smazel," said Kemy. Then she jumped up into the air and shouted, "No more Mr. Hyde!"

Aubrey was sixty-three. He had pains in his legs and skin that had fallen down. He told Mr. Hyde he was tired, some nights, and sat with Jack in the sun lounge looking out at stars. "Did you know," he remembered Judith telling him when he was a boy, "that stars die?" "Do they, Mother, is that true?" he'd asked, amazed. "Yes, Aubrey dear. And just before they die, they're the brightest that they've ever been."

The old man drove his youngest girl across London to the other side of childhood. Ida stood at the door and watched them go, while Nne-Nne whispered. They say the youngest child is the strongest child, because she had to make you love her, when you were tired, when you had loved the others first. Kemy had held on to Ida for a long time, to the old red shawl and history. Ida took one of Kemy's dreadlocks in her hand. "My God, child," she'd said, "I want you to stop this hair!"

When Georgia came home to visit she was struck by how empty the house seemed. She sat on the floor in the loft and listened dutifully to Bessi's reworked version of "Lucia Lover," and the beginnings of another song she was writing in a grand new effort to get out of Digger's. Bessi had been talking recently to the resident Spicey Riley's DJ,

Master Spice, and he had given her a profound piece of advice: *Make yourself seen.* This was now written in capital letters on a card by the mirror. Master Spice had also said he might give her a short slot at the club one night, in front of the music bods, if she was good enough. Georgia told her that she was. And some nights she spent at Waifer Avenue, just so that Bessi would not be on her own.

They lay in the dark, late at night. Bessi said, only half joking, "I'm surprised you can stand to be away from Toby for a whole night."

"He's got rehearsals—he's performing in Denmark soon," said Georgia. "Anyway, we're not stuck to each other."

"Practically. You're like a married couple, you two."

Georgia smiled to herself. "Shall I tell you a secret?"

"What?"

"I think I'm in love with him."

"That's a bit swift, isn't it—after two months?"

"Three, actually."

"That's ridiculous. It takes longer than that to fall in love."

"It didn't seem to take you very long to fall in love with that Pedro guy in Trinity."

"I wasn't in love. That was lust. He had muscles. I don't see what all the fuss is about with Toby."

Georgia turned to face the window. She closed her eyes and felt older than Bessi.

Then she said, "There are seasons in my head, Bessi, and sometimes it turns. Toby made it turn."

She brought Toby home with her on Boxing Day. They sat close together on the sofa, the way Georgia and Bessi might sit together, and Georgia kept a firm hold on his hand. Frequently she glanced at him, checking he was still there next to her, that he was comfortable. Toby chatted with Kemy a lot about his forthcoming trip to Denmark, and he was obviously amused by Aubrey swearing at his vegetables. Ida kept quiet apart from insisting that Toby eat more turkey stew and potatoes because he was "thin like a teenager." After lunch Aubrey asked, "What are your plans for the future, then, Toby? You'll be graduating soon, won't you?"

Toby and Georgia touched eyes. "I'll be staying in London for a while, keep working on my music."

Bessi raised her eyes.

"Toby plays the guitar," said Georgia. "He's really good too."

"Well, I'm no Hendrix or anything . . ."

They laughed a secret laugh, at exactly the same time.

"I do have a job as well, though," Toby added, with a hint of sarcasm.

"He makes clocks."

"I help make them, that is. I insert the batteries—"

"—in the backs—"

"—not that much to it really—"

"It's good for making music," said Georgia, "isn't it." She smoothed the back of his hair. She closed her hand over his knee.

In the kitchen Bel washed up, Kemy dried. Bessi had disappeared upstairs.

"I like Toby," said Kemy, "but isn't it *weird*?"

HE LEFT BEFORE the new year came in. He'd bought a necklace of amber beads and placed it around her neck. Georgia concentrated hard on her studies and tried to forget that he was gone. There were other distractions: She and Bessi were almost twenty-one and Bessi was planning a night out at Spicey Riley's to celebrate, seeing as she could get a discount on account of slaving next door, and more important, Master Spice had virtually promised her a slot.

It was a Saturday night. In the afternoon it drizzled as Georgia made her way from Seven Sisters to 26a. Without Toby, it had been a blue week with snatches of yellow and a moment of orange. She had gone out and bought a set of coloring pens. In orange, she had written a letter to Toby. It said, *There are always so many questions, Toby. How does someone live with all these questions?*

The loft was full of thumps and sisters and clothes and Soul II Soul. Bel had brought her red spike-heeled shoes, four feather boas, and everything she owned that glittered and clung. Bessi was standing hazel-eyed before the mirror and trying on a silver strapless dress with her white boots. "Hello, twin," she said. "It's going to be a night." She threw her head back and laughed the loud laugh. "Have some bubbly, go on. We are women."

Kemy, in her underwear and dreadlocks, gave Georgia a glass and filled it. "We've been waiting for you," she said. "Bel's doing eyes. You and Bessi have to wear something silver."

"But not *exactly* the same thing, innit," Bessi said.

"Yeah," said Georgia, "and I don't want to wear anything short."

"Come here, Georgie," said Bel. "Your eyes are the best."

She coated the lids in orange and blended it into green while Georgia sipped champagne. "You're good at colors," she told Bel, and closed her eyes. Kemy took a picture—Bel's enormous black hair, Georgia's face turned up. She called it *Rose and Mystic Bel.*

Georgia had eaten no dinner before she left so that her stomach would be flat. She put on a pair of shiny trousers and a crop top with tassels. Bel checked the afro puffs and slipped beads on the ends of plaits. There was much deciding and twirling and not being sure and changing and in the end there were four of them in feathers, bare-shouldered—the silver twins, their eyes in the shadows of green. Because of twenty-one, Aubrey ordered a cab and as they left Ida stood in the doorway and told them not to talk to boys. "Bel, make sure," she said. "Oh Mum," said Bel in her red shoes. "They're women!"

As the city came for them, Bessi whispered to Georgia in the back of the cab.

"I've got something for us."

"What is it?" said Georgia.

"It's acid."

"Is it? What for?"

"For being twenty-one. I want to take it with you. It would be amazing with you."

"I've never had any. Is it nice?" Georgia checked.

"Together it will be nice. It will be extra extra."

"Where did you get it?"

"From someone at work."

"Oh."

"Shall we?"

The West End was arriving. Streetlights and shadows and London's crooked beauty were crossing over Bessi's face. "Shall we?" she said.

"All right," said Georgia, "a little bit."

"A *tiny* bit," said Bessi.

They went straight to the toilets in Spicey Riley's and shared a cubicle. Bessi gave Georgia a quarter of a tab of something silver to put on her tongue. "Will you stay with me?" asked Georgia. "Yes, sweet," said Bessi. Together they swallowed and went out into the crowd.

Fluorescent lights put snow on people's faces, on their eyelashes, and electricity in their teeth. The floor was transparent and pools of light showed through. Beer trembled whitely at the top of beer. The dancers bopped and swayed against the scintillating lights. "Ladies! On the floor!" boomed Master Spice, and Bessi winked at him as she passed. Women swept by in their moonlight best, shoulder straps black and needle thin, hair thick with perfume, lips full, open, blazing with gloss.

Bel and Kemy were being what-ya-sayin'd by two men, one in leather trousers and the other in a suit and unnecessary sunglasses. Kemy was asking him why he was unnecessarily wearing sunglasses in the dark. "Can you see anything? I bet you can't even see me. Will your eyes fall out if you take them off?" The man was chuckling. He looked at Georgia and Bessi approaching and said, "More sisters! Where did they come from?" Kemy put her arms around Georgia. Bessi and Bel were moving out toward the dance floor with the leather trousers following. Kemy said, "There's four of us, and three of us are triplets, aren't we, Georgie." The man's sunglasses flashed. For a moment he looked exactly like Jimi Hendrix. Georgia didn't feel any acid yet. But she heard herself think, *He must be hot in those glasses,* and another Georgia think, *He must be hot in that suit.*

She saw Cynthia and Jo walk in and shake off their coats. "Happy birthday!" said Cynthia in a silky voice, and kissed her. The music got louder. Half an hour later, Anna arrived in the veil of her long falling ginger hair. And Reena, with a man much taller than her, then a friend of Kemy's, two friends of Bel's. They all were chattering and laughing with electric teeth. On the dance floor the dancers became witches, stumbling and cackling across the pools of light.

Spicey Riley's thumped.

The voices, the music, the lights and the dark slowed down.

Gladstone walked in wearing his dressing gown. He was bald now. He moved toward her through the lights and the witches and disappeared into her.

Where have you been all these years? she thought to him.

He said, *In the house. In the empty house. It never goes away.*

Georgia felt her arm being pulled. "Come and dance with me, love," said Bessi. She followed her white boots out to the witches. They danced to Shabba Ranks's "Mr. Loverman" and the rhythm in their bodies was the same. Their shoulders twitched in the same direction, they shook their hips on the same side of the beat; what one body did the other must follow. Kemy and Bel came back from the DJ booth laughing. Master Spice cleared his throat between the beats. "Gotta special request going out to da twins, twenny-one today, happy birthday, twins, and here's a tune for *you!*"

Bessi threw her hands in the air and squealed. She twirled to the music and Georgia thought she looked like Diana Ross, her hair foaming over her shoulders and the tiny dress shimmering. Her mouth was wide open. Bessi threw up her arms again and brought them down around Georgia.

"Can you see it?" The music was loud but Bessi was only whispering. Georgia could hear her clearly.

"The grass?" said Georgia. "Yes. Over there."

"It's pink!" Bessi laughed. "A pink field, and butterflies, hundreds of them! Can you see it? I *knew* it would be wild together. We can see the same things!"

They ran up the rosy hill to a large tree alone in the field. It had thick leaves and a swollen trunk. They climbed up it and sat in the branches and the sky was kind and blue. They heard the tree whispering and singing and did not know what it meant.

"I love you," said Georgia. "Let's stay here."

On the dance floor, Bessi started jumping around to Chaka Khan. "Come and dance, dance with me, Georgie!" she shouted, and Georgia climbed back down from the tree. Bessi's smile was wider than Georgia had ever seen it. She was laughing her very loud laugh but now it seemed to be coming from somewhere else. It turned into a giggle with two mouths. Georgia looked back over at the cool pink field. The butterflies had disappeared. In the distance, she saw two little girls moving toward her. They were doing cartwheels down the hill.

They stopped giggling, and concentrated on cartwheels.

When they arrived they stood on the dance floor. A space emptied around them. Georgia could see clearly now, their white dresses and the same face, holding hands. One of the hands was burned.

"I know you," said Georgia.

"Yes," they said. "You do."

Georgia looked back at Bessi and pointed at the little girls. Bessi laughed and twirled. There was the sound of drums, and inside the drums, a double heartbeat. The lights beneath the floor were headlights, icy suns. The little girls stared at Georgia, their dresses sweeping full in the wind, although the air was very still. They smiled sweetly and Georgia felt blessed.

She said: "Is it nice where you are?"

"Yes," they said, in only one voice. "It's the best bit."

Georgia giggled. "Isn't it," she said.

A restful breeze slid across her face. She heard the distant sound of fire. One of the girls turned and whispered to the other.

Holding hands, they faced her.

"Look what we can do."

Their smiles became wide and unsweet. Too wide. Georgia didn't want to look but she couldn't help it. She couldn't turn her head to get Bessi and she couldn't speak. One little girl opened her mouth until her face disappeared. Then, into the black space, the girl with the burned hand climbed. There was no mess. She didn't say good-bye.

Georgia cried for a moment.

She said: "Are you Ode now, or Onia?"

"Yes," said the little girl.

"Does it hurt?" said Georgia.

"Yes," she said. "But we forget."

Georgia cried again.

"If I ever wanted to," she said slowly. "Could I learn it too?"

The girl turned away and walked up the hill. They looked back once, and whispered: "You already know."

SHE WATCHED THEM until they were out of sight. The field and the tree were beginning to blur and there were other people, very close to her, other voices and the loudest one Bessi's, which sounded strange and labored as if it was being stretched. Just before the tree disappeared completely, Georgia saw someone walk out from behind it, a woman with thick black hair wearing a pair of red shoes, and reaching out her arms.

"What is it?" said Bel. "Why are you crying?"

Bessi's voice sang louder. Georgia lifted her arms and held on tightly to Bel. When she opened her eyes she saw Bessi on the other

side of the pools of light, holding a microphone. Her mouth was con-
torted. The silver of her dress had lost its shine. Georgia watched her,
struggling through her Lucia song, and she felt that she had not seen
her for a long and irretrievable time.

A HEADACHE CAME like a new country and stayed there. The
back of her neck exploded, volcanoes erupted at her temples, lava
boiled across her face and seeped into her ears. It left her when she
was asleep. She dreamed that she was in the boat, lying back, and
drifting toward the mountain. The sun shone down on her dress—a
white dress, with a yellow belt. She gazed up past seagulls and into the
silver mist, and felt it falling down upon her eyes.

"Guess what," said Bessi over the phone.

"What?" said Georgia. The headache was eating her eyelid.

Someone had offered Bessi a job in a record company, a man she'd
met at Digger's ("I knew it would happen!"). Bessi had insisted he
take her on, while drinking vodka and lime at four in the morning in
her uniform and reeling off the names and song titles of all the videos
on the screens above their heads. "I didn't get a single one wrong. He
was *well* impressed." And although she wouldn't be getting paid much
at first and the work was basically office work and she wouldn't really
be singing—and maybe she wasn't cut out to be a singer anyway—she
could work her way up, couldn't she, and eventually she'd get to travel
or something and meet *really* interesting people, and the office was
just behind Oxford Street. "Good, innit!"

Georgia's eyelid was throbbing.

"Yes," she said.

"Is that it?"

"I've got a headache. I have to go."

"What is it?" Bessi said.

"My head. I have to go."

"Georgia?"

She hung up. She dabbed rose and chamomile oils at her temples and went to bed for three days. In the timeless dark she woke up. There seemed to be a pressure, pushing her down into the mattress. It said to her, *We are here.* And perhaps it wasn't true (but what if it was?) that there were hands pulling the covers away from the bed. What if it was real? A stranger in the room, not a human stranger, a thing, a demon, watching her closely, leaning down to grip her shoulders and shake her, lay on her the hands of death. There was a voice, a horror voice. It said, *Get up, spin spin spin around, you will never find a sleep!*

I don't understand, she said to the dark.

She lay still. Be okay, be okay. Think of one good thing.

The two little girls, both of them in one of them, cartwheeled through the window. Their dress blew about in the no-breeze.

"Are you ready?" they said.

"No," said Georgia.

"It doesn't hurt," they said.

"No," said Georgia.

She fell back to sleep at dawn, when the light took the things away. In the long afternoon bath (three and a half hours, for the water was soothing and the water was safe) there was a lot to discuss:

The days are red. And what was the drill for red?

I don't remember.

What's the drill for red?

But why is it red? I want to know that.

Because you have a headache.

Yes.

And because you are afraid.

Yes.

And we must make you strong again.

Yes.

So. The drill for red?

I drink water. I restore my body to a state of purity.

Yes.

I eat apples and yogurt for breakfast and salad for lunch.

Yes.

I breathe and run through the trees and feel my heartbeat.

Yes. That's right.

And anyway, it will be better in the spring. It always gets better in the spring.

She decided to clean the flat to a state of purity. In the living room she pulled the cushions off the sofa and vacuumed underneath and then she pulled the cushion covers off the cushions (you could never be sure) and soaked them in a bucket. She mopped the bathroom and kitchen four times each with bleach, polished mirrors without looking inside them and cleared underneath her bed. She was lying there in the gloom on her stomach and a flash of something ran across the room.

At Middlesex she went to see the head of history. He always wore a thin brown pullover and he kept a peppermill next to his in-box. Georgia sat down in a blue chair across the room from his desk. She had an odd flicker of worry that she might suddenly shout something nonsensical to no one in particular. The history dean looked over at her and waited.

Georgia's chair was facing the adjacent wall. "It's just. Well, it's," she said. "Um."

"Ah," he said. "Yes."

"I was thinking. It's been, very difficult."

"Ah," he said, and touched a paper on his desk.

She huddled in the dark. "So I thought. Maybe . . ."

"Hmm?"

"Maybe I should intermit, for a year, for now, and come back when—"

"Any reason in particular, er, Georgina?"

"I thought it would get better. I can't cope with—"

The history dean said, "It's common at this stage, yes. But there needs to be a very good reason for it. We don't like to see talented students dropping out halfway through the course." He leaned back and glanced out of the window. "*Is* there a specific reason?"

She was sitting in a cave. There was no air in the cave. She tried to breathe. *Be okay, be okay.* A specific reason.

"Red," she said, her eyes getting wet (*Oh, not here, not here*).

"I'm sorry?"

She couldn't stop it coming now. She shook with it in the corner and sniffed and used her sleeve. The history dean's bookshelves, the blue door and the history dean were leaning away from her. She would have to be picked up and thrown out.

"Georgina, there are—" He rubbed his knees and stood up and sat down again. He touched paper.

What she had to do was get up and get out of here. Up. Out. It was not easy.

Through the corridors as she ran there were loud echoes. *Get out, spin around, get out, spin spin spin around.* She escaped into the unpretty day and ran toward the willow house. The winter sky was darkening as she approached. She was held in the moment of lilac becoming indigo, the in-between which had nothing inside it but the coming of rest. Night birds were singing. The earth smelled of old rain. She leaned against the trunk of a willow tree. She felt the pulse of peace.

In a very pale blue, she wrote it down, on separate lines:

I want to be dusk
I want to be
a lonely magic color
and fall and fall unstoppably
into darkness

A Cottage by a Hill

Later that year Bel had a dream she didn't like. A woman was climbing a flight of stairs. At the top of the stairs was a naked lightbulb hanging from the ceiling. The woman, whose face she couldn't see, was reaching her arm up toward the light. Her head was thrown back, her fingers wide apart. She climbed and climbed. Bel was afraid that if she touched the light she would burn her hand. When the woman reached the top of the stairs, Bel woke up.

She telephoned Georgia in Tottenham. She asked her about the colors.

Georgia said, "Don't worry, Bel, we're fine. Toby's helping me with my revision."

Bel reminded her not to study too much at night, it wasn't good for headaches. Before they hung up, Georgia asked, "Can I tell you something?"

"What, love?"

She lowered her voice to a whisper. "I have dreams. I want to walk toward him while he waits for me, holding a ring."

Bel had seen them, how they were. She had seen how alike they were in their distance from things, in their eyes. When Toby had returned in February he had virtually moved in. It was not always wise, Bel thought, to join yourself to another so like you. Colors could grow; they could double themselves.

"Think about it carefully," she told Georgia.

He held the back of her head in his palm. She thought about it. *I would like to walk toward you, and disappear there.*

Toby had come back with new songs and a memory of a cottage by a hill. It belonged to a Danish musician he had met and he had stayed there one night between gigs. He described it to Georgia as absolute peace—the sound of the birds, the quietness of dawn.

His hair had grown past his shoulders. They lay on their sides facing each other in Georgia's room, which was spotless. His rucksack had been left by the door for later, when he would take it home and unpack his things. She ran her fingers along his lips. She drew him closer until her eyelashes brushed his collarbone.

"Next time," she said, "take me with you."

She told him nothing of Spicey Riley's. Toby said she had lost some weight, that her eyes looked different, and he wanted to know what was wrong. "If you'd told me to come back sooner I would have," he said.

"I couldn't ask you that."

"Yes," he said, his hands stroking the skin on her back, "you could."

The nights were peaceful. On occasion, if he was not there, she slept with the light on. Toby worked more hours at the factory and helped her through the final year at Middlesex. She did not mention the cockroach she spotted in the bathroom, lying on its back with its legs in the air.

AT WAIFER AVENUE, absences swept through the rooms and flew up the stairs. They collected in the loft, where the air was heavy, and the saloon door was hanging off its hinges.

Bessi left for work in the mornings now rather than the evenings. The record company had promoted her swiftly from the girl who made tea to an assistant in the press office, where she was proving to be a gifted networker. She was especially gifted at attending photo shoots and taking people out to lunch, always dressed in the latest Oxford Street fashion, like a true and committed member of the music industry. Her hair was worn in corkscrew extensions applied in Bel's shop, and she had acquired some blue contact lenses.

Bessi was organizing a press campaign for a new artist called Leopard who had an unusual off-key quality in his voice that was being hailed as a vocal revolution in pop music (as she had phrased it in her press release). Leopard was very fond of fur coats, which he always insisted on being provided with when he posed for his photo shoots. To be kept satisfied and amenable to the press he had to be taken out for meals a lot, and Bessi took this opportunity, in order to avoid the drafty loft and the cloudy, solitary dinners with Aubrey and Ida, to stay out late as often as possible.

Ham had passed away on September 30, 1980. Bessi had forgotten the date but Georgia never had. It was not an anniversary, because anniversaries were for weddings. It was a noticing. The ones who had lost and who remembered closed their eyes and looked inward for a time, and then they carried on. On September 30, 1995, a foggy white Saturday with flecks of rain, Georgia came to Waifer Avenue to talk to Bessi for a specific reason. It was not a matter of permission. It was a matter of needing her blessing, which was a kind of permission.

In the sun lounge she stood by Ham's old table, closed one eye, then the other, and looked inward. Then she went upstairs.

The curtains were still drawn. Bessi had been lying in bed for two hours because she didn't like fog. She was still wearing her blue contact lenses from the night before. Georgia sat down next to her. They put pillows behind their backs and the covers over their knees. It was dark here, with the window on the other side of the room and the fog behind the curtains. And in the dark were other kinds of uncertainty.

"Have you decided what to do yet?" Georgia asked Bessi.

"What about?"

"Where you're going to live."

"No," said Bessi. "I've been thinking about it a lot, though. Definitely not south London, it's too far."

It's not as far, thought Georgia, *not as far as somewhere better.*

She said carefully, "Me and Toby have been thinking, too."

Bessi hesitated. "Have you?" She swallowed tea and looked at the end of her bed.

"I've had enough of London. It's no place to live. Toby says it's all madness and choking, and he's right. I don't know how you do it every day, going to Oxford Street."

"It's not that bad, the shops are fantastic." Bessi remembered a new pair of jeans she'd bought yesterday that were such a spot-on, music industry blue that she hadn't been able to resist them; she was about to ask Georgia if she wanted to see, but Georgia was speaking rather quickly.

"That's not what you said when you got back from Trinity. You said London was ugly and cold. You said you wanted to take us all back to St. Lucia and live by the sea, that's what you said."

"Well, I'm used to it now, aren't I. I've warmed to the fruits."

Georgia found this irritating.

"Anyway," she said, "we've been thinking, me and Toby, of moving away somewhere quiet, out of the city. We want to live in a cottage by a hill."

Bessi sometimes started singing when things disturbed her. It disturbed her, the emphasis Georgia had placed on "me and Toby."

"A little cottage in Negril," she said, "remember that song, Tyrone Taylor?" She began to sing.

"I'm serious, Bessi."

The singing stopped and was replaced by half a laugh.

"You want to live in a cottage by a hill? What hill? How far away is this hill?"

"There's hills in Brighton and around Brighton. I could see myself living in Brighton—with Toby, we've talked about it a lot. We might even go to Eastbourne, Toby says its gorgeous there."

"*Eastbourne!* Bloody hell! What d'you want to live in Eastbourne for!"

"It doesn't really matter where, Bessi," said Georgia passionately. "It's the idea, near the sea, open space, that could be lots of places. And anyway, what's wrong with Eastbourne? You've never even been there."

"Georgia, honey," said Bessi. *Honey* was a word she'd started using recently—Georgia felt a whip of fury. "Some dreams are just dreams. Cottages by hills are just dreams." Bessi shifted her position like a teacher about to explain something to her student. "It's like me with my singing, right? I dreamed of it for all those years and in the end it wasn't meant to be, it was something *similar,* but not exactly *it.*"

"That's not true!" Georgia pushed the covers off her knees and got out of Bessi's unbest bed. "You of all people should know that's a ridiculous thing to say. You went off to Trinity on your own—that was a dream, wasn't it?"

"Yes, but that was only for six months," Bessi pointed out.

"Yes, and six months can be a long time!"

"All right, all right, calm down."

Georgia opened the window and let in the fog. She breathed in and breathed out. "I'm trying to make my life easier," she said coldly, controlling her voice. "I'm trying to find somewhere I can fit. Isn't that what dreams are about, finding a way to fit? Just because you lost yours doesn't mean I should too."

Bessi winced. She covered it with a shrug, which agitated Georgia even more. All of a sudden it bothered her wildly that Bessi had never known the terror that could exist in buying milk, or making a cup of tea, or waking up alone in the middle of the night, or being happy right through and watching red crawl toward you to take it all away. She threw up her hands. "Honestly, Bessi, you have no idea, do you?"

"No idea about what?"

"Oh, forget it."

"What's wrong with you today anyway?"

It was then that Georgia let it out. The words toppled from her, they stumbled out, in an awkward voice: "Everything's so easy for you, isn't it, you just breeze through and it's all nothing, nothing, it's nothing—" Georgia shrugged and let her hands dance in gestures of nothingness, her voice went higher and trembled. "You go up the road and buy milk, you fly off to the other side of the world on your own, you hang around with pop stars and you hardly have to think about it, I know, I watch you, anything you set your mind to and it's done. It drives me mad!"

Bessi couldn't seem to take in all the aspects of what Georgia was saying. She crossed her legs and sat up straight. "Right, okay," she said mathematically. "First of all, okay, first of all, it's not easy getting a job, right, remember Digger's? Not easy, not easy at all. Secondly, getting a job is not the same as buying milk, and *thirdly*—"

"See?" Georgia threw up her hands again. "No idea!" She stepped toward Bessi's bed so that their faces were close together. She frowned into Bessi's false blue eyes. "Buying milk can be the same as everything else. Getting out of bed, getting to the front door, being out in the street in a crowd is all the same when—when you are so afraid that you can't lift your arm or take one step forward, not *one step*, do you understand? Of course you don't."

"I *do* understand!" said Bessi. "I know about sadness, we all feel it, not just you, because nothing is easy"—though Bessi had not quite grasped how buying milk wasn't easy—"and sometimes it *is* a struggle, so we get blue, *I* get blue. You're so far inside your own head, Georgia, that you don't—"

"No." Georgia was firm, her voice was loud but steady. She looked taller, as if a cord was pulling her up toward the ceiling. The loft listened as she spoke.

"Blue is not the only color. No. Everyone does not feel like this.

And especially not you. All this time, all this time I have carried and protected you so that it would stay easy for you always, so that you'd never have to feel like me. And you can't even see it."

Bessi's mouth dropped open. "*What?*"

Georgia turned back toward the window and saw the evergreen tree in the distance. She put her hands over her mouth and stared at the tree with her eyes wet and bulging. She turned back to Bessi, who had moved to the edge of the bed in disbelief.

"You *carry* me? Is that what you said?"

Georgia dropped her hands. "You don't understand, you can't . . ."

"Well, that's *one* thing you're right about."

"Listen to me, Bessi. You'll probably never understand this because you never asked for my help or my protection—"

"Protection?"

"I said listen!" Bessi flinched. Georgia continued; there were tears coming down her cheeks. "I needed somewhere that wasn't bad. I wanted to be light and happy like you, and I wanted never for you to see the dark. I was scared I would infect you with terrible feelings and pictures in my head of walking out in front of the traffic and—no. That's not for you, see? Not for you to hear. I needed you to be my sunlight, Bessi"—and here Georgia paused and her words became very small—"I lost mine, I lost it."

Bessi was glaring at Georgia but behind the glare was the wish to hold her and stop her tears and make her feel better. She held on to the glare.

"You're acting as if what I am depends on you or something, like, I can only be happy if you're not. That's just nonsense. We're two different people, Georgia, and what I feel does not depend on you."

"But *it does*. That's what I'm trying to say!"

Bessi stood up and snatched the tobacco from her dressing table. The desire to comfort her sister had disappeared. She was a whole person, on her own, she did things on her own, and she didn't depend on anyone. "Who do you think you are?" she shouted. *She* had roamed the streets of London and had a long cool drink of oneness. *She* had gone to Trinity and discovered her wholeness, and none of it did she owe to Georgia, none of it. Bessi furiously rolled herself a whole cigarette. She started shaking her head, curt, stubborn shakes. Georgia had the sudden urge to slap her twin across the face.

Georgia narrowed her eyes. "Elizabeth," she whispered. "I have made sacrifices."

Bessi had not been called Elizabeth since she was six and Aubrey had seen her scratch the side of the car with her bicycle pedal. She had almost forgotten, in fact, that her name was Elizabeth. She burst into an odd, hysterical laughter, and it was at this point that Georgia, unable to contain herself an instant longer, a reckless screech escaping her mouth, sprang forward and slapped Bessi with full force across the face.

"I have made sacrifices!" she yelled.

Bessi dropped her cigarette and fell back onto the bed. Nothing moved, nothing spoke. She looked around her as if she couldn't remember where she was, and then, at exactly the same time, the two of them burst into tears.

Georgia held out her arms and moved toward the bed.

"You *slapped* me!"

"I didn't mean—I'm sorry, Bessi—"

"You *slapped* me, that hurt, I can't believe you *hit* me!"

Bessi struggled up, the side of her face turning crimson. She said nothing. She pushed past Georgia, flung open the door and stamped downstairs to the bathroom, leaving Georgia alone in the loft with an ache arriving in her head.

After ten silent minutes, Georgia heard the sound of running water from the bathroom downstairs.

She sat down on the floor. She watched the fog fading away.

An hour later, Bessi was still in the bathroom. Georgia went down to the kitchen for the carton of tomato juice she'd left in the fridge, and drank it, and thought of Toby, a cottage by a hill, the musk of his hair, his hands on her back, his mouth on her scar. She thought of Bessi in the bath and muttered, "Won't you come out now?" She sat in the sun lounge and watched the garden. At the back by the shack of spiders the grass had grown to forest. Ode in Onia were standing in it, with leaves in their hair. Apples had fallen. They were rotting, bruised, among the blades.

Another hour passed and the bathroom door was still closed. Georgia told herself it was Ida in there, not Bessi. She knocked on Ida's door.

Ida said, "Come in."

Georgia's head throbbed. She clutched the beads around her neck.

"Nothing, Mum. It's Bessi I wanted."

"Bessi is in the bath," said Ida.

Georgia approached the bathroom, which was opposite Ida's room.

"Bessi?" she whispered.

Through the door she saw Bessi lying down in the water. The water was very cold. Bessi was under the surface with her eyes open. She was not moving at all. Above her, high up near the ceiling, a red mist was crawling across the air.

And Bessi did not know the drills for red.

Georgia thumped the door with her fist, twice.

"Bessi!"

There was no answer. The red was spreading down toward the bath.

"Bessi! Get out of the bath! Get out of the bath, please!"

On the other side of the door, Bessi sat up. Her cheek was sore and she was freezing cold.

"What is it?" she said.

"Come out." Georgia went weak with relief. "Come here. Please come out, won't you? You've been in there too long. I'm sorry I hit you."

"I'm cold," said Bessi, lifting herself up. "I was sleeping."

"It's dangerous, come out now."

Georgia waited for Bessi to unlock the door. When she came out, there was a tinge of gray in her face and crimson in one cheek and her eyes were hollow and dim. It frightened Georgia, that look. She had seen it many times before, in the mirror. It didn't belong in Bessi's eyes. It was essential that Bessi remain in a strictly yellow place. *I am a thief,* she thought as she climbed the stairs after her. *I have stolen from you. But it is also true that you have stolen from me. You are light, I am shade.*

Bessi sat back down on her bed. She had taken out her contact lenses but she could not look Georgia in the eye. Georgia put her arm around Bessi. "A cottage by a hill," she said. "It's only a dream."

"It's not," said Bessi. "You were right."

GEORGIA AND TOBY moved into a small first-floor flat in Bruce Grove, behind the Tottenham clatter. It was connected to Neasden by the A406. They painted the staircase leading up from the front door in lilac. On the landing there was a naked lightbulb hanging from the landing, which Toby covered with a paper shade.

The flat was on a hill and had lots of light. A wicker chair in the lounge looked out onto a green, and at the bottom of the hill was not the sea but a flower stall next to a shop where they could buy milk. For the bedroom they chose yellow. And on the door of the bedroom, on the inside, Georgia wrote in chalk, G+T. It was their house.

Once a week she sat down for fifty minutes on a chair opposite a woman whose name was Katya. She had gray hair at the front and she often said "hmmm" and threw her head abruptly to one side. The office smelled of many kinds of blue and next to Georgia's chair was a brass box with a slit at the top, a single tissue half pulled out.

Georgia told Katya about the fear and the figures in the darkness. She told her that she had many questions, that they were written in words in the air above her head, and they gave her headaches. She said that sometimes there were colors that made things difficult. Katya threw her head to one side. Georgia pulled out a tissue and a half and Katya said: "Hmmm." There were echoes of Italian in her voice. "It is possible," she said, "that sadness becomes something that lives, a monster, it has taken on its own flesh. And it is possible that the monster can multiply."

Georgia sat back in her chair and her heels lifted off the floor. She said, "But how will I stop it from multiplying? How can I make it die?"

Katya told her it might never die, but with acceptance and good management it could be eased. "It is an endurance," she said (*endurance* was a word Katya used a lot). "You overcome and chase it away, and you must be determined. You smash it to the floor. And if it is necessary you scream and tell it, 'I do not consent.'"

It got better in the spring. The herb garden Georgia had planted on the windowsill shot up to full bloom and she talked about looking for work in a flower shop. Toby remained at the factory, performing occasionally with Carl. In the evenings he sat in the wicker chair and sometimes played the song he had first taught her, a streetlight moon looking in from outside. When Carl came up with another gig abroad, he decided not to go. "I want to stay with you," he said, when Georgia asked him if he was happy. "I told you I would."

Some weekends, Bessi came to stay. She was living alone on the top floor of a block of flats in Kensal Rise. From her window she could hear double-decker buses going past and she could see a graveyard with a chapel and hundreds of trees. She told Georgia she loved the top floor at night because it was like living on the same level as the stars.

They sat next to each other on the bench in Georgia's kitchen ("Bessi's best bench"), lightly touching arms. Bessi told Georgia about a man she'd met in Oxford Street called Darel. He had irresistible shoulders like a basketball player or something and he drove a nice car, a convertible. He took her for long drives and played Louis Armstrong through the city, the wind making her close her eyes, and Bessi sighed in and out with pleasure and thought, *This—this is a life I love.*

Summer turned. It flickered through the rooms and turned away. Georgia told Katya that she was experiencing panic. She had been to

John Lewis to buy a birthday present for Ida and had taken a plate off a shelf. As she held the plate, which was made of clay, she became extremely worried that she would drop it. Her fingers squeezed the sides of the plate. She held it for half an hour, not moving. Then she bent both knees, concentrating, and went lower, put the plate on the floor, and walked out. Outside the shop, she had started running.

"Endurance," said Katya. "Tell the monsters they are not real."

But Georgia was losing her words. Something irreversible had happened. The panic was connected to the change in season, and the realization that neither warmth and light, nor the opportunity to merge into the darkness of winter, might save her. She fell with the leaves in autumn and in November she got a headache that would not go.

Toby placed a cold flannel on her forehead. She said, Come here, come closer.

Yes? he said.

Toby. Sadness is not a season. Now I understand.

He held the back of her head. Stay with me Georgia, he said.

And she closed her eyes.

She began to slip past him like mist. You are symmetry, he told her, remember. She smiled at that. But the next day, which was a harsh deep red day, she couldn't get out of the house. She took a plate off the kitchen shelf, smashed it to the floor and shouted, I do not consent!

The air in the flat became thick and stifled and Georgia noticed, in a haze of questions, that Toby had stopped playing his guitar. She could not allow it. She said to the ache in her head, *I must not kill his music.* He took her to the sea, they watched the indifference of dusk silently, like strangers would watch it, and the dusk told her, *You must not kill his music.*

At Waifer Avenue the Hunters and Toby sang "Auld Lang Syne" with their arms linked. Georgia was watching invisibles and Toby was trying to see them too. Bel was alarmed. She said to Georgia in their place on the edge of the bath, Talk to me. Georgia looked at the green in Bel's eyes, and said very little. She had discovered something, and she was trying to remember it until she got home. It was there in Bel's eyes, it was in Kemy's lively voice, in all of them, she had seen it as they'd sang. Most of all, it was in Bessi.

Me-ness, she wrote. *I am within them. And as long as they remain, I will remain.*

Georgia spent her twenty-fourth birthday with Toby, and she cried again that day, in the morning, which was the most dangerous time to cry.

Toby, she said, I feel like the old West Pier.

Don't cry now, he said.

In the bedroom, in their house they lay down. Come here, she said. There were shadows. The moon outside was turning red. Lie down with me, Toby, said Georgia.

She memorized his heartbeat. She said: Forgive me, my darling, I am a thief. You have to go.

See You Monday

ike a wizard you spin. Whole and new, spin spin spin. Tragic
magic, set me free. Your golden face will turn in the breeze of
spinning and there has never been such bravery, there has never
been such glory. You drift toward the rowing boat, across the water, the
bright open blue, and she holds out her hand toward you. From the
mountain up above, the silver mist is falling down upon your eyes. That
is how it will be.

On the way home from Bessi's this morning, Valentine's Day, 1997, Georgia stopped at the flower stall at the bottom of the hill. She bought two large lilies with gyp. It was not difficult, because there were no colors. The old man with a large tweed cap over his little head was putting the tulips in their buckets. She thought, I would have liked that, yes, to put tulips in buckets in the morning, wrap them up, choose how best to make beauty, and hand it to someone. Nothing more complicated. She said to the man, I would have liked that.

Before returning home she walked around the park opposite with the bunch of flowers in her left hand, held slightly out in front of her, the stems sticking out of the bottom of the paper. In her right hand she was carrying her bag of things (toothbrush, a book, a change of clothes). She wore a hooded anorak that made her look like a child, and her hair was in two messy bunches. For a moment she sat down on the bench, but stood up again quickly, and went home.

As she climbed the lilac stairs, Ode in Onia waited at the top. Their eyes had gotten very large, and their dress had gotten very dirty.

Georgia said: It's nice where you are. Isn't it.

Six weeks ago, after Toby had left, she'd sat in the kitchen on Bessi's best bench (where she is sitting now, at twilight, thinking, deciding, her head strangely tilted). She had the sensation that she was in some-one else's clothes, in someone else's home, and she had no right to be sitting there, with the kettle boiling and the alfalfa beans sprouting by the window and an empty salad dish in the sink, baffled, and the sugar bowl with the lid off. They had drunk final tea, he was a man of sugar. He had left, vanished, turned back once and waved.

Nights gave her sleep until the darkest deepest hours when she sat up in bed to the noises, definitely, someone standing on the landing outside the bedroom door dressed in black, there, footsteps, finger-nails on the banister, and she switched on the bedside lamp and waited for dawn to come back. (There is nothing slower than dawn.) And then she would bathe. And then she would go out walking, wear-ing a white cotton scarf with a dark blue pattern of figures, tied around her neck.

This winter was very cold. There was fog.

Bessi said, Come and stay with me. I'll look after you. Don't be on your own.

They slept in Bessi's bed by the moon, with the light on. Bessi held Georgia in her arms; she said, Sleep well now, think of good things. In the middle of the night, Georgia felt a knocking against her skull. It was a devil. He told her a story. The story was about a woman who lost her soul, she misplaced it one day, and couldn't remember where. Of course, said the devil, it was impossible for this poor woman to live without her soul, so she began to look everywhere for it. She asked everyone she knew, she searched high and low, she looked on this side and on the other side. And when she found it, she vanished. Isn't that a good story? said the devil.

No! Georgia shouted. It's a terrible story, I hate it!

Carol Fielding, Katya, *The Detox Bible,* and most recently, *Saving the Soul,* had no advice on what to do when the devil came.

Except, unless, there is a crucifix.

Bessi woke up. Georgia charging up and down, up and down in the moonlight, her hands over her ears shouting *Not this, not mad, not this!* Bessi called her name; it took eight times, with her thumb rubbing the skin between Georgia's eyebrows, smoothing the twists away. The devil shrank back. Bessi saw it fly out of Georgia's eyes, a distortion, something utterly without pity, and it made her shudder.

(Valentine's Day. Three o'clock. Someone dipped the afternoon in sun. She walked into Bel's shop in her bright yellow trousers and she looked as if the air had just made her. "You look wonderful today," said Bel. She had plaited her hair. Ode in Onia had helped.

Georgia and Bel said good-bye. They hugged and Bel held the back of Georgia's neck in her magic palm. The palm could not tell.

Now she gets up from the bench. *Spin spin spin,* she wrote, *like a wizard you spin.* She walks toward the stairs.)

The day after the devil came, Bessi took Georgia to Waifer Avenue, to Ida, and went to work. "I'll come back later," she said. Ida made chicken stew and eba because Georgia liked eba. She rubbed Vicks on the temples of the headache. "You'll be all right," she said, "lie down." Ida sat in the armchair next to the sofa and stroked Georgia's head. Her bracelets were very faint bells in the dream.

First she heard the seagulls calling, then she heard the water, it said, Lie back now and rest, dear, lie down here and rest. Georgia was sitting in the boat wearing a white dress with a yellow belt. She reached out her hand, which was too small for her wrist. She was more lovely than anything Georgia had ever seen. Softly, she said, You have to ask Bessi.

Ida's bracelets brought her back. The peacock on the ceiling, the rocking chair, the silver men keeping still. From the edge of her sight, Georgia could see Ida's long red fingernails as she stroked and stroked her hair.

Mum, she said, tell me the story about when you left the village.

Ida told Georgia about running from the house with her bag of things, and how she'd waited for the bicycle in the dark by the water pump, the sound of the trees, the sound of the moths.

Were you scared?

Yes. I was very afraid. I was leaving my family and my home.

Georgia lifted her head. How did you know it was right?

Ida stopped her stroking and nodded slowly as the right words came to her. My life is my own, she said. There was no future there for me and I cannot live for nobody else. She stroked again and added, Only you, my children.

Do you ever regret leaving? asked Georgia. Did it hurt?

No. Regret is worthless. And pain, it goes away, you see, it goes away. You'll be all right.

Georgia lay back down. Dusk was walking in through the bay window with a fearless slender stride.

She said, You were brave, Mum, to leave the village.

(Georgia is in the living room now. She is holding her scarf in one hand. She has decided that it is the right one: white, the restoration to a state of purity; and dark blue figures, because we know each other well. And will there be music? She is bending down, flicking through records with her right hand. What song? What music? Or should it be silence?)

One week after Ida and the eba and the stroking, on a vast, sunny morning, Georgia and Bessi went with Kemy and Lace to the airport, to see them off. They were going to the Trinidad carnival. Kemy had packed hot pants, gold ones, with sequins, she told them, and Lace turned the music up loud. Marcia Griffiths and Tony Rebel sang "Ready to Go" and Georgia and Bessi held hands in the backseat in case of the devil. Tony and Marcia sang,

come let us go to the land of love
where the love light shines so bright above
we will be so happy and free
all your pains will let you be

Georgia liked this song. It was tall and jolly, it had wings. She leaned forward and stared into it like Ham on his hind legs to "No Doubt About It." A sudden streak of sunshine bounced off the motorway and turned the road to glitter. She opened her face. They raced through glitter. Me and Kemy and Bessi with wings in the sun. It turns, how it turns, so easily and suddenly it turns!

Kemy hugged Georgia good-bye and dug her fingers into her back.

(Georgia leaves the records now. She has decided it will be silent. Night birds, outside, that's all. Except the phone is ringing. Bessi?)

And they drove back from the airport together singing all the way. Bessi said, You're back, I thought you'd gone, I was so scared. They stopped in at Georgia's to get more clothes, white clothes, because she was pure again. How it turns. "These are *my* clothes!" She laughed. She threw a T-shirt at Bessi and it landed on her head. She laughed harder and Bessi threw a pillow. Tops and skirts and flying hats danced backward and forward and afterward, they lay down, and Bessi whispered, Remember, sweet, how it turns.

(No. Bessi is out at the concert with Darel. It's Valentine's Day.
"Hello?"
"Oh, Georgie, thank God, it's Bel. Are you all right, love?"
"Yes. I am well."
"Are you sure?"
"Absolutely yes, it's a lovely night. Isn't it a ravishing night, Bel?")

The thing was, she couldn't sleep. She spent nights at Bessi's and Bel's and days with Ida and wherever she went the devil found her. One night she told Bel that she was lost. Bel led her to the mirror in her bedroom. They stood in front of it, stared into the glass.

Look at yourself. There you are, see?

No, I can't see her, said Georgia. She's not there.

Behind the doors they said, What shall we do about Georgia, oh, what shall we do about Georgia!

On a Wednesday afternoon, three weeks ago, she was sitting in Bel's leather armchair. She didn't move for a long time. Her eyes were miles and miles away. Jay, who was ten now, came and stood next to her. He said, "Auntie Georgia, do you want some chocolate? It's a treat." She turned to Jay and smiled for him a mechanical smile. "No thank you. It's too sweet." She had developed a strong aversion to sugar. Sugar was like amusement parks and love, music with words and lipstick with lip gloss, it was sudden motorway glitter and carnival hot pants, flapjack empires that weren't famous, wild fields and Hendrix in the forest, walking the clouds with Bessi, watching the sea with Toby, all of that, all of that outside. Sugar was alive. Sugar was an accusation.

Jay looked helpless. Not a quicker breath. Not a real smile. Auntie Georgia kissed him on the cheek as if it hurt and went to lie down in Bel's room inside joss sticks.

It was safe to lie down, because it was day. Georgia in the lake reached out her arm. She was holding a daffodil. She said, Ah it's so *peaceful* here, while Georgia, the untrue Georgia, the skeleton one, lay tossing into the evening, rubbing her chest with her knuckles—because there was something in there, something worse than everything before.

After work Bessi went to Bel's. She was very tired. Leopard's second album was about to be released and he was refusing to do an interview with *Melody Maker* because they had decided not to put him on the cover. Bessi had lunch with him, and as Leopard spouted on through his fourth Glenfiddich and she tried to get a word in about the success of his album being sort of dependent on the press, she had seen Georgia walking across the restaurant in her nightgown with her hands over her ears crying *Not this, not mad.*

Bel had lit candles. Silhouettes flared across the ceiling. When Bessi saw Georgia tossing like that, rubbing at her chest, her legs began to shake.

They stood over the bed. She was using her whole fist now, rubbing hard, into the bone.

What is it, Georgie, what's *in* there?

Half-awake, half-asleep, she said this: I see it, here, my gravestone in my chest! I can't get it out!

Bessi and Bel leaned forward and covered their mouths.

Nor did Carol and the others have any handy tips for what to do about gravestones sitting in the heart.

So, two weeks ago, in her notebook, Georgia wrote a letter to Bessi. The words of the letter came onto the page naturally. There was triumph in the ink. When she had finished, she smiled a real smile. It's good, eve.

She paid the overdue electricity bill of £44.12 with money borrowed from Aubrey. "You look well," he said. She looked the brightest she had ever been. Her hair was glossy at the ends and her cheeks were shiny. In her face was the glowing extremity of life on the edge of itself. Behind the doors they said, Thank God, she's back.

(She returns to the kitchen now, to the bench, and sits down. *To the edge, to the edge, let me sail.* She puts down the pen. Outside someone is whistling. She smokes a cigarette and picks a bit of tobacco off her lip. Ready now, she says, all ready. She rises up from the bench. She is fizzy inside.)

All that remained was to ask Bessi. It was ten days ago. They'd slept head to toe in Bessi's bed. Bessi was exhausted.

Georgia got up at dawn and went barefoot into the living room. By now the way she walked had changed. The outward feet had a daze, and tapped about, as if they were no longer interested in what was in front. Bessi found her standing by the window. Smile for me, Georgia, she thought.

Georgia turned. She rubbed her hands down the sides of her nightdress. It was a matter of permission.

My Bess, she said, I want you to let me go.

Her arms lifted away from her sides as if contemplating flying. Stillness was gathering, the inside lights retreating.

Go where? said Bessi, but she knew where.

Georgia mumbled. I've lost my flower, I—have to find Georgia, have to—

No. Bessi turned in a circle on her feet, her hands out, fingers spread. In a high voice she said, No, Georgia, you can't ask me that.

Please. Georgia's eyes were tattered now. They hung in their sockets like mildew on clothes.

No, Georgia. My God, no.

(We danced together last week, didn't we. I can still feel the heat and the bass and the storm beneath our feet. And I am sorry, darling, but I must go, for I do not fit. And you will understand, soon, that I must. Can you hear the birds?

She walks out onto the landing. She looks up at the light there. She touches her neck.)

This morning, Georgia watched Bessi not quite sleeping. The eyelashes trembling. One arm slung above her head. That pale mouth, closed.

I'm going now, said Georgia.

Where? whispered Bessi.

Home.

Georgia paused. She was afraid.

Can I come back tonight?

I won't be in tonight. I'm going out with Darel. Come back on Monday, then you can stay for a while.

Bessi's voice trailed off. Georgia didn't move. She breathed in, breathed out.

See you Monday, then, she said.

Bessi opened her eyes and saw Georgia in the doorway in her dark anorak. Their eyes did not touch.

Bye, said Bessi, see you Monday.

And Georgia went home.

It is eleven o'clock. The house is dark. Just before dusk, a rainbow happened. Did you see it? I am going to find the gold. Another shock, another scale, it all is history. She is on the water, holding out her little hand, and I can almost touch it. The wind picks up, the mist begins to fall.

Georgia climbs the stairs. She throws her head back and shivers and reaches her arm up to the light. The hand is outstretched, the fingers wide apart. Sweep me from my feet. Jump. Jump. Jump away. Like a wizard you spin.

And Bessi feels her face throb. Once.

The
Best
Bit

The Best Bit

1

The sign in the parlor window says WE CATER FOR ALL ASPECTS OF DYING.

It's Wednesday afternoon. Aubrey, Bel and Bessi stand outside in the rain looking at the sign initialed in the bottom right-hand corner, *JP Funeral Directors*. They are being watched by two blackbirds sitting on the branches of the sycamore tree in the center of the grass-topped roundabout opposite the parlor. There are red roses on the grass left over from Valentine's Day.

Bel lifts her head. "Let's do this," she says, and while Aubrey fiddles with his keys and Bessi rubs her ribs, she steps forward in her scarlet stilettos and knocks on the door. Bessi draws back—it's cold in there, it's cold and dark and full of coffins and corpses. Though standing before them now is a man with pink cheeks and whiskers, in a tweed suit and silk bow tie. He has a morsel of cornflake trapped in his mustache.

He says, "Good morning, Mr. Hunter. Jonathan Pole." Aubrey and Jonathan Pole shake hands and beam pinkly. In the last few days Aubrey has developed this beam for introductions that take place in establishments involved in the administration of death. He steps into the gloom with his wet feet and Bel follows, pulling Bessi in after her by the hand.

The stillness inside is unearthly. Bessi imagines the echoes of bodies being unloaded into the basement before funerals, of relatives knocking at the door weeping, of the coffins and memorial stones groaning inside JP's catalogs over many many years. A strange laughter begins to well up in her throat. She pushes the laughter back down toward her ribs.

"Won't you come through?" says JP, and he strides down the hall past a closed door on the left and a flight of soft gray stairs on the right. It's warmer in his office. There is a gas heater with three molten bars in the corner and Aubrey and Bel sit down in great gleaming mahogany chairs bound in dark olive leather. Bessi chooses a stuffed Victorian throne with descending arms. It's a rare piece, JP tells them, from an American antiques dealer in Seattle, the only one of its kind, which means of course that Bessi's chair is best.

JP lifts a bowl of candy off his desk. "Murray Mint, anyone?"

Although she is not quite in the mood for sugar, Bessi's hand moves toward the bowl. Her hand is not wholly connected to what she wants and she doesn't want; it is, for now, a homeless hand. Bel and Aubrey take one each to be polite and Murray Mints are unwrapped. The sound explodes in the stillness like sudden fizz inside water.

When JP speaks, the cornflake in his whiskers moves with him.

"You've been to the mortuary, then?"

"Yes," says Bel, "we just came from there."

"I see." He leans toward them over the desk and brings his hands together. "So," he says. "I think it helps to be as frank as possible . . . Are we thinking of cremation or burial?"

Aubrey and Bel both turn to Bessi, who is staring at a photograph above JP's head of Neasden Lane in 1902. They have discussed this already. Ida does not believe in burning bodies. Despite Bessi telling them that she knows for sure Georgia would prefer her bones to be ashes and tossed all over the South Downs and drift, and disappear, and become all of it—but Ida was adamant. There should be a stone and soil, a place to go, and maybe a bench nearby.

"Burial," says Bessi. She whispers it, and immediately afterward she thinks she hears a thump in the next room.

JP strokes his tweed cuff. He tells them that most of his clients use the main cemetery near Harlesden, which happens to be the cluster of trees and stones that Bessi can see from her kitchen window. Bel looks worried. "Isn't there anywhere else?"

"No, Bel, it's perfect!" says Bessi quickly. She feels another flutter in her ribs. There is something happening to them.

Bel studies Bessi for a moment, she is panting slightly, while JP flicks his eyes around at his guests, judging for tact and timing. "And would you prefer a single- or double-depth plot?"

"How's that?" says Aubrey.

"What is it?" says Bessi.

A secret smile pushes past JP's lips and he glances at Bessi. "As it sounds, my dear. A double-depth grave allows family members, spouses, what have you, to lie together, one on top of the other. Bunk beds, you could say. In this case it might be suitable, perhaps . . ."

Aubrey beams. Bel nudges Bessi. But Bessi is confused. Does this mean, she is wondering, that both people have to be buried together, and if so, how does—

"But how does—?"

JP is used to this. In his substantial experience of catering for all aspects of dying he promptly explains: the first person is buried, a space left blank on the nameplate for the second; years or months or what have you pass and the time comes; grave is opened; second person buried; grave closed for good; nameplate filled in; a bunk bed.

"Ah," says Bessi.

A double-decker grave. A double-decker sleep.

"Yes, please," says her voice.

She is thinking of her flesh and bones joining the same soil as

Georgia's, her body suspended within the thick wet earth and Georgia's belated body her foundation. It's good, eve, it fits us perfectly, thank you, JP.

"Now," he says. "Coffins."

He opens a drawer and gathers from it some loose sheets of card, which he spreads out on the desk. Photographs of coffins suspended on white backgrounds, beneath each one a blurb describing the model's credentials of wood, decor and value. "There's quite a collection to choose from, coffins and caskets in oak, walnut, pine, mahogany . . ." He points at one of the photographs. "The African olive is exquisite, they'll whip it over from Germany in a jiffy, and then there's a variety of linings and finishes. Please, take your time."

Bel and Aubrey frown at the cards. Bessi hears footsteps. There is a knock at the door.

"Pardon me," says JP. "Come, come!" he shouts.

A woman walks in, with wiglike hair and long arms. Her arms reach almost to her knees and she is wearing a long black skirt down to the floor that makes her arms look longer. Her voice is a drone at the bottom of her face.

"Would anyone like a cup of tea and a coconut macaroon?" she says.

Bessi's mouth laughs and then stops. She puts her homeless hand over her mouth. Aubrey seems bewildered but cannot refuse because he is a longtime fan of the coconut macaroon.

"Are there macaroons, Dora? Excellent!"

Dora lifts an arm, which takes a long time. She stares at JP and puts a finger above her lip where her mustache would be if she had one. She narrows her eyes. JP opens his mouth in recognition and wipes his mustache with the back of his hand. The cornflake bit falls and lands above a coffin.

Dora leaves the room.

Aubrey, Bel and Bessi huddle around the cards. They are not sure what to look for when it comes to choosing a box in which to store a lost one in the ground.

"Perhaps while Dora's getting the macaroons we can go upstairs to the showroom?" offers JP.

"Showroom?" says Bel.

"The caskets."

"Here?"

"Upstairs."

"Oh."

JP beams and rises and chants, "Follow me," with a new bass in his voice. He throws open the door and swings out into the hall. "We'll be along, Dora!"

The showroom is at the top of the stairs. As they climb, the sensation in Bessi's ribs becomes stronger. It's an odd whistling feeling, quick and spectral, like the inside of a flute. She follows Bel up the soft gray stairs and the flute is singing beneath her skin and she thinks that it might be more than grief, this feeling, as it grows, that perhaps she is becoming ill and she is going to die too, which would not be a bad thing now with the double-decker sleep and the promise of Georgia waiting, and she feels that she can almost hear her voice. It says, *Find me, follow me, and I will wait for you.*

The showroom is small and extremely cold. There are mammoth shelves of assorted coffins on either side of the room and an aisle in the middle for shopping, like Tesco. The hush of the empty caskets gives way to the sound of twigs trembling at the icy window.

JP minus cornflake opens his arms and backs toward the window. He shoves his hand into the smooth white lining of a glorious sand-hued six-footer on the middle shelf. "The veneered oak is our most popular brand, very traditional. Nickel-finished handles, this one, and we'll throw in the engraving on the nameplate for free." He gestures toward another model near the bottom. "This one's a darker oak, very similar except for the paneling on the sides here."

Then there's the brass-finished walnut. The woven willow with the raised lid that Bel quite likes. And a show-model-only of the African olive, which, frankly, is nothing to shout about.

Aubrey takes off his glasses and pretends they need cleaning. He bows his head and wipes his eyes with his handkerchief.

JP moves proudly on to a crimson, velvet-covered casket on the top shelf. He caresses it with his fingertips. "And here, the Garratt Casket. Solid fir. Just look at that velvet! This one's called the "ripe cherry" but we have other colors, of course—purple, gold, emerald green and what have you . . ."

It's grotesque. A monster of a thing and she's not going *anywhere* in that, thinks Bessi.

". . . and the lining's taffeta, nice if you're wanting an open casket?"

Bessi's ribs whistle. The feeling begins to climb, bone by bone, and carries on. "Yes," her voice says, "an open casket." This is melodrama. This is masquerade. The shell that held her will be lovely as she meets the earth to rest, spruced up, the eyelashes stroked along to the tops of her cheeks and the plaits splayed out on a white cotton pillow, as they lay the body down in the five-foot-five, feather-cushioned willow, that one, that one there with the varnished curlicues along the side . . .

"She wants this one," says Bessi, touching one of the curlicues. "She—"

Bel spins round toward Bessi. She sees a flicker of something in her face. Bessi is breathing fast and rubbing her ribs and looking baffled and thinking, *Is it? Could it? Could she? What is it?*

"No," says Bel, turning away, then turning back.

. . . and Bessi, there will be drums and soaring songs rattling in the sun-shocked wind as they take her down lower and lower to the hushed double sleep. They will sing, *Let us go to the land of love, where the love light shines so bright above,* lower and lower, and the flowers will be tossed gladly onto her in all their innocent colors. There will be no tears, no howling, only the joy, the relief, the laughter, and the peace, cascading down as she falls. That is how it will be.

"We'll take that one, then," Aubrey tells JP, "Bessi knows best." He pats the side of her head with his palm. He has never done this before. His palm is full of pity.

"It's a good choice." JP casts a quick, longing glance at the Garratt and leads them back downstairs, where Dora has left the macaroons on the desk. They drink tea and Aubrey and JP eat macaroons and discuss costs and arrangements. Aubrey remarks that the best bit of a coconut macaroon is the rice paper.

Bessi's ribs are quiet now. She sits still in the stuffed chair staring at the photograph of Neasden Lane in 1902, and Bel keeps looking at her as if she wants to ask her something.

"The coroners will be bringing her down on Friday," says JP, when all the aspects of dying are covered. "Why don't you come back then with a few things, something for her to wear, a favorite outfit perhaps, and there'll be the makeup to do—"

"I'll do the makeup!" Bessi leaps from her silence, because JP and Dora would get the colors and the foundation wrong, wouldn't they; and Bel can help too—Bel knows the colors.

"That's perfectly all right, of course," says JP. He now has a piece of macaroon in his whiskers.

The four of them stand. Aubrey and JP shake hands. Dora is out in the hallway and she purses her lips at them as they leave, which might be the way she smiles.

We will be back on Friday. Take care, JP, how you handle her. We have heard the parlor stories of bodies being thrown about like old bits of rubber, so handle her well, as a rose petal drifting on the lake.

Bessi, shall we?

WHEN THE POLICE lifted Georgia down she crumpled in their arms like fabric. The feet hung outward. She was wearing bright yellow trousers and a white top with a low neck and around the neck there were bruises.

It was half an hour toward midnight on Monday. The tips of the fingers were black. The sister was waiting in the flat downstairs where the neighbor of the deceased had offered her tea.

The police, one man, one woman, had broken in and gone upstairs. They saw her almost immediately, for she was swaying and
spinning over the banister above their heads. The man swung around.
He said to the sister: "Stay back. Get back."

The sister cried out the name of the deceased.

Earlier, while she was sitting on the wall outside waiting for the police to arrive, Bel had shivered in the cold and had thoughts, some of
which she said out loud, some of which she did not. She had left home
in a rush, with her slippers on, and her feet were coldest.

She said: I can see her. I can see her swaying.

And the cold and the wind answered: *Yes.*

The phone in Georgia's flat had been ringing since morning. Bessi,
wanting to make arrangements for coming back on Monday. Bel,
worried because she'd had a dream of a wedding in a big red tent and
a dog that wouldn't stop barking. Georgia did not answer. She was
spinning. By four o'clock there was no room left for messages. The
answering machine replied with a long dull note instead of her voice,
which used to say, quietly, with a guitar in the background: "Hello-ha."

All day at work Bessi had felt a stillness about things. It was a feeling of absence, of silence, despite the phones ringing all around her
and the smell of coffee and the clock on the wall. She felt gray inside,
as if she were made of dust.

She rang Georgia's flat every hour. She rang her every fifteen
minutes. And Bel rang. And Georgia spun. There was dread in the
afternoon.

On the way home Bessi prayed to God for the first time since the
apples. She shut her eyes: Please, God, let Georgia be waiting for me
when I get home, please, she has let herself in and she is sitting there on
the sofa with her bag of things, and I will say, "Where have you been?
I've been ringing you all day," and she will tell me that she went out for
a long walk and lost track and I'll say, "Well, here you are now, I'm
glad. Amen."

Bessi got home at six o'clock and Georgia wasn't there. In her head a voice said, What if?

Impossible, Bessi replied. Absolutely most definitely impossible.

She cooked giant mushrooms and sweet corn with olive oil and pasta shells. She made enough for two because Georgia might be hungry when she came and she *would* come and Georgia liked giant mushrooms. She decided to wait until she arrived before eating.

At eight o'clock, in Kilburn, Bel was at home with Jason. They had just finished eating dinner, during which Bel had gotten up twice to answer the phone when it wasn't ringing.

Bel went to wash her hands in the bathroom. She used soap and rinsed. She watched the water falling off her skin. Then she left the bathroom without turning off the tap and returned fifteen minutes later to water spilling over the top of the sink. She turned off the tap and stood still.

Georgia, she said. Oh my God.

She left the house with wet hands and there was a hole in her right slipper. The drive to Tottenham was slow red lights in dark streets. The stars were hidden by rain clouds. Bel held the steering wheel very tightly because her hands were shaking, and as she approached Georgia's flat she held it tighter.

All the lights were off. She walked up the stairs to the front door and knocked. She stepped back from the door and looked up. From the streetlight moon she could see the top of the bookshelf and the light hanging from the living-room ceiling. Nothing else but the dark, and something around the edge of the dark, something that was so very still.

"Bessi," she said into the phone. "I'm at Georgia's. She's not here. I'm getting the police."

"Where is she?" said Bessi. She sounded parched, as if there was no moisture in her mouth. "I'm waiting for her. She was supposed to come. Where is she?"

"I'm getting the police."

Bessi waited in her bedroom. She was wearing a thin red nightgown with wide sleeves that Kemy had made her out of silk. She placed the phone in the center of the bed. She lay down next to it and the sky was red tonight and each moment waited for the next. She fell into one of the moments. Georgia was standing in the living room with mildew eyes. *Let me go,* she said, and her arms lifted from her sides.

Bessi got up and walked into the kitchen. She saw the cemetery out of the window. She opened the fridge and closed it. She said out loud, to the air that was beginning to buzz: I told her to come back on Monday.

Just before the phone rang, Bessi was drowsy and she allowed herself to imagine what if. She saw herself alone in a tunnel, turning around in circles and falling to the ground. She saw herself get up and walk down the passage, without a face.

Her last thought was this: *If she has gone, I will not forgive me.*

Then the phone rang. Bessi picked it up. Bel spoke the words.

And in the red night, Bessi screamed.

She dropped the phone and kept on screaming. Afterward, she sat cross-legged in the middle of her bed. She didn't understand what to be.

But only last week, she said to the dust, we were dancing!

At one o'clock in the morning Bel arrived at her door instead of Georgia. They sat on Bessi's unbest bed and held each other in the dark.

"I told her to come back on Monday," said Bessi, "as if she was the milkman."

"I saw her swaying," said Bel.

All night Bessi tried to remember something. The moment before the scream. How exactly, *exactly,* did it feel, all those years, being alive with Georgia alive? What was it like? She wanted to hold it in her hands, the warmth and the tenderness of it. She sensed that if she couldn't remember she would have lost everything including herself; and that she would never quite remember it because of what she had lost.

She fell asleep in a crooked position next to Bel. By dawn, she had words for the questions.

First: *How do I talk to her?*

And this: *Oneness in twoness in oneness—forever? But how?*

THEY ARRIVED AT Waifer Avenue and let themselves in. Ida was on her way down the stairs in her old champagne wrapper to have some bread and black-eyed beans. Bel and Bessi stood in the hall looking up at her.

Ida was pleased to see them. And then she was not pleased.

She looked at their faces and she could see dust. And she thought it was odd that they were here, suddenly, on a Tuesday morning, when they should be at work. And where was Jay? And what was wrong?

Ida said: "Where is Georgia?"

Bessi began to cry.

Ida screeched: "But where is Georgia!"

Neither of them could speak but Ida could see it. In Bel's face, in Bel's memory, she could see the echo of a fatal sway.

She heard Georgia's voice then. It said, *Were you scared? How did you know it was right?* She saw the scar across her daughter's stomach and the faraway eyes and she felt her legs dissolving beneath her. In a compulsion toward dying she did not grip the banister to stop herself falling, and she did not shield her head from the danger. She fell. She tumbled. She landed at the bottom of the stairs at Bel's feet and screeched, "You bring her to me! When she is sick you bring her to me!"

The fall damaged her leg. Bessi had to go upstairs and find Baba's walking stick with the snake carved around the middle that Ida had brought back from the funeral in Aruwa. Through the afternoon she limped about and said, "All on her own." She said, "You bring her to me." She limped into the hallway and looked up the stairs at the eyeless black mask with straw hair and said, "The devil he tek my child."

That evening the dining-room table changed. It experienced something it had forgotten many years before.

That evening, the dining-room table witnessed Ida and Aubrey in a mutual embrace for the first time since the 1970s.

Aubrey got home, the cold wafting off his coat, and Bel immediately made him a large cup of tea because tea was the way to make things manageable even if no one drank it. She put sugar in the tea and the sugar was uncomfortable. Aubrey took a long time taking off his tie, opening and closing his briefcase, walking up and down the hall. He straightened the pens on his desk, he went upstairs and came back down, he wondered about dinner.

Bel said, "Will you sit down, Dad."

Aubrey was getting nervous. They looked like blackbirds, standing about like that, waiting. What were they all waiting for? He was getting spooked. Bel's hair was a mess, and this was unusual, and Bessi was flitting around in the middle of the living room like a wasp.

"What the blast is going on?" he said.

"Sit down!" went Ida.

"What's wrong with your leg?"

Ida pulled out a chair from the dining table and pushed him into it by the shoulder.

She said: "There is bad news. About Georgia. I fell down the stairs, she—"

"Georgia fell down the stairs? Is Georgia here?"

"No," said Bel, "*Mum* fell down the stairs, this morning."

"What for?" said Aubrey.

"Oh, Mum, *tell* him."

"Georgia—"

"Is she all right?"

"Georgia tek her life."

Aubrey looked up at Ida as if she'd punched him. He tried to stand up but failed. A little boy gasped like a man, threw his arms around

Ida, and buried his face in her stomach. Ida bent over him. She held him and stroked his white hair. There it was.

"Hellfire Jesus God almighty! God help us, Jesus Christ al-*bloody*-mighty I say, what? What? How? But what the dammit do you mean?"

Bessi started to howl. It was deep and clawing and not quite human. All the house joined in. From far off, as she swiftly traveled, Georgia could hear them calling.

Aubrey peeped around Ida at Bessi. He said, "It must be worst for Bessi, poor thing," and howled, and held on to his wife.

THE POLICE HAD taken Georgia's body to the mortuary in Hornsey. On Wednesday morning, in preparation for the identification, the body was laid out on a narrow table behind a wall of glass. On top of her, covering the neck, they draped a heavy velvet cloth embroidered with a gold cross. The cross reached from her chest to her feet (she was a little one).

The parents and two sisters arrived with raindrops on their shoulders. In the reception area the mother and father sat next to each other in their very thick glasses, and the sisters sat adjacent. The woman who welcomed them noticed that one of the girls, the one in the blue coat, looked the same as the one on the table.

The mother and father went in first.

While they were waiting, Bessi looked into the office leading off the reception area. There were two women in blouses typing. Every so often their fingers stopped and they sipped coffee, which Bessi could smell. She wondered if they were writing something about Georgia, and what the coffee tasted like; she wondered whether coffee tasted different in a place like this and whether it cooled down quicker than in other places.

Aubrey and Ida came out. They looked smaller than they had when they went in.

Bel took Bessi's hand and led her inside. It was spacious and without time. It occurred to Bessi that today—this—might be the reason why Wednesdays were what they were, the tumbling and tossing, the oldest thing she knew, because Georgia was lying over there at the end of this bare room, behind glass, underneath a golden cross.

They concentrated on getting to the glass. In the center of the room was a rectangular indoor garden outlined by a low brick wall. The leaves were green, but there were no flowers. Bel and Bessi walked around it, bent forward like old women, Bessi around one side, Bel around the other.

They came back together a meter away from the glass and looked into a very bad dream. She was wax already, preparing to disappear. The eyelids were closed forever. The mouth was a darker, harder shade of ruby than the moment before, which Bessi still couldn't remember. The cheeks were falling, all the muscles in the face had breathed out. Her neck was hidden beneath the cloth.

Did it hurt a lot? How did you bear it? Bessi wanted to ask. But she didn't know how to talk to her.

She stepped forward into the dream. She pressed her thumb against the glass, in the place between Georgia's eyebrows, and moved it upward, over the forehead. She felt cool air, around her ribs.

Bessi leaned her whole body against the glass now. She fell into the dream and lay down on the table next to the rest of her, and slept for a while beneath the quiet velvet. It was a long and hopeless sleep, and when she woke up the body beside her had gone. She tried to get out, but the glass would not let her.

From behind her, Bel said: "It takes a soul to make a body come true."

2

It's dark outside and the rain and the moon have turned the streets to glass. On the short drive from JP's back to Waifer Avenue, Bessi looks out through the car window and there are questions in her head. Is it you? she asks. Her ribs are aching now, as I shift and climb, as I struggle to arrive completely. She begins to feel hot and asks, Am I going to die too?

Ida is sitting in her rocking chair and all the lights throughout the house are off except for the sun lounge. We come in through the back door and the bells ring. "Dammit!" says Aubrey, because Ida doesn't like the bells now. She says they're too loud. The house should be quiet. It is no longer a real place with real sounds. When someone speaks, it is as if they have spoken in their sleep.

Aubrey turns on lights.

"The funeral's next Tuesday, Mum," says Bel.

"We're doing the makeup ourselves," Bessi adds.

Ida shakes her head. "You bring her to me." She is wearing a head scarf and lots of layers of fabric, a wrapper, a dress, a black crocheted shawl. Baba's walking stick is leaning against the radiator next to her.

Behind the rocking chair, I can see a stooped figure with an ancient face. Her shriveled hand is resting on her daughter's shoulder. She is hazy but I know her immediately. Nne-Nne leans forward, and squints at me.

"All on her own," Ida whispers. Bel steps out of her heels slowly, and goes into the kitchen to make tea.

Nne-Nne says to me, How did you come?

I try to tell her, about the forest and the running and how it was just like Baba said, but I am weak still, and my words will not reach her.

Aubrey asks if Kemy has phoned from Trinidad and Ida says no. He is full of coconut macaroons. He sits down and does not switch on the television.

Bessi leaves the room and goes upstairs to 26a. She wants to see. The beds are stripped. The saloon door has finally fallen off. It smells musty and there is nothing in the wardrobe except for the two white corduroy coats that Dad said to keep because of wasting not and wanting not. There are beanbag ghosts in the alcove and a smell of strawberry that is not a real smell.

Bessi looks in the mirror. Her eyes flicker. She almost sees me and she shrinks back from the glass.

Is it you? she thinks again, and crawls back toward the face. It is her face, as much as it was ever her face.

Is it? You?

I lift her hand to the glass because I am not yet strong enough in her eyes. We touch the cheek with the fingertips. I am tired. I am so very tired. The hand drops and Bessi gasps.

There is more to climb. The aching in her ribs gets stronger. The heat is filling her head and throbbing inside her fingertips, which begin to dance of their own accord. I move up toward her shoulders where it is tight and I cannot quite enter. I push and clamber around the bones. Inhabitation is not an easy thing.

From the staircase below comes the sound of footsteps approaching the loft. Bessi stands up and concentrates on keeping her fingers still.

Bel puts her head around the door. "Dinner's out."

"I'm coming," Bessi says. I can smell rice and fish. I can smell the tomatoes soaked around the fish.

Bel waits. She is staring intensely at us. In a swing of light as Bessi turns toward the door, her eyes catch mine. She suddenly seems as if she is about to cry. "For a moment," she says, "you looked just like Georgia."

Ida and Aubrey are sitting in their places at the table opposite each other. Before sitting down, Bessi moves her mat and plate to the right so that she can sit in my place. Ida stops eating. "Sit in the middle like your sista."

"No. I want to sit here."

Aubrey clears his throat. "Let her sit there if she wants."

They eat their rice and fish in the evening and the echoes. The rice is a little bit soggy. Outside there is rain still falling on the sun-lounge roof.

Ida says, "At home a woman will not live by herself, she lives with her family. They look after her. They ask you how you are."

"Yes, Mum," says Bel.

Bessi feels something new in her neck and at the top of her head and in the veins throughout her body. I shake myself loose throughout her. It is a feeling much sharper than the flute and the aches, it is very close to pain. A tightening of the skin and a sense of being filled up, of teetering on the edge of bursting, like the top of making love. It makes her tremble and drop her fork. I have moved fully into her legs, her arms and feet, into her eyes, and I am almost comfortable now. I almost fit. It has been harder than I imagined it would be, to find a way to fit her.

Oh, sweet, thinks Bessi, it's *true*!

I move, finally, into her heart, and I tell her yes.

"You should slow down when you eat," Aubrey says. "You're out of breath, look."

Sweat has broken out on Bessi's forehead and there is glitter inside her cheeks. She's eating the fish and looking at her hands, rubbing her stomach, rubbing her heart. Bel and Ida are staring. I can see Nne-Nne clearly now, sitting with Mum, virtually inside her. Nne-Nne is staring too, as if we are under a microscope. She squints at me again, then she turns to Ida and says, "All the stories Baba told were true. You see it."

She turns to Bel and points at me with her long shriveled finger. "You see it."

Bel sinks back in her chair, astonished.

"Georgia?" says Ida.

"Bessi, you mean!" Aubrey is distressed. "It's *Bessi*!" Yesterday he accidentally called Bessi Georgia and afterward he went upstairs and hid in the bathroom.

Ida looks down at her plate, refusing to see, her voice strange and cracked as she tells Bessi, "Go and lie down."

"I'm going home soon." Bessi smiles. She takes her plate into the kitchen. The feet walk neither inward like Bessi nor outward like Georgia; they face the front. She laughs in the silence, and in the laughter, there is a trace of fear.

"Why don't you stay here with Mum?" Bel says from the kitchen doorway. "You shouldn't be on your own." For a moment Bessi does not recognize her. It is as if she were standing a long way away from her, in another place.

"Don't worry, Bel," she says. "She's all right now. I know she is."

BEL DRIVES US home through the wet glass streets. The houses and the sycamore trees are upside down and twice themselves. At Lanten Road, Bessi says she'd like to walk the rest of the way on her own because the night is ravishing.

It has stopped raining. The sky is washed and the stars can see us clearly: a woman in a blue coat, half skipping. She passes the bus stop and the petrol station. She picks up speed down the hill. She is almost running.

Bessi asks the most urgent question.

Did it hurt?

A little bit, I tell her.

I'm sorry. Oh dear, I'm sorry.

Let's not talk about pain. That pain was less than the pain before.

The pain before, she says, that is even worse to think about! I should have done something!

Like what?

I should have stayed with you in the nights, all the awful nights, I should have looked after you—

I am not a child, I tell her, and you are not my mother. The pain is over.

I am so glad it's over.

We skip and we run with forward feet. Bessi says it feels like flying. We reach the flats. We take the stairs.

What happened after? she asks.

I'm not sure.

I try to think of it. Bessi's muscles and ribs feel very warm, like the beginning of fever. Her head is light. I tell her this, I imagine this:

It was like flying, just like that. A flash, a jump. I became white light, silver flesh and galactic bone.

Did you?

I got to the water and I lay down in the water.

Yes.

I heard you scream and I ran.

Yes.

Miles and miles through the forest. I was carried in the body of a child and her dress had turned to rags and her name is Ode in Onia. There were birds crying in the trees above my head and the howls of witches in feathered skirts. There was fire in the distance.

I remember that story.

The thorns on the ground cut my feet as I ran and I could hear you all in the house, all the howling. I tried to shout but my voice would not carry. I began to wonder whether I would make it at all. But then I found you.

You found me.

I climbed up your ribs.

Moved into me.

Yes.

Bessi unlocks the front door. It is our house. She takes off her coat and puts down her bag in the living room. The door to the balcony shakes in the wind and creaks.

"I don't like that noise," she says to the door. "It sounds like rope, twisting and untwisting."

The phone rings; Darel leaves a message asking where Bessi has disappeared to. She ignores him, washes and goes to bed. Tomorrow is another big day, she tells me. We're going to the cemetery to choose a double-decker bed. And we're going to get your things.

The room is dark except for the moon, which sends the vase of daffodils on the windowsill across the ceiling in long bold shadows. The shadows ripple and Bessi thinks of ghosts.

Are you a ghost? she asks.

I do not answer her.

She gets up and turns on the lamp. She lies back down, turns onto her side facing the window, draws up her legs and holds one hand in the other hand.

I've got an idea, she thinks.

What is it?

You are the right of me. I am the left.

The balcony door creaks. Bessi's words quicken.

I give you my right hand and right leg and everything on the right, and when I want to touch you I take your hand in my left.

Okay, that's a good idea.

I am both of us.

Yes. Like a flame. It flickers Georgia, it flickers Bessi.

We will be fire.

She is almost asleep. She can no longer hear the balcony door.

It's not true, is it? she says, nearly dreaming.

What?

It's not worst for Bessi. It's best for Bessi. Isn't it. Will you stay forever?

I do not answer.

We sleep a deep double sleep, holding hands.

THE KEEPER OF the graves lives in a cottage by the dead. He carries a stick and wears a cap. Under the morning sun he leads us along the silver beech avenues, through the elms and the ash, the blackberry bushes and the mausoleums. There's an open tomb in the walkway of the chapel. I can smell the flowers of lavender and hyssop and rosemary.

At night, in the cemeteries, the ghosts are said to wander among the stones. They are white and murky, with see-through empty selves. They pass through the cemetery walls and stand motionless in people's bedrooms. It is not true. We are lace shining around the living who still need us. We are the glitter in their faces that is close to madness. We lift them up, and pull them onward.

Some of the monuments here, the keeper of the graves is telling Bel, date back to the 1700s. There are Greeks and Russians, Ethiopians and royalty. There are stones big enough to live in with statues on the roof of birds and cats, and stones that are crumbling and mottled and forgotten.

On Sundays you can get a two-hour guided tour, for under five pounds.

Bel and Bessi follow the keeper of the graves to the vacant plots. Bel is wearing Wellington boots to protect her stockings.

It should be somewhere with lots of light, I tell Bessi. Yes, she says. And not too near the wall.

"Here?" says Bel, on a hill near the chapel.

"No," Bessi says. It's cramped, there's too many weeds.

We carry on. There is a site overlooking the keeper's lodge, and another close to the entrance, visible from the main road. We pick our way through the sleeps.

On a level plain at the bottom of the hill we find an evergreen tree with a bench nearby. There is room for us between two crumbling stones. A throng of butterflies are sifting over the long grass as flocks of cloud pass over the sun.

Bel says, "Is it here?"

"Yes," we say.

Here, then, thinks Bessi. This is where they will take me—what a thing to know. She is getting a rash on her neck. She keeps scratching it, with her left hand, and I tell her to stop it with my right.

The administration of death is a thing of work and activity, journeys and signatures, telephones and composure—yet the world has changed. Flowers become louder than concrete. All the colors are extra. Bessi watches a woman with auburn hair striding along Neasden Lane past the station, swinging a purple umbrella by the hook. She sees two boy twins in their pram, asleep, with black hair, under a white quilt. They are facing each other. It occurs to her that these streets will never again carry Georgia's outward-walking feet, my own walking body, and that is why they have changed.

Ida is pleased we chose a grave near a bench. "That's it," she says. And she approves wholly of the cemetery being visible from Bessi's window. It is as it should be, like Cecelia under the washboard in Aruwa and Baba by the vegetables. They should remain with us, in our domesticity.

Neither Bel nor Ida will address me directly, but they know I am here. They look at Bessi with suspicion, with amazement. They look at her twice, thinking hard with their eyes. It is the same expression that mounts on Toby's face as we walk toward him, in the empty street in Bruce Grove, outside the home we shared.

He has cut off all his hair. Tufts of it are jutting out from his skull. He looks thinner than ever, wrapped up in his coat with his bootlaces undone, so thin and dirty that I feel something close to regret. The flame flickers Georgia. I move toward him. There's a trace of terror in his eyes.

"I'm sorry," he says. "Bessi . . . I still can't believe it. I'm so sorry."

"It's not your fault, Toby," we tell him.

He looks away from me. Bessi makes herself very small so that I can take, for a moment, the left arm as well as the right. I put these arms around him and feel him shivering against me like a little boy. "What did you do? What happened?" he says. He takes the back of my head in his palm.

"Have you been waiting long?" asks Bel.

Toby breaks away and drives his hand through the clumps of his hair. "Not long," he says. He looks around him frantically, as if about to run. "Let me take some of those."

Laden with empty boxes and plastic bags, we climb the stairs and Bel unlocks the front door. The air inside is barren, there is a lack of waiting. A home waits, it expects, it waits for knocks or rings or voices; this home waits for nothing. In the lilac shadows off the hallway my white coat brushes Toby's cheek and he twists away from it. "Come on," says Bel, "come on." Bessi clutches Toby's arm up the stairway. She hears the sound of rope, twisting and untwisting; she imagines the little body swaying up there, above their heads.

I try to talk to her. Do not think of it, I say. But she will not listen. Do not think of it, the spinning, think of what I told you last night, white light, I ran to you, the pain is over.

Toby goes straight into the bedroom and sits down on the bed. I watch him through the crack in the door, staring at one of the pillows, not moving. Bessi goes past into the living room. The record stack is open on Roberta Flack, the wicker chair is facing the window. She wonders how it was that night. Was there music? she asks me, but I will not answer. Was it like this? Did you sit in the wicker chair and look at the street moon and rise up, and look through the records for the perfect sound? She wanders out onto the landing and runs her hand along the cold banister. Like this, did you walk out here, quiet in your heart? Were you very sure, were you very clear, that you were going, that you were leaving, exploding beyond yourself? What was it like, Georgia?

I was a wizard, I tell her faintly. I was magic.

Or were you chased away, biting your fist and clutching your clothes. While you were choking, did you regret? Because breath takes a time to leave, doesn't it, Georgia? The body will not let it go. It jerks and twists. It cries until there is no breath left, only a final push, a whisper that says I was equal with this air. How can I know for sure? Bessi stamps her foot on the floorboards.

Regret is worthless, I say. I was spinning! The spinning set me free. She unplugs the phone. She turns in a circle. She wants to spin too. No! I tell her. You can't!

From somewhere else in the flat, Bel calls out Bessi's name. Bessi rushes toward the kitchen and finds Bel standing by the best bench, holding open a notebook. She passes the notebook to Bessi, and leaves the room.

We sit down at the bench.

It was here, wasn't it? she thinks to me. You were sitting here.

There are whole pages colored in red and entries written in yellow, blue and orange. There are letters to God and to someone called Carol. There is a letter that starts *Dear Bessi.* It is dated two weeks before Valentine's Day.

Bessi reads the letter. *Believe in me,* it says. *Believe in me until the end.*

I DISCOVER THAT I can leave her when she sleeps. I stretch out and enter the mouths of the night birds. I paint the night with the flowers and discover that I am all of this, everything my body made me forget.

I visit Bel in her dream. She is standing in the garden in Sekon, waiting. I walk into the garden in pajamas and a cardigan and I am much younger than I was. Bel says, Come here, little one, let me protect you. Sedrick creeps out from the bushes. Bel begins to shout at him. She's flinging her arms around and swearing. I point at Sedrick and shake my head. No, Bel, I say, everything was strange to me.

In the morning there are two pigeons sitting on Bessi's balcony rail. She sits up in bed feeling blank, and studies them. She wonders what they are talking about. The birdsong was very loud this morning. It woke her up.

When I get back (I am late) the pigeons fly away and Bessi yawns as if she has just come to life.

I had a dream that you died, she tells me.

Oh.

You were dead and I was upset about it, so I cried all night in bed. In the morning I got up and went into the living room, and guess who was sitting on the sofa.

Me?

Yes! Imagine how happy I was. Your hair was tied back and it had a yellow rose in it and your cheeks were shiny. I made a big fuss but you acted as if it was nothing. You seemed older.

Forty-five minutes?

Older than that. Much older.

She gets up and starts tidying the bedclothes.

What are we doing today? I ask.

We're going to paint her, she says.

Bessi packs a bag of makeup. We walk in the sun along Kilburn Lane—it is an unnatural level of sunshine for this time of year. She walks swiftly, swinging the bag of things. The blood is charging up and down her legs, swirling around in her head, and she scratches her neck with her left hand. She does not wait for the cars to stop before crossing the road. I am invincible, she thinks, the worst nightmare is true and anything after is lesser. If I were a soldier, and called into the deadly center. I would run to it because whether I live or die, I am invincible.

Bel is waiting for her at the parlor. JP has an oat in his whiskers and he offers us Murray Mints to which Bessi says no thank you; she is hot and her mouth is dry and she is feeling bad toward sugar.

JP warns them about the embalming, which may have altered her features. He warns them about the fingertips.

THE WHITE CURTAINS rustle as the door is shut behind them. On the wall there is a bare silver cross; beneath it on a table, a vase of long white lilies.

Georgia is lying down. A doll in a box. They have prepared themselves for the cool of porcelain.

Bessi holds the bag with both hands. Her right side feels weak, all of a sudden, and when she entered the room there was a fearful tugging within her skin. Now she feels this heat, this fever, crawling up both sides of her face into her hair.

They stand around the coffin, looking in at the peculiar face. The skin around the nose, chin and forehead is turning gray. From the chest down she is covered in a white brocade, so they cannot yet see her hands. The curtains sigh again and seem alive.

Bessi moves her fingertips toward the face. She touches Georgia's forehead, then draws away. She touches it again, and stays there, and moves the fingers up and down by an inch. "Cold," she says.

She lays out foundation, lipstick, Vaseline and Vicks that Ida has insisted is rubbed into Georgia's chest to protect her from angry spirits who might disapprove of what she has done. Aubrey overheard this and muttered, "Haddock."

Bessi takes the sponge and dabs it with foundation. She rubs and blends until the gray is gone. *There,* she thinks, *that's better,* and breathes in and out, and feels the fever spreading through her. She touches the lips, which are hard like cobbles, and her fingers scuttle away for the Vaseline.

"I'll do it," says Bel. Bessi leans back against the wall, getting hotter.

Bel makes the lips ruby again. She rubs Vicks over the heart. Then Bessi takes one of two silver rings out of her pocket. "Help me lift her arm—the right one."

They pull down the brocade and lift Georgia's right hand, whose fingertips are black at the tip. Bessi thinks, *It's a very heavy arm not Georgia's arm it's too thick to be Georgia's real arm, isn't it!* The fingers, the black ones and the alive ones, jostle with one another. *Stay still stay still! With these bands of silver, let us marry across the graves.* Bessi pushes the ring down. She puts the other ring on the same finger of her own left hand.

Now I live for both of us, as you sleep for me, wait for me, in the double earth.

They look down at their work. Bessi thinks the face is smirking at her. Gradually, she notices a red tinge at the edges of her sight. The area around the coffin is beginning to turn red. It starts with a tinge of fever rose and becomes stronger. It hovers over the coffin and casts a mocking rosy shadow on the face.

Bessi backs away, clutching the bag. The red begins to buzz. It sucks her breath away and travels across the room and flares up the white curtains. Bessi drops the bag and her hand flies to her throat.

"Bessi, what's wrong!" cries Bel.

She gropes behind her for the door and bursts out into the hall. JP rushes out of his office: "What's happening here?" Bessi spins around in a circle. "Red!" she cries. "Red!" She runs out into the street. She sees Kemy walking toward her in an orange jacket and the orange makes her weep. Ida and Aubrey are walking on either side of Kemy and the three of them begin to run. Bessi's legs disappear. She reaches out her arms toward Kemy and falls down in the burning street. "Bessi's dying Bessi's dying!" says Ida's voice, which also disappears.

They are in the loft, the two of them, and they are standing face-to-face. There is grass beneath their feet and flowers lying down. They are wearing their summer dresses, which are dusty and torn. They have arranged that they will go now. Bessi will go first and Georgia will follow, and they will meet at the evergreen tree. Bessi ties the scarf and jumps. She runs to the evergreen. But when she arrives, Georgia is already there.

"SMAZEL?"

"Sssh," says Bel.

"She's waking up," says Aubrey.

"People knock on your door, they ask you how your body."

Bel's hands are stroking her head. There are people on the ceiling in the loft. They are all enormous people with blue in their faces.

"Thank God—help us," says Ida.

Bessi's lips are stuck together. Kemy hands her a glass of water with a slice of lime floating at the top. You fainted, she says. You were spinning round and round on the spot. It was pretty freaky."

"You were overwhelmed," says Aubrey.

"But you're all right now." Bel tests her palm against the back of Bessi's neck. "You're not so hot anymore. Let's leave her be for a while."

Kemy remains with Bessi in the loft. She has Trinidad coffee in her skin and smells of coconut oil. They lie on their backs and look up at the ceiling. They are two-thirds of three.

"I knew she'd do something," Kemy says. "When I hugged her at the airport, I could sort of feel it. I said to her, 'You won't do anything silly, will you?' and she said, 'No, silly!' She never listened to me about anything, the stubborn cow." Bessi starts laughing and Georgia is in the laugh. "Then when Bel phoned that morning, I was getting ready for the carnival and I just knew. As soon as the phone rang, I knew it was Georgie."

Kemy thinks about Georgia's eyes. She thinks about how they were always somewhere else.

"She never really liked it here, did she?"

"No," says Bessi.

"Where d'you think she is?"

Bessi shuts her eyes. There are bits of red left over in the dark.

"I don't know."

Kemy turns to face Bessi. "On the plane on the way back from Trinidad, I looked out of the window at the clouds. I looked for a long time and thought about her. Then I saw her. She was sitting down on a cloud all to herself and dangling her feet over the edge. She waved at me. I think she's everywhere."

"Not all the time," says Bessi.

Kemy looks at Bessi's eyes, and sees that they have changed.

ON TUESDAY THEY sang in the church as candles danced in lakes of heat. Before the lid was fastened over the box, Bessi and Kemy had their last look. Bessi bent in toward the body, and kissed the cobbled lips.

They put her in the ground after that, JP in his coattails, the keeper of the graves directing the digging, and they sang again, and lifted her memory to the sun. Bessi looked down. The box was beneath the soil. She forgot, for a moment, that Georgia was not in there. She thought: *I want to go down. I want to go down and get you out of there.* Toby ripped the plastic off the flowers so that their stems and leaves and petals were free. She was smothered in flowers, the yellow velvet roses and the lilies lying down, lilac stems and shoots of tulip spilling over the hump of double earth. JP explained that it would take a year to sink level. After that, they could bring her stone.

Aubrey stood by the mound of flowers. He fumbled with his tie and cleared his throat. "There's butties and macaroons back at the house," he said to the congregation.

The house was surprised by the noise, the voices, thick in the living room and kitchen and all the way up the stairs. Kemy put on Michael Jackson and Bel kicked off her shoes to dance with Jay. She said it was bad luck for the departing spirit if no one danced at their funeral. Aubrey clapped his hands to the music, slightly out of time, and said, "God bless you, Georgia!" He didn't drink a lot. Mr. Hyde was not invited to the party.

That night, as they lay in bed, Bessi and Georgia agreed that it was a wonderful funeral. Bessi asked Georgia very delicately what the gravestone was like that she'd seen in her chest, the evil stone, so that they could choose one that was nothing like it. Georgia said she couldn't remember exactly, except that it was crumbling. She was concentrating on keeping the bad memories to herself. It was proving difficult, since she was not entirely herself.

It was very quiet tonight except for the balcony door. No voices, no wind, no sound of traffic. The administration period was over. There was nothing more to be done.

3

Bessi went back to work with the rash still there on her neck. The corkscrew extensions were gone and her hair was plaited into cornrows with beads at the end the way Georgia liked to wear it. One afternoon she picked up the phone and accidentally dialed Georgia's old number. A man said, "Rob speaking?" And Bessi said, "Who the fuck are you?" "No, who the fuck are *you*?" said the man. With her right hand, Georgia made her hang up.

Bessi felt, for the first time in her life, that the music business was composed vastly of fluff. She sensed that Leopard was perhaps not a genius pioneer of a new vocal movement destined to change the face of pop, but someone who couldn't sing. She tried her best to be dazzling but spent a lot of time daydreaming, and more time in the bath. There were days that she felt she should call lilac and she liked those days, and there were others when she was upset by the color orange. Sometimes the nights were red, which Georgia couldn't help, much as she tried, and on those nights Bessi sat in the center of her bed and begged Georgia to come back here properly.

Once a week with flowers they went to the cemetery. Bessi touched the evergreen tree and stood for a while by the wooden cross with the number on it. She wasn't sure whether to talk to herself, the Georgia part, or the cross, or the tree, so she usually didn't say much. Unlike Kemy, who always had a lot to say. She would sit down and tell Georgia all about the vegetable dyeing and how she was planning a market stall with Lace and a friend from college. She told her about a dream she'd had of a tiny mint green bird that flew in through the window and tapped her on the shoulder with its beak. She told her that she wished she was still alive but she understood that she couldn't hack it.

Bessi reminded herself, as she watched Kemy chatting with such ease, that it was best for Bessi, even though it was complicated and sometimes hard.

"Kemy," she said once, "Georgia's inside me." For three months she had wanted to say this to another human being.

"I know," said Kemy, looking up at Bessi. "Of course she is. You're twins." She turned back to the cross. Bessi did not know what else to say.

She visited Waifer Avenue more often than before because Georgia was concerned about the roses. They watered them with her right hand. They sat with Ida, who said, "You bring her to me," and sometimes, when it flickered Georgia, "Why you didn't come to me?" Ida had started going to church regularly, every Sunday without fail, to a place in Harlesden with her friend Heather from the Brazilian cookery class.

Bessi's rash began to spread. It sneaked into her wrists and made them red. It found her elbows. She only ever scratched with her left hand because Georgia firmly refused to let her use the right. Kemy monitored Bessi's itch. She said, "Stop scratching!" whenever she caught her, and she concocted a cream involving melon juice, Vaseline and granulated oats, which didn't work. Bessi could no longer remember what it felt like to be rashless.

She woke up one morning and the two pigeons were sitting back on the balcony rail. Behind them was clear blue sky, the air could smell the coming of summer. Bessi felt limp in her right side. She waited and nothing happened. Eventually, she got out of bed and put on a dress of Georgia's that didn't help with the limpness. The pigeons were still sitting on the rail, their heads close together, twitching. She decided to go to Gladstone Park with nectarines. Her feet were pointing inward. She took the 52 to Neasden, bought two nectarines from the greengrocer's, then walked unevenly to the park to sit by the duck pond next to Gladstone's house. She heard the ducks chatter as they moved across the water. Down on the hill below, a man and a woman were sitting back-to-back eating sandwiches.

Bessi took a nectarine from the bag but did not eat it right away. First, she concentrated on what she had to remember: the moment before. The moment before—when it was possible to sit with her back against Georgia's back—was in the nectarine. It was soft and sweet and it was ready to be eaten.

She brought the fruit to her mouth. She took a bite. The juice of the nectarine slid down her chin and she caught it with a finger. She concentrated on chewing and tasting. It was a perfect nectarine, but there was something not right. Bessi could not taste the sunset. If Georgia was sitting next to her as a whole other person, she would be able to eat the sunset.

"You made the world taste better," she said out loud.

Georgia didn't get back until late in the afternoon as Bessi was walking home along Chamberlayne Road. She climbed up the ribs and spread out. The feet faced forward again. The right side was equal with the left.

Bessi said, Where have you been? You've been out all day.

Sorry, Georgia said, I lost track. I was in Kemy's dream last night and I think we went swimming somewhere, I can't remember exactly. Isn't it a beautiful day?

You remember the bad things but you don't remember the good things, Bessi said bitterly.

Georgia was silent. The right side stiffened.

I didn't mean it, Bessi said. I thought you weren't coming back, that's all. I was getting frantic.

Do you want me to go? asked Georgia.

No. Never. I just wish you'd never gone.

They did not speak the rest of the way home. When they got in they wanted to be in separate rooms, like people do when they have argued, but this was not possible.

The rash got worse with the heat. It flamed up and down Bessi's arms and the backs of her legs. Georgia said it was unbearable and started scratching too; there was scratching with the left hand and with the right, there were blisters, cuts and sleeplessness, there were a thousand knives gnashing under the skin. Bessi had not had an outbreak of this scale since the egg lumps in Sekon after Nanny Delfi's fish cakes. She checked her diet for eggs and peas and spinach; she went to the doctor, who told her that severe outbreaks of eczema were common under these circumstances. And Georgia got back late more often.

On the phone now, Ida said "How's your rash?" instead of "How are you?" She had started going to church with Heather on Wednesday evenings as well as on Sundays. It was a small Baptist church with a local Zionist twist. Ida encouraged Bessi to come with her because God would save her. She had been reading the Book of Job and she was convinced that Satan was attacking Bessi the way he had attacked Job—the itching, the fever, the sadness in Bessi's face and the dark shadows gathering around her eyes—and therefore God (and Vicks) were the only possible remedies. She was also trying to get Aubrey to come, to cleanse his soul of Mr. Hyde for good. Georgia, said Ida, was the sacrifice for all the sins of the Hunters and it was our duty to purify ourselves of the evil that had driven her to tek her life. Aubrey was not ready to put on a white head scarf and sing hallelujah in Harlesden and instead started redecorating the bathroom, which meant he had an excuse when Ida started haranguing.

He wanted to paint the bathroom walls in Georgia's favorite color, but it occurred to him that he did not know what this was. He blamed Jack, and he developed more and more disgust for Mr. Hyde. On a cool summer night while Ida was in her room reading the Book of Job, Aubrey walked up to the apple trees and smoked a cigarette. He looked up through the branches at the stars. He found the brightest one, and he said, "Forgive me."

A single green apple dropped to the ground.

That's the color, thought Aubrey.

In the madness of the rash it took Bessi a few weeks to notice that something inside her was different. Georgia's voice was getting quieter. Bessi asked, How are you, at the center of me? And Georgia replied with a fainter heartbeat. Bessi began to speak more softly and to spend more time alone, so that there was less interference when Georgia wanted to talk. She took long silent walks through the cemetery and the shopping expeditions on Oxford Street came to an end. Instead, Saturdays were spent at Bel's house, babysitting Jay while Bel was at work.

They sat together on the floor in front of the television, Bessi, Jay, and (faintly) Georgia, and watched gymnastics. Bessi sipped ice-cold water and rubbed lashings of cortisone cream into her arms. Jay had decided that when he grew up, he was going to be a gymnast; he had little muscles growing in his arms and held his back very straight. It was the most exciting job in the world, he said, apart from the tights you had to wear if you were a boy. He liked the vault a lot but he and Bessi agreed that out of everything the beam was the best.

Jay sometimes felt, when he was with Bessi, that she was more like Georgia now. She was a quiet one, and she was somewhere else.

"Auntie Bessi," he said, "are you still a twin?"

Bessi's face crumpled. She scratched her right hand roughly and snapped, "That's a silly question, Jay. Of course I'm still a twin."

A little girl from Romania did three somersaults in a row and landed in a split. A man in tights flew off the bars and twisted in the air. A girl from Russia who was only thirteen years old hopped up onto the beam. She stuck out her chest and stood straight and proud and ready with outward feet. Her balance was perfect. She threw up her arms after the jumps and didn't wobble. Then, with her hands outstretched, she did a cartwheel. The cartwheel happened slowly. And inside the cartwheel, there were grassfeet memories and a cockroach army and a scream.

Bessi felt very itchy indeed. There was a jolt in her ribs, she fell back onto the floor, and burst into tears.

"WHAT A MESS now," says Bel. "I knew this would happen."

She takes off her coat and lights joss sticks. Bessi is lying on the floor with her legs pressed closely together. An ugly shadow is resting on her face.

"It's Georgia, isn't it?"

Bessi clings to my right hand, digging the fingers into the palm. She nods and squeezes her eyes shut.

"Bel. Why didn't she talk to me?"

From a shelf Bel takes a bottle of lavender oil and dabs our temples. "I think she didn't want to spoil things."

"We were in the garden," says Bessi. "Such a beautiful garden. We sat down by the orange trees and there was fire in the distance."

The shadow walks across Bessi's face. It is still a face where bad things should never happen. She scratches the back of her knee. There is pain again in her ribs.

"When she is ready," says Bel, "she must leave you. You know that, don't you?"

"Leave me?"

"Yes, Bessi. And both of you will be well."

"But she can't leave me!"

"Why? Don't you remember Baba's story?"

"Yes, I remember."

"One year, for the soul to leave the earth?"

Bessi forgot that bit. "But *no*," she sobs, "she *can't.*"

"Why?"

She whispers it. She grips my hand and says: "No one taught me how to be alone."

IN SEPTEMBER, ONLY a few weeks before Ham's noticing, Diana was carried in a box to Westminster Abbey. The procession was four miles long and the flag on top of Buckingham Palace was lowered to half-mast for the first time in history.

She was buried at the family estate in Althorp, on an island.

While two and a half billion people watched.

The country was thrown into an unusual state of mourning. The palace at Kensington was choked with bouquets, the traffic slowed down, the people took notice of moments before, until they forgot. Charles and his mother became grave, their faces older, and concerned. In spite of it all, they carried on as normal.

Bessi began to panic. She said to Kemy, "I've not seen her since February, Kemy, I've not seen her properly in eight months." Bessi's body was eight months older. Georgia's body had stopped. Did this mean that Bessi was older than Georgia, or that Georgia was older than Bessi? At work Bessi had picked up the phone as she still did and started dialing Georgia's number; she was alarmed to find that she had forgotten the second-to-last digit.

On the strength of her position as one third of three, Kemy had appointed herself Bessi's best friend. She had also offered to be her twin if she ever needed help making a decision or fancied making flapjacks. Kemy heard Georgia's voice clearly sometimes coming from Bessi's mouth, and it comforted her. As a Christmas present she made Bessi a citrus beanbag in remembrance of strawberry. She'd soaked the beans in the zest of a hundred limes and left them to dry for two weeks. On Christmas Day, they sat on it together in 26a, back-to-back, and shared a Viennese whirl.

"It's not the same without her, is it?" said Kemy.

"No," said Bessi, and Georgia sat between them, thinking about the icy stars of winter, and how delightful it would be to languish in the edges of an icy star for a long long time.

Bessi signed all her Christmas cards *Bessi and Georgia*. During lunch she wasn't allowed to have Christmas pudding or cream or turkey because she'd been to see a homeopath, a Chinese herbalist and an allergy doctor about her rash, as well as sampled many different creams from many different pharmacies—and she had collectively been advised that sugar, birds, dairy products, strawberries, wheat, oranges (the acid), mushrooms (the fungus) and red peppers (the heat) were to be avoided at all costs. She was becoming a waif of herself. Ida, who now went to church three times a week, said that God was calling Bessi's name and she had no choice now but to answer. Aubrey had escaped baptism by going on to redecorate Ida's bedroom and the kitchen. He raised his eyes and told his soggy button